White Oak Summer

Artemisia Rae

Earthly Delights Press;

ISBN: 0615971113
ISBN-13: 978-0615971117

1

WANTED: Full time intern on organic farm in West-Central Oregon. Mar-Oct. Two daily meals and rustic lodging provided. $50/wk stipend. Applicants must be willing to work in all weather and to follow orders. Must enjoy getting dirty.

Slumped in the teal overstuffed sofa amid the 1990s retro of Heavens to Java coffee shop perusing the want ads, I slurped my coffee a little too exuberantly as I read this one, splattering an abstract line down the front of my blouse.

"Damn it!" I muttered aloud.

The only two other people in the place, both regulars like me, glanced over indifferently before returning to their worlds of afternoon coffee and whatever they were reading.

Isn't it odd? I see these people every day and never talk to them. It's obvious we're all here for the possibility of social interaction, but for some reason we keep to ourselves. The stains metastasized to consume even more of my shirt, in the process highlighting one nipple. *Great.*

I reread the ad. Something about it intrigued me. For years, I had passed through the farmer's market on my way to and from work at the Sunrise Café, a greasy spoon breakfast joint near the Capitol Mall complex in downtown Salem. There was vibrancy about the market, a liveliness I liked but that intimidated me. You couldn't just walk up and grab a tomato as if you were in a supermarket—here, you actually had to talk to the farmers. They seemed to me to be wholly possessed of a certain type of knowledge I hadn't the faintest idea about.

As I would scurry by late for work, I'd glance sideways at the rows of booths with their rows of wicker baskets and colorful signs. I didn't even recognize half the foods on their tables. I guessed people must eat that leafy stuff, but the whole thing seemed so overwhelming that I would not have dared even to walk up to one of their booths, let alone ask what the weird spiky-looking green thing was that looked like a clump of weeds. One morning a girl offered me a sample of sugar snap pea.

"No thanks, I'm trying to quit," I joked to her as I rushed past flushed-cheeked and ducked into the crowd.

This ad offered the terrifying opportunity not only to approach those tanned, toned people behind the booths, but also to actually live and work with them and learn their secrets. The title "intern" implied that I need not already know anything about their business, and they would be paying me accordingly. $200 a month? Sheesh!

They did provide room and board, though, which added a bit. I did need a place to live since my live-in boyfriend and I had recently split up. Plus, I was sure my managers were fed up with my lack of enthusiasm at the restaurant, as evidenced by the last conversation I had with Charlene, the day manager. She didn't understand why I had no desire to move on from bussing tables to being a server where I could earn more money and presumably rise in social status in the restaurant. I personally liked the lack of interaction with customers that comes from being a busser. I really did not want my paychecks to be dependent on somebody's willingness to tip me. But to management, that reads "unmotivated," and that translates into not being a "team player," which they care deeply about.

When I really looked at it, I didn't have one stinking thing keeping me from picking up and moving to the country for nine months and, in fact, the more I thought about it, the more it seemed like exactly the right thing to do.

I called the number on the ad and a woman's voice answered, "White Oak Farm."

"Um," I stammered. "Can I speak to Craig or Dana, please? I'm, um, calling about the internship."

"Wonderful!" she exclaimed. "Can you come out to the farm this afternoon at 3:00? Craig and I will show you around and see if you're a good fit for the position."

I had to work this afternoon at 3, but something in this woman's voice told me not to blow this.

"I'll be there," I blurted out.

"Take the I-5 south of town toward Albany and connect with the 20 east." I scribbled furiously to keep up with her. "Look for the sign for

Lacomb and take the 226 east. Follow the road past Lacomb for about 8 miles until you come to Sweet Well Road on the left. Turn there and go another three miles. You'll see the oak before you arrive. It's the tallest thing for miles. You'll see the greenhouses as you approach the driveway. Turn in and follow the dirt drive back past the farmhouse and park in front of the greenhouses. You'll find us in the greenhouse."

***

I returned to my friend Caroline's apartment, where I had been crashing for the past 3 weeks since Jeff and I broke up. She was heating up a can of soup on her tiny stove when I blew in the door, threw down my bag, and announced that I was driving to Lacomb this afternoon to interview for an internship on an organic farm.

"You're what? Don't you have to work this afternoon?" she asked, stirring her bean with bacon.

"Yeah, but I really think I should do this. I'll just call in sick. If I get the job, I'd have to quit anyway. Plus, I think Charlene's planning on firing me."

"I never knew you were interested in gardening," Caroline questioned.

"Neither did I!" I exclaimed. "In fact, it scares the hell out of me. I just feel like I need to do something different, you know? Get the hell out of here and try something new."

"Now, wait. So you'd move?"

"Yeah, you live on the farm. You get meals and $50 a week."

"$50 a week! Kelsie, are you crazy? That's slave labor! How much do you have to work for that?"

"I don't know. But I'll find out this afternoon." I giggled nervously. "Now help me figure out what a person is supposed to wear to an interview on a farm."

"Shit, girl. You are out of your mind," Caroline muttered as she started rummaging through my duffle bags full of clothes.

I tried to think of the people at the farmers market, how they dressed. I couldn't remember much, except for that there were a few young people with tattoos all down their arms.

"I have no idea what to wear..." I trailed off.

"Well, jeans are a must, right?" What goes better with farmers than blue jeans? Too bad you don't have a straw hat..."

"All my jeans are too tight," I complained. Breaking up with Jeff had certainly rekindled my love affair with beer and ice cream.

"The more curves, the better," Caroline said, shoving a pair of low-rise boot cuts into my arms. Looking through my selection of shirts proved more challenging.

Finally, Caroline decided on a fuzzy V-neck sweater in warm autumn colors. "This seems agrarian enough to me!" she stated, satisfied with herself.

I pulled on the sweater and noted that my breasts, already large to begin with, had swelled up along with my ass after weeks of binge eating to stave off depression. Plus, I was about ready to start bleeding, which always makes my boobs balloon to the point of bursting.

"I can't wear this!" I exclaimed, looking down at my exploding chest. "I look like a hooker!"

"Whatever!" Caroline answered. "Who ever saw a hooker in a sweater before? You look great."

I didn't have time to argue about it, so I put a thin white tank top under the sweater to cover the cleavage peering up through the v-neck. Then I searched for some shoes. Most were good for work and for going out, but the ad said, "Must enjoy getting dirty," so I figured they were all too dressy. I finally settled on a pair of running sneakers I had bought thinking they would motivate me to work out more. Judging by their stiff whiteness, it hadn't really worked. However, it was the best I had, so I threw them on and drove out toward Lacomb to find White Oak Farm.

The February day was chilly and overcast, as per usual in this part of Oregon. After I found my turn for the 226 and left the freeway, things looked desolate. There wasn't much out there but farmland and farmhouses surrounded by tall, naked trees. The fields all blended together in a mass of open ground with patchwork lines of trees between them. The road curved gently over the rolling hills, each new vista looking similar to the last one. What am I doing out here? I wondered. After miles of this, I finally came to the sign for Sweet Well Road and made my turn, zeroing out the odometer to keep track of the last three miles. I saw the oak tree from a distance, as Dana said I would, and slowed to approach a small cluster of buildings set back from the road. As instructed, I pulled down the drive and parked in front of the greenhouses. The wind whipped at me as I stepped out into the chilly air and looked around.

Here goes nothing.

I shyly approached the greenhouse door and could see obscure figures moving around inside. Straightening my sweater, I knocked timidly.

"Come in," a male voice said.

I opened the door and a blast of hot, humid air bellowed out, filled with an earthy smell.

"Come in and shut the door behind you. We don't want the heat to escape," he said gruffly.

"Right!" I stammered and fumbled with the door latch behind me. I turned around to an outright assault on my senses. Separated from the gray, barren early February landscape by only a thin sheet of Plexiglas, I stood in an oasis of verdant greens and reds, of rows and rows of green plants stacked high from the ground to chest level, with long chains of pots hanging from the ceiling filled with more plants. The place was hot and wet, drops of water condensing and dripping off every surface. Pungent smells of earth, of life and death, filled my nose.

Right in the middle of it all stood two people, both almost naked, staring at me with an intensity that almost knocked me over.

I gasped for air, filling my lungs again with the thick heaviness of this lushness.

"Hi, I'm Dana," the woman said warmly, stepping forward. She was about ten years older than I, tall and lean, with long brown hair pulled back in a ponytail and rich skin that looked tan even in the middle of winter. She wore short cut-off jean shorts, a strappy brown tank top, and a myriad of silver necklaces, earrings, and bracelets. Her deep brown eyes looked directly into mine as she reached out and took my hand. Her hands were strong and rough and covered with dirt.

"You must be Kelsie."

I nodded nervously, the sweat already beading up and dripping between my breasts. It trickled down my stomach and caught on the lip of my jeans.

"This is Craig." She motioned to the shirtless, dark-haired man whose piercing blue eyes had been staring at me since I walked in.

"Hello," I smiled weakly and gave a feeble wave, as he made no move forward to shake my hand. I had never seen so many muscles on a human chest before, at least not in real life.

Craig's eyes flitted over my entire body, pausing briefly at my sneakers, and moving back up slowly over my legs, my belly, my breasts, and settling back on my eyes with the same intent stare. I was burning all over.

"It's really hot in here!" I blurted out, flushed. My stomach sank. *That's* what I thought of to say?

"You got that right," Dana laughed. "We don't wear much in here for exactly that reason. Isn't it great to be so warm and surrounded by living, breathing plants when everything else is so cold and dead outside?"

"It really is," I breathed, letting myself relax a bit.

"You'll probably be more comfortable in here if you take that sweater off," she continued.

I must have looked panicked because she added, "Don't be shy. We're all very comfortable with flesh around here. After all, we've all got the same stuff under these damn clothes society tells us we have to wear anyway, right?"

"I'm really fine," I lied as sweat trickled down my leg.

"Take your sweater off," Craig ordered in a slow, deliberate voice, still looking directly into my eyes.

"Uh..." I stuttered, taking a small step back. He made no change in his demeanor.

Unable to think straight, I started to lift the heavy sweater up over my head. The thick air rushed across my sweaty arms and neck, tingling every bit of my skin and cooling me instantly. My nipples tightened and popped through my bra against the thin fabric of my white tank top. I quickly pulled the sweater off and crossed my arms over my chest, but my breasts just bulged over the tops of my forearms. Craig glanced down momentarily and they swelled even more. His eyes met mine again and the corners of his mouth turned up slightly.

"Now that that's out of the way," Dana said matter-of-factly, "let's get down to it. The farm is on 10 acres of certified organic ground. We raise vegetables, herbs, fruits, flowers, and seeds for sale at two farmers markets, area restaurants, and through a 200-member CSA. We keep bees and chickens here and, occasionally, pasture our neighbors' horses or goats. We offer farm tours and B&B accommodations to people who want to come spend the night on the farm. Craig calls them agri-voyeurs," she smiled.

"I also offer workshops for women and men to further their sensual connection with the earth. Each year, we take on four interns who will work alongside us for the entire season, learning everything from seeding to planting to tilling: weeding, harvesting, marketing, seed-saving, beekeeping, chicken care, and other farm-related tasks." She paused. "Do you have any questions about the farm?"

My mind raced. Tilling, weeding, harvesting, seeds, bees, chickens—I didn't know where to start with my questions. "What's a CSR?" I asked.

She looked confused. "Oh! You mean a CSA?"

I glanced over at Craig. He was full on smiling now, showing gorgeous white teeth that set off his dark skin. He obviously thought I was a complete idiot.

I blushed. "Yeah. CSA."

"CSA stands for Community Supported Agriculture. People subscribe to the program by paying a set amount of money in the beginning of the season that guarantees them a share of the farm's harvest every week through the growing season. They either pick up their box of vegetables from the farm or get it at one of our farmers market booths."

I nodded.

Craig butted in. "Have you ever worked on a farm before?"

"Uh, no," I replied. "My experience with food has mostly been serving it in restaurants. I work at the Sunrise Café in Salem right now," I added.

"And you'd give up such a glamorous career to come live out here and dig in the dirt with us, huh?" he teased.

Before I could think of a retort, Dana asked, "Why *do* you want to learn how to farm, Kelsie?"

Shit. Up to this moment, I hadn't thought about it at all. How could I not have prepared an answer to the most inevitable question they would ask? A gnat buzzed by my ear. I reached up to swat it away. I opened my mouth:

"Well, I guess I need a new direction in life. Any direction, really. I feel like life is just happening to me and I'm just going along without playing any real part in it."

I looked along the hundreds of rows of seedlings waving gently in the breeze from the fan at the other end of the greenhouse. "I'd like to learn how to *do* something. To put my body and my mind and my energy to good use."

Wow. Did I really think all that? They both smiled.

"Let me give you a tour, Kelsie." Dana said, stepping into a faded pair of dirty coveralls and pulling on a beautiful light blue and silver winter hat. I grabbed my sweater and wrestled it over my head, all the while feeling Craig's eyes on me. "Nice to meet you, Kelsie," he said as he gave me a wink. He turned around to face the trays he had been filling up with soil before I showed up. His back was just as luscious as his front. "Maybe we'll see you again out here," he called over his shoulder.

Dana and I stepped out of the greenhouse and into the windy gray day, which felt even harsher after the warmth of the greenhouse. She led me past the farmhouse with its wide front porch, tucked away from the rest of the farm by a giant tree that, even without its leaves, was one of the most stately and impressive things I had ever seen. Dana told me it was an Oregon white oak. "We've seen over 35 species of birds in this tree. This entire valley used to be dominated by Oregon white oaks, but a century of agriculture and overuse have left less than 2 percent of native white oaks living. Even a single tree like this one is a crucial stop for hundreds of birds, providing shelter and food for them where none else exists for miles in any direction. Also, if you look on the branches you'll see some green mossy-looking stuff hanging from them. It's actually more than 30 different species of lichen, all living out their lives high up in her branches. She is the lifeblood of the farm. She's estimated to be over 300 years old." A tire swing hung from a rope tied to a branch 20 feet off the ground. I felt tiny as I trailed along after Dana, skipping to keep up with her long, graceful gait.

Just beyond the house was the barn. Part of it had been converted to a henhouse for the farm's laying hens (the *chicas,* Dana called them). They were merrily scratching around on the ground outside the barn, having a wonderful time it seemed to me. I had never really been around chickens before, and they amused me greatly with their peculiar lack of arms that made them look out of balance as they teetered forward and backward.

"Ay, chiquitas linditas, las preciosas de mi vida," Dana clucked as we strolled by several of them under a tree.

"Why is that one so big?" I asked her, pointing to a particularly massive one in the distance with an impressive assortment of feathers pluming out from its tail.

"Oh, he's a rooster. The only one of the bunch. *¿Que tal, galloto?"* she called to him.

"So all the rest are girls?" I asked.

She nodded. "All the rest are girls. Chicken sex is kind of rough, and I feel the *chicas* prefer not to deal with somebody chasing them around all the time, pinning them down and forcing them whenever he sees fit. Still, there's a biology to it, and I don't want to deny them their ability to procreate, so I just make sure the females greatly outnumber the males so that they can have some peace and quiet some of the time."

As if on cue, the rooster let out an enormous crow, craning his neck as far into the air as he could as he cock-a-doodle-dooed, nearly lifting himself off the ground. After his refrain, he did a little hop and ruffled his feathers, looking quite pleased with himself. He was comical. I laughed. "He seems to like being the only guy," I said.

"Yeah, most of the men around here enjoy the male to female ratio," she said with a wink. "Come on. I'll show you the intern housing."

We walked through a large garden area with several giant plants that had wide silvery-green leaves as well as an assortment of dried stuff. There was straw all over the beds and a wandering maze of pathways led us between them. "These are the demo beds," Dana said. "This is where we keep pretty little gardens for the people who come to tour the farm and stay in the B&B cabins. We also grow small seed crops in here."

I nodded as if that was the most sensible thing to do. She pointed out the small cabins they rent out. Beyond that, we came around a small grove of trees to a grouping of four trailers like the ones I see old folks towing behind their vehicles when they go camping at the beach, only more run down. Dana explained these were the interns' quarters, one per intern. *So I would be sleeping in a trailer*, I thought.

"Each of the trailers has its own fridge, stove, and electricity," she went on. "There is a composting toilet in the outhouse over there," she pointed to a small wooden building off to one side, "and a wood-fired hot tub and solar shower over there." I looked in that direction to see a newer building, bigger, with a window on one side. "In the center here is the communal kitchen, which interns can use and hang out in. We also make farm lunches there. It has roll-up doors so it stays relatively warm and protected in the winter and airy and open in the summer."

Beyond the large wooden deck that housed the kitchen area, I could see miles of fields that I assumed belonged to Dana and Craig. All of them were covered in what looked like green grass. I was overwhelmed. How could food come from these flat, grassy fields? How did they even know where to start?

"How long have you two been farmers?" I asked her.

"Craig grew up on a farm," she said. "Only it was a big farm that raised cotton and soybeans in the south. So, this was quite an adjustment for him. I learned to farm when I was in college on Vancouver Island. I cared so deeply for the earth but I had a hard time with the environmentalist-students who insisted that humans are always a problem, a cancer on the earth. I happened across an amazing woman, Alice Marshall, who took me in as an intern on her farm, and taught me the secrets of the garden. From her I learned how we gain the strength to heal ourselves, our neighbors, and our planet through sustainable farming. I've been farming ever since."

Craig's bright blue eyes flashed through my mind. "Um, how long have you and Craig been together," I asked, trying to sound casual.

She laughed. "Craig and I aren't 'together' as you mean it. We each have different skills that fit together nicely on the farm, and that's why we farm together."

"Oh," I stammered. I felt so naïve out here in this place just a few hours from where I lived, where everything felt so foreign and unintelligible, including the relationships of the other humans on the farm. So they lived out here together but they were not together? Why not?

"I think you would get a lot out of the experience of being here, Kelsie, and I think you'd fit in well. So, if you like it, the position is yours."

I nodded.

"Sleep on it," she said. "And get back to us when you've made up your mind. We'd like you to start in a week."

Dana picked up some stray branches off the ground and tossed them into the wooded area to the right of us. "Over there is the bee yard," said, pointing to a cluster of white boxes in stacks of two or three at the edge of the forest, behind the greenhouses. "The bees are all tucked away in their hives right now, trying to keep warm and waiting for the spring to come." She laughed. "Aren't we all?"

I smiled, too, though I had never really given the coming of spring much thought before.

2

"So let me get this straight," Caroline said, clutching her wine glass and slurring her words ever so slightly. She gets drunk faster than anyone I know. "You would be living in a trailer, shitting in an outhouse, and working in the dirt 10 hours a day, 5 days a week. And you'd have to make a fire to take a bath."

I leaned back in my chair and took another swig of wine. "Don't forget working the farmer's market on Saturdays." I wound a few strands of my sandy blonde hair into a braid. Dana's long slender legs and her graceful stride kept moving through my mind.

"What I don't get is how he ordered me to take off my shirt and I fucking *DID IT!* How could I have been that complicit? How could he have had that much power over me?"

"Well, you *were* in a job interview," Caroline suggested. "Didn't the ad say you must be willing to follow orders?"

A snapshot image of me on my knees in front of Craig flashed in my mind. Whoa. My heart pounded. I grabbed the bottle of wine off the table and swigged directly out of it.

"I don't know what the hell happened. I did mention he was incredibly hot, right?"

"Yeah, you've mentioned it a few hundred times."

"Sorry."

"Hey, I'm just jealous I didn't get checked out by a hot, buff farmer guy."

"I'm seriously thinking about doing it. I mean, it's only for 9 months, right? After that, I'm a free woman again. Women are pregnant for 9 months and then end up with a kid for the rest of their lives. This is a one-time commitment that could change my life forever, but it doesn't have to. If I decide I don't like it, I can always come back here and get another shitty restaurant job."

Caroline poured herself another glass of wine.

"Besides," I went on, "wouldn't it be kind of nice to get me off your couch?"

"I wouldn't miss your hair in the bathtub, but I don't really mind my living room turning into your breakup hostel." We both laughed and clinked wine glasses.

"I can always come visit," I reminded both of us. "On my one day off."

"On your one day off," she echoed. "Be sure to fire up that hot tub before you make your way back into town, eh? I don't allow dirt bags to sleep on my couch."

***

I called Dana and Craig the following day and got their answering machine. "It's an incredible day at White Oak Farm," Dana's purposeful, sultry voice began. "We'll get back to you when we find our way in from the garden."

"Hi Dana and C-Craig," I stammered after the beep. "This is Kelsie, from the other day. I think I would like to come and be your intern this season, um, if you'll still have me. You can call me back at 503-375-5634. Uh, thank you. Bye."

I hung up with a pounding heart. I had just taken the first step at changing my life, though I had no idea what that change would look like.

Dana called me back later that evening and gave me a short list of items I would need to get for the internship. Work boots, gloves, and a rain jacket. She recommended something called muck boots, but the other items already totaled 2 days' pay and I decided I could make "work boots" serve as "muck boots" considering my newly attained $50 per week salary. She asked me to start in a week.

"I'll have to see if my job will let me go without a full two weeks, but I imagine it shouldn't be a problem," I told her.

When I told Charlene I was quitting the café, she seemed relieved and assured me that there was no need to complete my final two weeks. In fact, I didn't need to come in tomorrow. I told her that indeed, I needed to come in tomorrow, and every other day I was scheduled for the week because I needed the money, and she reluctantly agreed. They trained my replacement while I was finishing out my shifts, and nobody seemed too bummed when I walked out the doors for the last time.

Packing was easy enough, since I had not really unpacked at Caroline's. The morning I left, she and I went out to breakfast. Afterward, we said our goodbyes, gave hugs, and I drove away in my stuffed-to-the-gills Honda. The sun was shining (a rarity in Oregon in February), and I felt lighter and lighter the further I got from the city, and the further I got into the country. This was going to be a new leaf for sure.

***

When I arrived, Dana came out of the farmhouse to greet me. She showed me to my trailer (the furthest one from the outhouse, but the closest one to the bathing area). The outside was quite dilapidated, but as we opened the thin door and stepped in, I was relieved to see it was cozy inside—tiny but cozy, with dark brown wood cupboards and table, and soft gray upholstery on the couches. To the left of the doorway sat a little kitchenette and a table surrounded by fuzzy gray benches. She said the table lowered and connected with the benches to form a bed, if I ever wanted to have a friend come and visit. I wondered what Caroline would think of sleeping in a trailer in the woods. The bathroom was through a door that way, but Dana said not to use it, since it wasn't hooked up to water or sewer. She pointed out a cupboard to the right that held bedding—blankets, sheets, and pillows, all I would need to keep warm in any weather. A table attached to the wall could fold out between the couches below it, or they could be slid together to form a king sized bed. *I have never slept on a king sized bed.* Windows surrounded the couch-bed area in all directions, with views of the demo garden beds, the communal kitchen, and another intern's trailer.

Someone had obviously cared for the place. Homemade wooden shelves held various small jars with handwritten labels—oregano, chives, parsley, cumin—and larger, intimidating glass jars of powdery flour and dried beans and multi-colored grains. Next to the couch-bed sat a small shelf of books. It occurred to me that I had never lived in a place by myself before. My trailer was love at first sight.

"You remember where the outhouse and the bathhouse are?" Dana asked me.

I nodded nervously.

"Inside both, you'll find instructions on their use. Take some time to get yourself familiar with them before nightfall, so you'll know what to do in the dark. If you have any questions, feel free to ask me. We go to town on Saturdays for the market, and even if it's not your turn to go, you can request us to pick up bulk items you might need for cooking, like oil or grains or flour. Just make a list and give it to Craig, me, or anyone else who will be working the market that weekend. There's some provisions here already," she said, pointing to the rows of half-filled glass jars, "and some root veggies in the fridge. That should last you for awhile."

She turned to go.

"Um,—"I began.

Dana whirled around again.

"When do we begin work?" I asked.

"Oh, I'm sorry. Take the rest of the day today to settle in. We'll begin at 6:30 tomorrow morning. Meet me by the henhouse, and I'll introduce you formally to the *chicas.*" She turned to leave.

"Will I just be working with you, or with Craig, too?" I quickly spurted.

"You'll have your fill of both of us before the season is over, don't you worry," she said with a smile, and closed the door behind her as she took off in her long stride toward the greenhouse.

I looked around at my new home. It was cozy, but cold. What looked like a heater hid underneath the refrigerator, of all places. It had an on/off switch that was turned to Off. I clicked it to on. Nothing happened. *Shit.* After a moment of panic, I noticed a hand-written label over the stove that gave instructions for lighting the pilot lights on the heater, the stove, and the oven. In one of the drawers, I found a lighter, along with an assortment of kitchen utensils. I followed the directions to light the pilot, including holding down the bright red ejection-looking bubble-button for a full minute before attempting to turn the heater back to "On." When I did, it took a second, but the thing fired up with a grumble, and I felt the heat radiating from it almost immediately.

I set about unpacking my car. It was a bit of a trek to get from the parking area to my trailer, and I started hauling loads of clothes and personal items through the demo beds, dumping them all on the couch as I walked in. It occurred to me that I maybe should have been a bit more deliberate about what I packed, since I would be living in such a tiny space. Nevertheless, I hefted load after load past the greenhouses, through the gardens, and into the trailer. Carrying one particularly precarious load, I thought I saw someone watching me from the greenhouse window. A tank top fell off the top of the pile into the cold dirt. I bent over to pick it up and lost a bra. I waddled around, butt up in the air, trying not to drop anything else as I collected the lost items. Finally, I rounded it all up on top of the pile again, stood up with a wobble, and glanced toward the greenhouse. I didn't see anyone.

Back at the trailer, I struggled to find a place for everything. There was a closet in the bathroom, which I quickly filled with clothes, and then decided I could go ahead and use the shower, too, since I would never bathe in it. The tiny bathroom became my walk-in closet, another amenity I had been bereft of up to this moment. As I started to unpack my only box of knick-knacks, I smelled the unmistakable smell of marijuana wafting in through some unknown crack in the trailer's armor. I looked out all the windows, but saw no one.

Finally, curiosity got the best of me and I stepped out on the trailer's small stoop to investigate. Still no one, but I heard a cough in the woods just behind the trailers.

"Hello?" I called out.

"*Cough, cough,* Hey!" a female voice called back. "Do you want to smoke a joint?"

I headed around back to find a small, pixie-looking girl with short, crazy dark hair sitting against a stump. She was wearing a leopard-print parka with a black-and-white striped sweater underneath, and tight black jeans and sneakers.

"I'm Cleo," she announced. "Dana's niece. Do you want a hit?" She offered me her joint.

"Uh, no thanks," I said, trying to sound cool. Her hair was wacky, heading in every which way at once.

"Oh, you don't smoke?" she asked.

"No, it's not that," I replied. "I just got here, and I don't really know the ropes yet. Do Dana and Craig care?"

"Hell if I know," she retorted. "They smoke for sure, so I don't see why they'd mind if we do, too. What's your name?"

"Kelsie Thompson. I'm from Salem."

"Ever worked on a farm before?"

"No. You?"

"I've worked here for a couple of seasons, but I'm not convinced I want to make a lifetime of it, if you catch my drift."

I nodded. "So why do you keep coming back?"

"Not much else I'd rather do," she mused. "Either I work here or I work somewhere shittier in the city, with less interaction with the vegetables."

"I really love the vegetables," she added.

"I don't know if I love the vegetables or not," I confessed to her. "I've never even tried half the stuff I see people selling at the farmer's market."

She took a long drag off her joint, which was dwindling down to a nub.

"You'll love them, too. I can tell."

"How can you tell?" I prodded.

"You're ripe," she stated matter-of-factly. "I can just tell."

She finished her joint and flicked the roach into the woods.

"I'll see you around," she said. "I'm getting hungry. Think I'll go make myself dinner."

With that, she headed into the trailer farthest from me. I watched her walk away, a red handkerchief hanging out of the back pocket of her jeans.

I returned to my own trailer and got back to work organizing. My stomach started growling about a half hour later. Dana had said there was food in here, but all I saw were those jars of dried food. I opened all the cupboards. Not much in them, except some coffee and teabags. The fridge looked equally dismal. A tub of butter (Hand-packed at Meadowlark Farm, it said on the container), and more jars with handmade labels—tomatillo salsa, sweet and sour sauce, green tomato chutney. In one of the refrigerator drawers was a bag of dirt-covered rock-looking things. Some were purple, some white, and some yellowish. They sort of looked like potatoes, but none I had ever seen. Then there were some that looked like carrots, but they were white. *This is quaint but what the hell am I supposed to* eat?"

I looked out the window toward Cleo's trailer. The lights were on and I could see her stirring something on her stove. I considered knocking on her door and asking if she would share what she was making, but she had not offered before, so I decided against it.

On the bookshelf, I noticed a couple of cookbooks. I thumbed through the *Student's Vegetarian Cookbook* and found the chapter "The Perfect Pot—of Grain, Of Course," which detailed how to make a pot of rice, something I had never actually done before. I followed the directions, dumping rice from the jar above the stove into a pot of water and boiling it, then turning down the heat to simmer for 45 minutes.

I got this. Now to tackle the toilet.

I put on my jacket and headed out into the evening, passing Cleo's trailer, where she was sitting at her table reading a book. Loud music with a girl singer screaming leapt from all the pores of the rickety thing, and her head bobbed in time with the song.

On the door of the outhouse, someone had carved a small cutout, like in the Wild West outhouses you see in the movies, only instead of a half moon, it was a carrot. Once inside the outhouse, I got my first look at the "composting toilet." It was a five-gallon bucket like the one the mayonnaise came in at the restaurant, sitting underneath a plywood platform with a toilet seat attached to it. *So we shit in a bucket?* I reluctantly sat down and tried to relax, but all I could do was pee. I thumbed through the 10-page primer on how to use the toilet.

"Welcome to the White Oak Farm composting toilet!" The pamphlet began. "By following a few simple steps, managing your own waste will never be a shitty job!" I read on to learn that we were to poop in the bucket and then cover our poop with a handful of duff from the nearby woodland. When the bucket was full, we emptied it into its own compost pile about 20 feet away from the outhouse, and then put it back in the outhouse with a layer of duff at the bottom so it was ready for the next user. The pamphlet said they used that compost on non-food-producing beds after it was "finished."

Finished doing what?

I peeked into the bucket as I stood back up. There was definitely "duff" in there, which must mean there was poop underneath it. I was surprised to find that it didn't stink. In fact, it smelled like the forest.

When I opened the door to my trailer, a welcome blast of warm air enveloped me and I climbed up inside. The cooking rice smelled wholesome, and I looked around at my new home with a sense of satisfaction.

After the allotted 45 minutes, I lifted the lid on the rice and fluffed it with a fork, as the cookbook suggested. I didn't know what to put on it, so I opted for some of the hand-packed butter and some salt and pepper. I threw in a dash of spice from one of the jars for good measure--rosemary. It was not the best meal I had ever eaten, but it was certainly the first time I had ever cooked rice from scratch.

After dinner, I washed my dishes in the little sink and spread them out on a towel to dry on the counter. I pulled the couches together to make the bed and spread the thick jewel-toned blankets I found in the cupboard on top. Snuggling in between them, I glanced over the bookshelf. Titles like "Four-Season Harvest" and "The Unsettling of America: Culture and Agriculture" stared back at me. I thumbed through another cookbook entitled "From Asparagus to Zucchini" from the Madison Area Community Supported Agriculture Coalition.

"CSA," I mumbled to myself. "*CSA.*"

"Central to community supported agriculture is eating locally and seasonally," the introduction began. "To be a CSA member is to take a revolutionary step and try changing one's eating, which often means changing one's lifestyle and daily practices..."

...I drifted off to sleep.

3

At 6:00 am, my alarm went off, and I woke with a start in a moment of panic. Where was I? Oh yeah. In a trailer in the woods. It was raining outside. Excellent. *Good thing I bought that rain jacket*.

I pulled on some clothes and looked for the coffee pot. I found a French press. *Perfect*. I boiled my water and ate a few bites of leftover rice. My stomach had a few butterflies as I thought about my first day of work. What would it be like? Would I just be working with Dana, or would Craig be around too? I hadn't seen him at all yesterday. What would we be doing all day?

After slurping down some delicious coffee, I threw on my rain jacket, laced up my new work boots, and headed through the demo beds to the henhouse to meet Dana. I could hear her singing to the chickens inside the henhouse.

"Good morning, Dana!" I called to her.

She stuck her head through a small hole in the wall of the house. "Kelsie! Good morning! Come on in and help me get everybody fed!"

I climbed through a door better suited to chickens than humans and joined Dana in a small room full of straw. Cut branches laddered up one wall, and straw-lined boxes filled the other. "Over there is where they sleep," she said, pointing to the branches, "and here's where they lay their eggs--their precious gifts, *gracias linditas!*"

"¿Quieren su desayuno, mis amores?" she cooed as they circled around our feet making odd revving noises. She opened the lid on the metal trash can that held their food and began scooping it out onto the straw floor. At least a dozen more came running when they heard the lid clank. I laughed aloud. They were *funny* when they ran!

"Aqui, aqui, mis lindas." Apparently, Dana only talked to her chickens in Spanish. I don't know what she was saying, but the *chicas* certainly seemed to like her. I wondered who else gets her Spanish-speaking side.

"After we fill up their water, we've got to repair a hole in the roof. It just started leaking, and I want to make sure they can always get out of the weather in their little *casita*. No sense in having a henhouse if it leaks like a sieve," she stated. "Part of your duties here will include gathering the eggs from the nesting boxes each afternoon. You can put them in these baskets," she pointed to a few in one corner of the barn, "and bring them to the wash station for packing."

I nodded, and we headed outside to fix the roof.

It was really raining hard now, and Dana had me climb up onto the roof with her, hauling a host of scrap metal and tools. The metal was slick, and I opted to crawl over to where the hole was, thoroughly soaking my jeans in the process. She had me hold a piece of sheet metal in place while she screwed it in with the screw gun. As I held on for dear life, I watched the muscles in the small swath of forearm tense up as she pushed the screw through the metal. Her face held an intent concentration, and a thin strand of hair fell down on her cheek as she guided it in. She was stunning. I had never met such a capable woman before. I wanted to soak up everything she had to share with me.

After she screwed in enough screws to keep the metal from sliding, she had me try a couple. She showed me how to change the speed of the drill by easing off the trigger if I started to lose control. It took me several tries before I could keep the screw perfectly positioned over the metal with enough force for it to break through. When we were done, we cleaned up our mess and clambered down off the slick roof. I was completely drenched, but somehow Dana seemed only slightly wet.

"You're soaked already!" she exclaimed. "Where are your muck boots?"

"I thought I could do without them," I admitted. "I can see now why you recommended them."

"Well, never mind that now. I'm taking Cleo into town today to help me load up a truck full of straw. Why don't you help Craig do some seeding in the greenhouse this morning? That will give you a chance to dry off. Cleo's making us all some breakfast, so go over to the greenhouse until it's ready. She'll call when it's done." She flashed me a big smile. "Cleo's a great cook," she said eagerly.

My stomach leapt fully into my throat. *Back into the greenhouse with Craig? Us alone? What would I wind up taking off this time?* I nodded and started walking, dazed, toward the greenhouse, where I could already see his figure moving inside.

"Dana," I called to her as she walked away, "Thank you for teaching me how to use the screw gun."

"Of course," she smiled. "That's what you're here for."

My stomach was doing somersaults as I approached the greenhouse door. I didn't know whether to knock or walk right in, but I decided that I had to get it together and not give this man any power over me. If I was going to be here all season, I could not be all weak-kneed every time I got around him. He was just a human being, like anyone else. I grabbed the handle and flung the door open.

I saw him look up as I quickly turned around to latch the door behind me. I took a quick, deep breath and turned back to face him.

"Dana sent me in here to help you until breakfast is ready," I said way too fast.

He looked at me with an amused grin on his face. Thank God, he had his shirt on this morning.

"You look like a drowned cat," he said.

I glanced down at my rain jacket, which was literally dripping.

"It *is* raining outside, you know," I retorted. I removed my rain

jacket. The rest of me was just as soaked. *Damn it!*

His blue eyes stared a hole right through me.

"Well, what do you want me to do?" I asked in exasperation.

"Come here," he said.

I caught my breath. "Um--" I started.

"I want to show you how to seed these *Brassicas*," he said with a slight irritation.

"Oh," I stumbled. "I'm sorry. I thought—"

"Never mind," he cut in. "There's a lot of work to do in here, and you'll likely take awhile to get up to speed."

Ouch. I walked up beside him. He smelled like the ocean.

"That wasn't so hard, was it?" he asked, smiling sideways at me. "I'll show you my seeding technique. Dana and I have different styles, and the thing you need to know about mine is that I am very particular. I like things to be done a certain way, and I have very little tolerance for mistakes."

No problem.

"First thing you do is fill the cell tray with potting soil until it's level, then scrape off the excess into this pile. You'll be seeding *Brassicas*, which are small seeds that need to be covered by ¼-inch of soil. You'll load some seeds onto this stake, roll them down one by one into each cell, one seed per cell. Then, sprinkle a thin layer of soil over the top, and label your tray with the variety of the seed and today's date using this tape and marker. Got it?"

"I've got it," I assured him.

***

"SUUUUUUU-EEEEEEEEY!" a voice rang out.

"What was that?" I asked.

"That's Cleo, calling us for breakfast. She insists on calling us like pigs." He smiled. "It's well worth it, though. She makes a hell of a good breakfast. We'll pick up here afterward. Let's eat. I'm starving."

We walked back to the communal kitchen area where Cleo had a feast on the table.

"Sit down, sit down!" she urged. "I don't want it to get cold."

We obliged, Dana on my left and Craig across. Cleo brought out

a gorgeous quiche, "made with the *chicas'* eggs, collard greens, spring onions, sundried tomatoes from last year, and feta cheese from Joshua's goats. And, of course, Beth's flour for the crust." She proudly set the pie in front of us.

Dana dove in with a knife, cutting us all fat slices and serving each one. Cleo brought a small bowl of chopped cilantro to sprinkle over the top, for pizzazz, she said. She also brought a pot of that delicious coffee, which I immediately helped myself to.

Despite my fear of the green chunks in the quiche, I cut myself a wedge off it amid the moans of contentment coming out of all of their mouths as they devoured theirs.

"Incredible, Cleo," Craig said. "You've done it again."

"We're so glad to have you back!" Dana chimed in. "We don't eat half this good without you."

I took a bite. It was delicious. I couldn't taste the green stuff specifically, which relieved me.

"Seriously, Cleo," I told her. "I worked for years at the Sunrise Café in Salem and their quiche never tasted anywhere near this good. You should sell it!"

She smiled. "Glad you like it. I enjoy cooking."

The conversation stopped as we stuffed ourselves, giving muffled groans of approval. After breakfast was over, Dana and Craig excused themselves and left Cleo and me to clean up.

"You know what you're doing in the greenhouse when you're finished up here, right?" Craig asked me.

"I got it," I assured him.

***

After breakfast, I returned to the greenhouse in my still-wet jeans. The temperature was noticeably warmer inside than it was before breakfast. Without Craig there stealing all my attention, I was able to look around at all the plants. A lot had changed in the week since I'd been inside. There were about twice as many filled trays on the shelves, and the plants were definitely bigger than before. *How incredible. They're just growing away in here while it rains and sleets outside.*

On my way back to my workstation, I brushed against a tray of what looked like grass. The smell of onions wafted upward. *Whoa!* I bent down and smelled it. It smelled like onions. *I'll be damned. Grass that smells like onions. Who knew?*

Hoping to impress Craig when he came back in, I quickly got to work on my trays. I did it exactly as he said, filling the trays and inserting the seeds one by one into the cells. It took a long time to fill a tray—200 cells in total.

The truck outside grinded to a start and took off down the gravel driveway. Dana and Cleo were off to town, and I was alone on the farm with Craig.

A few minutes later I heard the greenhouse door open and felt the blast of cold air outside come rushing in. It had really gotten warm in here. Craig immediately walked up and inspected my progress.

"Very nice," he said, nonchalantly removing his t-shirt.

Very nice, indeed, I thought. I tried to remain focused.

He took up position to my left and began the same job.

His speed was amazing. Before I finished my second tray, he had already seeded three and was onto his fourth. As I finished my second, I realized I had not labeled my first.

"What did you say goes on the label again?" I asked him.

He looked over at my two finished, unlabeled trays.

"Why didn't you label your first tray after you seeded it?" he asked sternly.

"I forgot," I shrugged. I felt his mood shift.

"Kelsie, I told you, I'm very particular about how I want things done."

A knot tightened in my gut. "I'm sorry," I said. "I know which one is which, though."

"Of course, you do," he snapped. "You've only done two. However, the seeds look so much the same that they're easy to mix up. If they get mislabeled during seeding, down the line we may plant them wrong and either waste space in the field spacing them too far apart, or plant them too close together to get a good crop."

"Oh, I see..." I started to apologize again.

"Take off your shirt, Kelsie," he interrupted me.

I gasped. *"What?"* I choked out. Regaining my voice, I countered, "You think you can just order me to undress and I'll do it?"

He took a hold of my shoulders and turned me around to face him. His eyes looked straight into mine and he said, "Yes. Take off your shirt. If I'm going to have to hold your hand through this process then I want to be able to look at those gorgeous breasts while I do it."

My nipples tightened furiously. *This cannot be happening.* But a warm, wet feeling welled up between my legs. Something about this man made me want to see where this could go.

I looked straight into his eyes and I could tell he would not hurt me, even if he were telling me what to do. I turned around and, with my back to him, slid my t-shirt up and over my head. I took a deep breath and turned slowly back around to my seeding station. I could feel his eyes all over me, but I did not turn to look back at him. My heart was pounding. I picked up the little stake of Cabbage seeds and started working on another tray. My hand was shaking as I directed the seeds one by one into the tiny holes. I could feel Craig watching me, watching all of me. It was so hot in the greenhouse that the sweat from my face was dripping onto my breasts.

I accidentally dropped two seeds into one of the holes. I kept going, hoping he wouldn't notice.

"Kelsie," he began.

"I'm sorry!" I exclaimed. "If you'd stop staring at me maybe I wouldn't make mistakes!"

"Take off your pants," he ordered.

"Craig," I pleaded, turning to face him. "No."

"Do it."

Between my head, my heart, and my cunt, I was throbbing so hard at this point that I could not see the cell trays in front of me. Unable to believe what I was doing, I unbuttoned my jeans and slid them over my ass and down to my ankles. I had not considered when I got dressed this morning that a man would be staring at my undergarments a few hours later, so I hadn't put much thought into my choice. I was relieved to see I did not have on a pair with a hole in the

crotch. Just simple white cotton, high cut, with a little lace ruffle along the top and bottom. I stepped out of my jeans and stood back up to face the counter.

Craig was breathing a little faster, too, I noticed.

We both went back to work. Even in my underwear, it was a lot easier to do the job without Craig just staring at me.

What would it be like to have that much power over a woman? Why did his power turn me on so much? Furthermore, how on earth does this hard little round red-brown seed make a cabbage? I didn't even know cabbage had *seeds. They must grow underground.* I made a label for my finished tray, "MAMMOTH RED ROCK CABBAGE: 2/26."

The fan kicked on and sent a cool breeze across my bare stomach. I glanced sideways at Craig, who was filling up trays at an incredible pace, and lining them up on the shelves on the other side of the greenhouse.

"Kelsie, bring your finished trays back here one at a time and I'll show you how we organize the greenhouse to keep track of everything."

"Ok, sure," I agreed, and then remembered I was almost naked.

Hell of a first day on the job, I thought.

I picked up my tray of cabbage and came around the corner with it, wearing only my work boots and my silly white lace undies. The 20-foot walk to the other end where Craig was standing felt like an eternity. He watched me intently the entire way with a little grin on his lips, his eyes consuming every part of me at once. As I approached him, I could not look into his eyes. Instead, my eyes looked down at the trays near his waist.

"Where do you want this?" I asked him.

I could feel him staring, but he didn't say anything.

I looked up. He was grinning. He obviously loved this power trip, too.

"Put it up here." He pointed to a high shelf on the other side of him, but did not move even an inch to let me pass.

Burning, I reached across him and over his head to place the tray on the top shelf, moving slowly so I wouldn't tip the tray and spill

the seeds. Who knows what would happen then? My arm brushed his right shoulder. My left breast brushed against his smooth, bare chest. I had to stand on tiptoe to reach the shelf from where I was standing, and Craig seemed to be enjoying every second of our awkward exchange. I came back down to earth, so to speak, and he continued his lesson on greenhouse organization as though nothing was out of the ordinary.

"Newly seeded flats go on these shelves, where the temperature can be controlled better. Many seeds require different temperatures to germinate than they do to grow," he added. "Peppers, for example, need temperatures of 70-90 degrees to germinate, but will grow at lower temperatures once they're up."

"After they've germinated, we move the flats to one of these other benches, depending on when we'll be transplanting them out. The first crops we seed are the *Alliums*—onions, shallots, and leeks—and then we begin with *Brassicas*, which is what we're doing now. We'll be starting our Solanaceae family plants—peppers, tomatoes, eggplants, et cetera—next week."

I nodded, trying to keep up. "So "*Brassica*" is the same thing as cabbage?" I asked, trying not to sound too dumb. In my underwear or not, I came here to learn something, and I was not going to let a little exposed flesh stop me from figuring out the secrets that made this world so sexy.

"Cabbage is one of the many *Brassicas*," Craig began. He seemed eager to share what he knew. "*Brassica* is the genus, the first part of the cabbage's Latin name, *Brassica oleracea*. Believe it or not, cabbage, cauliflower, broccoli, kale, collard greens, Brussels sprouts, and kohlrabi are all the same exact plant, or rather, they come from the exact same parent plants. All of them are the same genus and species."

"Broccoli and cauliflower and cabbage are the same thing?" I struggled to understand. I didn't even recognize some of the vegetables he just rattled off. "But they're *not* the same..."

"I know, I know," he interrupted. "They don't seem the same, but they all share a common ancestor—what we know today as the kale plant. Centuries ago, along the vast lineage of farmers, a guy here or there noticed a certain kale plant that got a flower like a tiny cauliflower

or broccoli or cabbage. They saved seeds off of that plant, growing it out each year and selecting for that trait in each succession, until a plant grown from that seed could reliably produce the same trait, like a bigger, fuller head of cauliflower or cabbage."

"Huh." I shook my head. There was so much I did not know about plants.

"It's amazing, isn't it," he said, his eyes gleaming. "Humans play at agriculture and after decades of hard work and diligent observation become co-creators with the earth. A human being can help to create something that millions of people all over the world enjoy without a second thought to how it got to their table, simply by agreeing to enter into a game played by nature's rules. Our work needs us as much as we need it."

I didn't know what to say.

"Let's finish up here," he interrupted his own reverie, possibly a little uneasy about having just shared such an intimate part of himself. "I believe you have some chicken eggs to attend to this afternoon."

***

After my steamy day in the greenhouse, the rain felt even colder as I made my way to the chicken coop to collect the eggs, my mind racing with what just happened. Oregon winters comprise a penetrating gray that invades bones and chills a person's insides far more than the snowy wonderlands to the east where temperatures are a dozen degrees colder. I stepped inside where the *chicas* all huddled up together in the house. It seems they didn't want to be outside in the rain either. *I don't blame you one bit.*

Away from Craig, my thoughts became my own again. I collected the eggs one by one out of their little straw circles, noting that even chickens make nests for their eggs. I guess they just pop them out and get back to whatever it is chickens do with their days, because the boxes were empty.

The girls watched me curiously, their heads cocked to the side. I noticed that their eyes are on the sides of their heads, which must mean they can't see directly in front of them. One *chica* rammed her beak into the metal container that held the food.

"Nice try," I told her. "You'll have to wait until morning."

That evening Cleo invited me to her trailer for dinner. Out of a desire to escape the looped playback of the events of my first steamy day on the job and the flood of bewildering self-reflection it unleashed on my brain, as well as my own inept cooking, I happily agreed. I threw on my rain jacket and sneakers—I would *have* to get muck boots—and trudged through the still pouring rain and barged in the door before I could soak another pair of jeans.

"Welcome to my lair," Cleo giggled, turning down the volume on her music as I took off my jacket. Her trailer was laid out much the same as mine, but with windows only on two walls over the bed area. The third had an additional bookshelf packed to the gills with books, CDs, stacks of papers, and a bread-loaf-size velvet figurine of a horse. Every inch of her walls was covered with some type of poster or painting or drawing. It looked like she'd lived in here for years.

"How long have you been here?" I asked her.

"This year, about a week. Why?"

"I don't know—your place looks so *lived in,"* I responded.

"It's the Cancer in me," she shrugged. "I need to have a cozy nest."

The girl in the punk rock band blaring from her stereo was screaming, "Lips! Tits! Hips!" A giant piece of fabric hung from her ceiling with a silk-screened image of a city in ruins with the caption, "LIFE is ecstatic intercourse between destruction and creation." A poster of topless women with Mohawks and electric guitars standing around a horse in a dirt barnyard covered her entire refrigerator. Postcards and photos covered every available inch of the tiny space.

Cleo pulled a bag from the bottom drawer of her refrigerator and began unpacking its contents. I recognized some of them from the bag in the bottom drawer of *my* fridge, and I crept up behind her to catch a glimpse of how she was going to handle them.

"I thought I'd roast these root veggies. Does that seem okay? How do you prefer them?" she asked, diving in without waiting to hear my response.

"Cleo, can I tell you something? I don't know what a single thing in that bag is, let alone how to use it." *There, I said it.*

Cleo smiled her cockeyed smile and shrugged. "Good thing you're here," she replied. "Don't worry. You'll learn quickly. I love to talk about food, in case you couldn't tell."

"This," she said, pointing to a purple and white globe-shaped one," is a turnip. Here's a rutabaga. See how it's yellower than the turnip? That's how you tell the difference, although they both have some purple in them. This long skinny one is a parsnip. In my opinion, it's a little early for parsnips. I like to dig them fresh in March and April, when they're sweetest and there isn't much else fresh to eat. They're like candy then."

"Huh," I replied. "I would have thought that was a sick carrot."

"Just wait 'till you try it," she twinkled, her wild hair bobbing with her nodding head. That hair was so incredible. Half of it looked curly, the other half looked straight. I couldn't tell if it was an inch long or a foot long, as most of it stuck straight out from her head in a dark mass that could either have been a joke a drunken friend played on her or an advertisement for a hip hair salon.

"I'm going to cut all these roots up into bite-sized chunks and toss them in salt-and-peppered olive oil with chopped onions and whole garlic cloves. Then we'll spread them out in a baking dish and roast them in the oven. You'll love it."

As I helped her chop the veggies, I continued to notice little trinkets and treasures tucked into every nook and cranny; a precarious stack of small, flat stones on top of the toaster oven; a snapshot of Cleo kissing a short-haired girl on the cheek, both of them with cans of beer in their hands and happy, swimming eyes.

"These are all your friends, in these photos?" I asked her.

"Yeah, I guess you could call them that," she said. "It's hard to outgrow people you used to be close with, you know? It's not that there's anything wrong with them, really. It's me that changed, or is changing, I guess."

"Uh-huh."

"What about you?" she asked. "What brings you here? Did you leave anybody behind?"

"Kind of the same, I guess," I replied, taking a seat and doodling on a piece of scrap paper. "I was dating a guy for a few years but we recently broke up. He was my longest LTR."

"LTR?"

"Long term relationship. That's what my friend Caroline calls them. Anyway, I've been living with him for the past year, but we sort of mutually decided we weren't into each other anymore. He was getting serious about his career path, and I think he thought I lacked the same ambition."

"Do you think you lack the same ambition?" she asked.

"Not really. I just haven't found anything I'm interested in learning about yet. I think that's why I wanted to come here. I've always had sort of a secret fascination with the young farmers I see at the farmer's market. They seem like they know something I don't."

Cleo sliced expertly through an onion, and the smell of it filled up the tiny trailer.

I went on. "Even just in the two days I've been here, I've already learned so much from Dana... and Craig." I hesitated. I hoped Cleo did not sense it. "There's so much to learn here. This might be the first time I've wanted to learn anything since high school." *What was I talking about?* "Or ever, really. I've never really felt interested in anything to speak of, except maybe art."

"I have the opposite problem," Cleo confessed. "I have so many different interests and I can't ever focus in on any of them for long enough to really get good at them."

"You're a really good cook," I noted.

"Yeah, but that's not a hobby or a career," she said. "That's a matter of life and death. We have to eat to live."

She tossed her veggies in a bowl of oil and spread them out on a baking dish.

"Let's go out and grab some collard greens before it gets too dark," she said, throwing on a pair of well-worn black muck boots with yellow spray paint slashed across them.

Collard Greens—a "Brassica!" I've learned something already!

I put on my jacket and followed her out the door into the rain, which had slowed down to a drizzle. I was curious where we would find food to harvest at this time of year, when everything seemed so dead.

Cleo's tiny stride quickened as she led us to the demo gardens and pointed at the huge silvery-green plants I had noticed on my tour with Dana. "There they are!" she squealed. "They stay lush all year long, even through the winter. You can eat collard greens in every month, if you take care to plant them at the right time. What an amazing vegetable you are!" she gushed as she snapped leaves off the bottom of the plant that were as big as her torso. "You harvest the leaves from the bottom first," she instructed me. "That will keep the plant growing up and up and up."

"Take a hold of the stem and snap it off," she instructed.

I hesitated.

"Just do it!" she said. "You won't hurt it!"

I grabbed hold and pushed down. The huge leaf snapped off in my hand. It was as easy as that.

"We only need a few, seeing as how they're so *voluptuous,*" she announced with pride. "Oh, and let's grab some green garlic. I saw it poking up over there."

We walked over to an otherwise bare patch where strappy, grass-looking leaves poked out of the ground about a fist-length.

"This is baby garlic hiding under here," she said, grabbing a blade of the grass-looking stuff and coaxing it out of the ground. Sure enough, a whiff of garlic filled my nose.

This really is magical. A mysterious world with garlic grass and onion grass, and we eat humongous leaves off a voluptuous collard green plant.

On our way back to the trailers, Cleo pointed out a patch of tall dried up stalks. "Jerusalem artichokes," she informed me. "Some people call them sun-choke, and they're the only vegetable I haven't been able to fall in love with. Yet."

"I'll get there someday," she assured herself, as we climbed back into the warmth of her trailer. A warm, savory smell filled the tiny cabin. She pulled the veggies out of the oven, turned them over in the pan with a spatula, and stuck them back in.

"Want a beer?" she asked. I nodded.

"I picked some up from town when we were there today. Didn't exactly point it out to Aunt Dana. It's not that she has a problem with it exactly, but I think she and Craig don't want to see the farm turn into a party place for the interns."

"I could see that," I agreed.

"Yeah, well, I don't want that either," Cleo stated. "That's what I left, and I don't want to bring it out here with me. Still, there's nothing wrong with a beer after a hard day of moving straw bales.

She handed me a bottle and began chopping up the green garlic we harvested. "I'll sauté this in a pan with a little oil, then throw the greens in and add some salt and pepper."

I took a seat on her couch-bed and perused the bookshelf. There were some of the same books that were in my trailer amid a bunch of others. Right in the middle, she had a whole collection of thin paperbacks entitled *Herotica*. Was that what I thought?

I casually took one off the shelf to read the back jacket, turning my back to her slightly so she wouldn't notice what I was looking at. *"Erotic short stories for women,"* the jacket said.

"Aren't those great?" she asked. I whipped around, trying to hide the book. "Uh, I don't know..." I said sheepishly. "I've, uh, never seen them before."

"Oh, I love them," Cleo gushed. "Written for women, by women. There's something for everyone in there. You should borrow one," she said, raising her eyebrows at me.

I giggled. "Yeah? I've never read porn before."

"It's not porn," she stated plainly. "It's erotica. There's a difference."

"I guess I'll find out," I said, putting one of the books by my jacket. My heart was pounding once again, though less than earlier with Craig. There was sex all over this place, and although I'd never really considered myself a prude, I was learning very quickly that there was a lot I did not know about it. Namely, what I liked and didn't like, what I wanted and didn't want. Here on this farm, in the middle of the country, I was feeling for the first time that it was really okay to ask myself that question.

"Dinner's ready," Cleo announced excitedly.

We sat down at her tiny table to our feast of roasted root veggies, sautéed collard greens and smuggled beer. The roots were buttery and delicious, and as nervous as I was about eating the collard greens, I found I actually liked them. We cleaned up and I thanked Cleo and headed back to my trailer to prepare for another early day.

***

My own trailer was cold. I hadn't turned the heat on while I was at Cleo's, so I cranked it up, hurriedly brushed my teeth, and jumped in between the chilly sheets and blankets. Lying there, the play by play of my afternoon in the greenhouse with Craig began rolling through my mind again, and I started to tingle and get butterflies for the dozenth time that day. My hand slid down between my legs and pushed the button of my clit. I replayed the scene again, from removing my jeans to walking in my boots and underwear to where Craig was standing to leaning over him to put the tray on the top shelf. I let myself imagine dropping the tray as I reached, seeing Craig's frustration grow and, with it, his desire to further expose me. He grabs my arms and my shoulders and shoves me against the shelves. He rips off my bra and looks hungrily at my breasts as they flap out. He grabs them firmly in his hands and bites down on my nipples, hard but not too hard. My hands trace the curves of his back and he pushes himself against me. I move my fingers faster over my clit, and then my mind shifts to Dana, to her capable hands, covered in dirt on the first day I met her. I picture her moving them over my belly, sliding them inside me. I think of Cleo and her mess of wild hair and the rooster pinning the hens down one by one and I tighten fully and release, throbbing as I spill the whole of my juices onto my now-warm sheets. *Not a bad start.*

4

The next afternoon, after a delicious lunch of wild rice and kale soup, I wandered back to my trailer and noticed Dana and two women climbing out of the trailer next to me.

"Kelsie," she called to me. "I want you to meet this season's other interns." She motioned to the taller woman a few years older than I, probably about 35, with shoulder-length dark hair and a lean but sturdy figure. It was obvious she knew how to work. Her being held the same inexplicably wise energy as Dana and the folks from the farmer's market. I liked her immediately. "Jessi Ramone came from back east, where she has worked on several farms, but wanted to come try her hand at Western Oregon growing." She smiled at her. "I wasn't sure we could teach her anything she doesn't know already, but she seems to think we've got something to offer, and we're glad to have someone with experience. She'll be a huge help to you novices." She motioned to the other, a petite girl with bouncing blonde curls. "Shantel is a fellow west-coaster. She's been living in California, and doesn't have much experience with farming. She is eager, like you, and I think she'll fit in well here. I'll leave you to get acquainted, and please do remember to collect the eggs this afternoon, Kelsie."

"Will do!" I nodded as she walked away.

"I'm so incredibly excited to be here!" Shantel exclaimed after Dana left. "I've wanted to learn how to be an organic farmer for so long!" Although she had never worked on a farm before, this girl exuded a confidence that did not match her lack of experience. "Still," she continued, "I can't believe we'll be spending our summer sleeping in trailers."

Defensiveness welled up inside me as I thought about how much I loved my trailer and all its cozy idiosyncrasies. "Yeah," I mused. "I guess it's the best they can do."

"I sure hope it's worth it," she retorted. "I took a season off from my massage job at a Monterey resort to come out here and learn how to grow vegetables—oh, hi!"

I turned to see Cleo walking toward us. Shantel bounded up to her with a huge grin on her face and stuck out her hand.

"I'm Shantel. I'm from Santa Barbara."

"Cleo," Cleo said flatly. I could tell she wasn't feeling friendly. Maybe she had overheard the conversation about the trailers.

"Kelsie, could you give me a hand with these last couple of loads?" Shantel asked, batting her long eyelashes at me.

"Uh, I guess so," I replied, following her back out to her car, trying not to think about how she was a massage therapist. I had mistrusted them ever since my second boyfriend cheated on me with a massage therapist only a couple weeks after we had moved to California together. She handed me a box with paisley wallpaper covering it, and grabbed a matching one for herself to carry, rolling a lime green suitcase behind her through the mud as she headed back through the demo beds to her trailer.

***

It was Tuesday, the day of Dana's monthly workshop on deepening your sensual connection to the earth. Cleo offered to make dinner for the four of us. It wasn't raining, but it was still chilly outside as I made my way over to her trailer and barged in the door. A sweet and savory smell overpowered me before I even stepped all the way inside. Jessi was already there, chopping up the ever-present kale and collard greens. Even the addition of one extra person pushed the overfull trailer to the point of bursting.

"Welcome to Summer-In-Winter, Kelsie!" Cleo squealed as I squeezed past her and threw my coat into her bathroom. A surfer punk band with a female lead recklessly leapt from the stereo in the background. When I turned back around, Cleo was holding a large necklace out to me. "It's a lei! I made it from old magazines and newspapers Dana had in her recycle box." She placed it over my head as if welcoming me into a secret club. I noticed Jessi was already wearing one. "We're having sweet and sour chicken with gingered rice, and *this* for dessert!" She lofted a small, whole pineapple triumphantly into the air like a trophy.

"I couldn't help it. I splurged!" She seemed at once delighted and ashamed. "It came from Mexico," she said, "but it's organic...I'm getting so tired of greens and root veggies...I can't *wait* for the fruit to come!"

"What kinds of fruit do y'all grow here?" Jessi asked.

"Berries are the real specialty in Oregon," Cleo began. "Raspberries, strawberries, gooseberries, marionberries, blueberries, you name it. We also have a small orchard on the farm with a couple of apricots, pears, apples, peaches, nectarines, Asian pears, cherries, and plums. In fact, I made this sweet and sour sauce last year from our apples and peaches, along with a bunch of other stuff."

"Cool," Jessi said. "Canning is one thing I've never gotten into. You'll have to teach me when the time comes."

"Sure, I'd love to," Cleo said. "It can get real tedious and lonely when you're doing it by yourself. The more hands the better at canning time."

"I'd like to help out, too," I butted in.

Cleo smiled. "Yeah! We'll can the shit out of the farm this summer!" Her lei had somehow lodged itself in the spiky part of her hair, giving her a slightly disheveled look.

She grabbed a bottle of red wine out of her cupboard and uncorked it.

"I always like to have a little wine in me when I attend Aunt Dana's workshops," she said with a laugh. "Connecting with Luscious

Earth and the Magic Presence is easier when you're a couple glasses down."

A knock came at the door. "Hello?"

"Come in!" Cleo yelled, though the door was an arm's reach away and a normal voice probably would have been audible from outside.

Shantel stepped into the trailer, trailing perfume. I thought it smelled wonderful. Cleo coughed. The little house on wheels bulged at the seams with all of us crammed in there.

"Sorry I'm late!" Shantel continued. "I had to figure out the bathtub. Pretty nice, once you get the hang of it."

"You needed a bath already?" Cleo asked her. "You haven't done any work yet!"

"Yeah, well, I like to freshen up after a day of driving, don't you?" she asked.

"Sure, sure," I answered, jumping headfirst into the obviously tense conversation. At the same time, Cleo retorted, "not really." Shantel did not seem to notice any tension, and continued chattering about her long drive and how much colder and grayer it is here than in Santa Barbara.

"This is nothing," Jessi shared, pouring herself a glass of wine. "It was 10 below in Massachusetts the day I left."

I shuddered. "I hate being cold," I said. I helped myself to a glass. Soon we were all packed around Cleo's tiny table, sipping wine. Cleo threw a lei at Shantel. "Welcome to summer in winter," she said unconvincingly.

Her mood brightened when she pulled the chicken from the oven, beaming at it as though it was her first born. She set it dramatically between us on the table. We ooh-ed and ahh-ed appropriately, and dug in. It was delicious.

"Man, Cleo, I feel like I hit the jackpot!" Jessi commented.

Cleo blushed a little.

Shantel chimed in, "Yeah, Cleo. It's really scrumptious!"

"Mmm-hmm," I nodded with a mouth full of food.

***

After dinner, we headed for the barn. I hadn't actually been inside the main part of the barn yet, and as we entered, I was shocked to see how huge it was. A web of dark boards climbed high into the air, crisscrossing in intricate angles to an arch in the center. It felt like a cathedral. The rich smell of old wood and the expanse of ceiling far above made me feel at once intimidated and protected.

Cleo led the way to a staircase at the far end, past a tractor and various implements, climbing up to a partitioned room about halfway between the ceiling and the floor.

I trailed along behind them, gawking at the ceiling and finally followed Shantel's tight little butt as it wagged pertly up the stairs with a pang of jealousy as my own thighs rubbed at the jeans between them.

Cleo opened the door and, one by one, we followed her into the workshop. The stout lacework of the barn roof loomed closer now, and the scent of the wood filled me.

The warmth wafted out into the chilly barn as Dana welcomed us inside.

"Welcome, Women!" she greeted us, taking each of our hands briefly in both of hers.

"Did you two get settled in okay?" she asked Jessi and Shantel.

They nodded and I took the opportunity to glance around. A few other workshop attendees had already arrived and were seated on the jewel-toned rug in the middle of the floor. Dana had decorated the space with a variety of dried flowers in gorgeous vases. An enormous wood and metal sculpture of a female with one foot planted in the ground and the other leg reaching for the sky covered one wall. Candles of all sizes and shapes lined the various tables and ledges around the room, casting licking shadows onto the walls. A huge stack of pumpkins occupied one corner.

This incredibly visceral space was already awakening my "sensual connection to the earth," and it terrified me. I glanced nervously around to see if I had some solidarity among my new comrades, but all seemed to be enthusiastically soaking in the scene. I thought I saw a brief flint of something in Jessi's eyes, but when she saw me looking at her, I realized I was much worse off. She patted me on the back gently and said smiling, half-laughing, "Relax, Kelsie. This isn't gonna kill ya."

She kneeled to the floor and patted the ground beside her. Grateful for her invitation, I scrambled into position to her left in the great circle. Cleo and Shantel had already joined, about as far away from each other as they could get. By this time around twenty people of varying ages filled it in, mostly women. Several had long, silver hair and wrinkled faces and hands. A group of 20-something women sat together, leaning familiarly on each other as they chatted and laughed. Some folks sat still with their eyes closed and their palms turned up on their knees.

"I think we'll get started," Dana began, sealing the door back up against the chilly air outside in the barn. She stood to the side of the circle, her long hair flowing over her strong, bare shoulders and slender torso. She wore a gray, knee-length cotton dress that clung to her incredible body.

"Welcome to all of you, and a special welcome to this year's White Oak Farm apprentices." She nodded at all of us. "They are a capable group of women, and we're incredibly thankful to have them."

Me, capable? Flattered, my face flushed and I shifted uncomfortably on the floor.

"Tonight, our workshop activity will be to harvest the winter squash seeds that will grow our crop this year."

That did not sound so bad.

"Native Americans will wait several months before breaking open the squashes they intend to save seed from, as a way to prepare the seeds for planting."

Glancing at all of us individually as she spoke, drawing us in, she continued, "Many plants that have seeds that grow inside a fruit, like tomatoes, melons, cucumbers, and squashes, make a gelatinous sack around each seed to protect it from sprouting inside its warm, wet fruit of a mother. When the fruit begins to rot, various species of fungi and bacteria eat the gel coat around the seed so it can go forth, swell, and burst open when water is added!" She spread her hands wide into the air. I tried to follow her passionate explanation as best I could.

"By leaving the squash seeds inside the squash as it begins to rot, the sac is broken down. Now, we must remove the seeds before they start to grow inside their mother."

With a twinkle in her deep brown eyes, she said, "That's where we get to have our fun. I figured there's no sense in hogging this pleasurable job for myself. Thus, all of you will be helping us collect our seed. So thank you."

The group smiled.

"What I'd like you to do," she continued, "Is to pick a squash that calls to you. You will engage in seed removal with it. Then, return to your seat on the floor, removing any clothing that will separate your legs from the flesh of the squash as you place it in your lap."

I panicked, whipping my head around toward Jessi. *"WHAT?"* I rasped to her, my heart thumping. She shot me a humongous smile and laughed as she pulled me to my shaking feet. "You can do it, Kelsie," she chuckled.

A nervous excitement electrified the air as the group made its way to and from the pile of squash. *So now, Dana was ordering me to take off my pants? In front of 20 other people, no less! I cannot believe this is happening!* I wailed to myself. Several younger women were laughing as they unearthed especially odd-shaped specimens and thrust them toward each other. "He's calling to you!" one said to the other.

The older women quietly gathered their specimens and causally rolled their long dresses to their hips as they eased themselves back onto the floor, exposing weathered thighs. They smiled knowingly at each other.

Most people remained in their own private worlds, looking at the ground as they teetered on one leg to remove pants and shoes, some serious and some smiling. I was totally mortified, but I couldn't leave now. Dana would be so disappointed!

I hurriedly grabbed a red-orange, lumpy squash about the size of a basketball.

"That one's a sweet meat," Dana smiled at me as I hurried back through the litter of pants and shoes, unsure of where to put my eyes. I slid my jeans off and plopped down quick, placing them and my shoes within easy reach behind me.

Dana walked around the circle, handing each of us a large knife and a bowl to hold our seeds. I watched the muscles in her calves taut and slack as she stepped, finally taking her place in the circle, lifting her thin dress up to her hipbones, exposing lacy black underwear as she slid down and wrapped her legs around a giant, slate-blue pumpkin.

She wrapped her arms around it, too, and gave it a squeeze, her eyes lit up like the candles on the walls.

"We'll begin by opening our mother fruits." She stabbed her knife into the top. "Surely you all are familiar with this from jack-o-lantern making. Just jump on in and get to work!"

I grabbed my knife and plunged it into my "sweet meat." It was softer than I imagined and I was able to make my way around it without too much trouble. The knife jabbing so close to my bare leg sent tingles into my clit, and the rough skin of the squash rocking against the sharp blade as I cut did not hurt either.

Breathing heavier now, I finished the cut circle and pulled up on the scratchy umbilical cord that had linked my squash to its mother plant. Seeds dangled from the sinewy flesh.

"You can guess what's coming next," Dana continued, grinning. "Be careful to keep the seeds from your own squash in your own bowl. Do not mix them with any other seeds. We want to keep the varieties separate and pure, so we keep all the strains alive and viable. Diversity is a vital component of food security."

Her tone shifted. "I purposely didn't give you any utensils to remove the seeds from your mother fruit. This is so you can connect your body to this sacred act. Use your hands, and as you remove your seeds, pay special attention to the smells and textures, the way they feel on your fingers and on any other exposed flesh." She sparkled out a mischievous smile.

"Inside the womb of your incredible mother squash resides hundreds of seeds, each of which could grow a plant that could produce dozens more fruits that each contain hundreds more seeds, and on and on." I glanced sideways at Jessi. She stared rapturously at Dana as she spoke. I pushed up my sleeves and plunged one hand into the pulpy abyss of my mother squash. The pulp oozed between my fingers and thumb as I brought a handful of seeds to the surface and placed them carefully in my bowl.

"A seed is the lush essence of abundance," Dana continued, her sultry voice muffled slightly as she reached into her enormous blue squash with both hands and extracted handful after handful of huge seeds. "It contains all ingredients necessary to sustain life, once you add water. Like women's wombs that explode to spark to life our species, the wombs of these squash nurture future life, life that in turn feeds us and keeps us alive! This abundant process connects us to generations of humans who also have carefully kept the different squash species going year after year. It's what connects us to the earth itself and to the Magic Presence that creates it daily."

I slid my other hand into the cavern of the fruit, as Dana was doing, and though I felt shy, it was fun. I don't know if I was sensually connecting or not, but I sure did feel more free, like a little girl who ran around topless without a thought to who might see her.

Dana went on, "In these workshops, we call it the Magic Presence, but you can call it God or whatever else speaks to you. We are the flesh of the divine. We take in the flesh of the earth, and the cycle continues as it has and will, beyond our imagination's capability."

"Amen, Aunt Dana!" Cleo blurted out across the room. She had orange squash flesh up over her elbows, smeared all down her black-clad front and over her legs. I noticed one of her legs was completely tattooed from the knee down, foot and everything. She seemed to be thoroughly enjoying herself.

I had been avoiding looking at the men in the group but as I removed the slimy seeds from their birthplace, my curiosity got the better of me and I glanced up to examine my counterparts. The men seemed to be shyly enjoying themselves, too.

Dana got to her feet and globs of squash flesh tumbled down her thighs and onto the floor. She grinned, wiping her hands on her bare legs as well. "Once you've extracted your seeds, let me know and I'll come around with a label for you to stick on your bowl with the name of your squash. As you leave tonight, please carry your now-emptied mother squash downstairs and place her in the chicken yard if you do not wish to take her home to eat. Consider thanking her for the hundreds of life-giving seeds she produced, and for her allowing you to help her disseminate them. The *chicas* will greatly appreciate your gift when they awake tomorrow morning also. For tonight, please leave with my gratitude for your help with this process, and for your willingness to put your inhibitions aside to come and connect with each other and with the sacred sensuality of the earth. It is by our loving, connected energy that we create the kind of world that we want to live in."

One by one, the participants slid stiff pants and shoes over their now slimy legs and sloshed down the stairs with their mother squashes in hand. I rushed to finish and hurriedly threw my jeans back on, still shy at the prospect of others seeing my naked, white thighs. Cleo, on the other hand, seemed in no rush to get dressed, sauntering around the room in her black boy cuts, peering into everyone's squashes to examine their process. She squatted next to Jessi, just finishing hers.

"What's that one again?" she asked.

"Hubbard," Jessi and Dana answered in unison. They smiled at each other.

"Right, Hubbard." Cleo echoed. "They make great enchiladas."

"Squash enchiladas?" I asked her.

"Oh yeah! They're amazing!" she cooed. "I know what we're having for tomorrow's lunch!" She glanced at Jessi, who nodded excitedly.

"Sounds good to me," she said.

I looked across the room at Shantel as she was standing to put her jeans back on. She was so small, with a perfect little figure. She wobbled on one leg as she slid her tight jeans up over her red lace panties. I wondered if she had been a cheerleader in high school. She walked over to join us, and Cleo rolled her eyes at me as she went to collect her pants and boots.

"Well, that was amazing, huh?" Shantel asked as she approached. We nodded as she went on. "I never knew all that stuff before, but it makes sense. The seeds in a squash would grow more squash plants. It's so simple, but I hadn't ever thought about it!"

"You ladies ready?" Cleo butted in.

We nodded. "Cleo, aren't you going to put your pants back on?" I asked her.

"Nah," she replied. "I'll just walk back to the trailer in my boots. It's kind of nice to be half-naked outside in the winter, eh?"

"Whatever, Crazy." I shook my head. "You're a braver woman than I."

"Thanks for coming, ladies!" Dana called to us as she crossed the room to say good-bye. She gave each of us a long, heartfelt hug. "Cleo, you going pantsless for the evening?"

Cleo nodded, and Dana grinned. "That's my niece," she said, rumpling her hair. Cleo pulled her head away with playful exasperation. "Take care of yourselves tonight," she said. "Do breakfast on your own, and meet me at 9 near the greenhouses, okay?"

"Thanks, Dana," we nodded as we gathered our mother squashes and lugged them down the stairs.

With every step I took, the squash flesh that stuck to my thighs squished and slurped against my pant leg. Cleo's skinny, stark white legs bounded along in front of us, her muck boots covering up all but the top of the massive tattoo on her right calf. The part I could see was unmistakably a collard green leaf. "Sorry I doubted you, Cleo!" I called after her. "I think you have the right idea tonight! My jeans are covered in squash slime!"

Jessi laughed. "Mine, too!"

"You know, I bet the water in the tub is a little bit hot still, from my soak earlier. It wouldn't take long to heat it back up again," Shantel chimed in.

I smiled as we passed by the collard green plants, immortalized on Cleo's calf, braving out the winter, waiting for sunny weather. The chill of the evening seemed less intense than it had been the past several days.

"I wouldn't mind cleaning up before bed," Jessi said, "especially if we make it an early night. I want to be rested for work in the morning. Can all of us fit in there?" she asked Shantel.

"We've fit 6 people in there before," Cleo asserted. "I'm not saying' I'd want to do that again, but I'm saying' it's possible. Four's no problem."

"I'm in, then," she replied.

"Me too!" Shantel and I answered in unison. I felt relieved. I had not tried to tackle the tub yet, and I was starting to smell like it. I was glad to have someone else show me how to do it.

While Cleo ran ahead to her trailer, the rest of us crammed into the bathhouse, which was surprisingly warm. A shelf underneath a deep, round, wooden tub held the remnants of a fire, red outlines of logs that crumbled to ash when Shantel put another log on.

"So, you build a fire under here," she told Jessi and me importantly, "and it heats up the water above." She felt the water with her hand. "It's pretty warm now, almost exactly body temperature, and it didn't take long earlier to get it hotter, so we'll probably only have to wait a few minutes, if at all." She threw a few more large logs on the fire. Through the window you could see the woods behind our trailers, the stars visible above the jagged tops of the trees.

"Looks like it's clearing up," Jessi observed.

A possible warm-ish day of work on the farm? I wouldn't know what to do with myself.

"I hope so," I retorted. "I swear I've been drenched ever since I got here."

Cleo burst in the door then, with an open bottle of wine in her hand. Without warning, she stripped totally naked and climbed up onto the platform to enter the tub. I watched a small streak of pale white, haphazardly tattooed flesh sink into the water. She raised the bottle above her head as she sank, head and all, under the water. Bubbles broke the surface, and she slid back up again, coming to rest with only her head and shoulders above the water line.

"Feels great!" she declared. The water tamed her wild hair into a choppy bob, with several longer chunks clinging to her collarbones. "Not quite hot enough, but I'm still a little warm from the barn. It was sweltering in there!"

Oh, Lord, I fretted. *Here we go again, damn it!*

Jessi followed suit, stripping off her squishy jeans and snap-button plaid shirt and climbing in to join Cleo. She had a muscular build and small, perky breasts. I noticed a patch of dark hair under her arms as she slid into the tub. Both women seemed completely comfortable getting naked in front of strangers.

Flashbacks of gym class invaded my mind, trying to sneak in to shower before anyone else was off the field so I could avoid being seen by the other girls. I hated situations like these. One of my best friends in high school's parents had a hot tub at their house, which automatically nominated her place for parties whenever her parents went out of town. I both dreaded and looked forward to those parties. Growing up in a "don't ask, don't tell" family, my parents never had "The Talk" with me. Instead, they shifted the responsibility to the public school system to educate their daughter about bodily changes and the mortal dangers of intercourse. These parties, more than anything else, taught me the ropes about male-female relations and the woes and ahhs associated with different body types. My tiny friends wanted to be curvy like me, me and my big, curvy friends wanted to be tiny, and on and on. I preferred to hang out in the house by the stereo, nursing a beer with any other uncomfortable partygoers, than to get right into the action in the hot tub, though I would sneak a peak at others when they entered and exited it, trying to figure out where I fit. Occasionally, when I'd had enough to drink, I would join them in the tub, amid a raft of unsolicited comments about the size of my breasts, from both the guys and the girls.

Snapping back to my present reality, I glanced over at Shantel, who had removed her shirt and seemed to be posing for a fashion magazine, her legs offset and one hip in the air. Her breasts swelled over a red lace bra and her tiny, smooth stomach curved into bell-shaped hips as she leaned forward and slid off only her jeans, rising up to look like a damned Victoria's Secret model. She had an amazing body, and she knew it. She wanted me—or us—to know it, too.

Fuck it. I tore off my sweater and jeans and splashed into the water with Cleo and Jessi, who were taking turns swigging off the bottle of wine.

"Would you like some?" Cleo asked.

"Don't mind if I do. It'll ease my discomfort about this whole situation," I told them, grabbing the bottle.

Cleo dismissed that with a wave of her thin wrist. "We've all got the same shit underneath," she said.

I nodded. Shantel was now making a slow show of sliding her bra and panties off and I heard a small guffaw from Cleo. Finally undressed, she sauntered up the stairs and sunk into the now-hot water. There we were, the White Oak Farm crew, naked in the hot tub together. My leg brushed up against someone else's and I jerked it back, hitting another.

"Cleo, can I have another swig of wine, please?" I asked her.

She handed over the bottle.

"So how long have you been farming, Cleo?" Jessi asked her.

"Three years. But I don't think I'd be ready to do it on my own yet," she replied.

"Yeah, I've been farming for 6 years, and I'm just now getting to the point where I feel I'm ready." Jessi offered. "There's so much to it, so much to keep track of and learn and know."

"I know!" I butted in. "I've been here for 3 days and I swear my head is packed full of stuff already! I don't know how I'll make it through the season."

"You'll make it," Cleo grinned at me. "Think how far you've come already! You didn't even know what collard greens or turnips were a week ago!"

Nor did I know I'd be undressing in front of my new bosses. Or my coworkers.

"I'm so excited to learn from Dana and Craig," Jessi said. "They're widely-respected farmers. One of the farmers I worked for back East knows them, and says I will learn a lot from both of them. That they have a very unique approach."

"I'd say that squash seed thing tonight was pretty unique," I giggled.

We all laughed together. "Yeah, Aunt Dana really knows how to engage people," said Cleo. "Folks drive for hours to attend her workshops."

The wine and the hot water were making my head fuzzy.

"Cleo, does Dana have a boyfriend?" I asked her, immediately questioning my boldness. Cleo seemed undaunted.

"Two or three, I think," she giggled. "There are a couple men I've noticed come out a few times a month and their trucks don't leave until the next morning. One calls her *Dana Reina*, Queen Dana. Plus, I think she sometimes helps out the folks who rent out the cabins, if you know what I mean."

"Really?" I asked, shifting a bit on the slippery bench and passing the bottle to Shantel, who took it eagerly. The water felt so soothing on my body.

"Yeah, she's got some pretty strong ideas about relationships, as you might imagine. She says her love is too great for one person. I think it caused some problems between her and Craig early on."

My heart thumped in my chest. "So they *did* date, huh?"

"They dated for awhile after they met in Canada. The way Aunt Dana says it is that Craig can't walk his talk, which I think means he's fine with himself having lots of lovers but not with Aunt Dana doing the same."

"So they're polyamorous?" Jessi asked.

I hadn't ever heard that word, but I could guess what it meant.

"In their own ways, yeah, they are, but their relationship with each other has evolved to more of a familial one. This year continues the tradition of the all-female apprentice crew, which I'm pretty certain plays into Craig's version of polyamory."

My face must have turned the color of the wine in the bottle Shantel was slugging next to me. I could feel the blood pounding in my cheeks so hard I was certain my eyes must be bulging in time with my heart throbbing. I had to change the subject, lest I explode.

"So, Shantel, why did you want to come here?" I asked her.

"Oh, gosh," she began. "Through my massage I've been learning more about holistic healing and nutrition, and I see food as *so* important to the mind-body connection."

Cleo coughed. I thought she was being a little hard on Shantel.

After all, they both shared a love of the food. But what did I know?

"Plus, Craig is so incredibly hot!" She added with a gleam in her eye.

Maybe I would take that back.

"I mean, don't you think?" she asked, looking around at each of us.

I squirmed uncomfortably in my seat. *Would it be too awkward if I just got out and left? I could say I had to pee...*

"No offense, but he's kind of like my uncle." Cleo said. "So no, I don't think he's hot. Besides, I've never really been into men anyway."

"Me, either," Jessi replied. "Well, not recently anyway."

I saw Cleo's mood brighten a bit. She looked sideways at Jessi for a brief second before grabbing the wine bottle from Shantel and taking a nonchalant swig.

That declaration from the other half of the hot tub seemed to disrupt Shantel's thought process a bit, thankfully. However, it also changed the mood in the tub a little.

"Well, I don't know about you ladies, but I'm pretty tired after a long, long day, and I'd like to turn in." Jessi said. "It's weird to think how I woke up this morning on the east coast!" She pulled herself out of the tub and dried herself off with her shirt. "Air travel is crazy like that," she mused.

"Good night! I look forward to working with y'all," she called as she lit out into the night toward her trailer lugging her squash, the cool air wafting into the steamy bathhouse. Cleo made her way to her feet, too, and I quickly followed, not wanting to be stuck with Shantel in a conversation about how cute Craig was. Without drying off, I grabbed my clothes and my squash, mumbled a quick good-bye, and practically sprinted toward the safety of my trailer. The lights were on in the one next to me, which I was relieved to see. *That must be Jessi's trailer, then. Good.*

***

The next morning, after I cooked myself a breakfast of eggs scrambled with greens like Cleo had shown me, I made my way toward the greenhouses, per Dana's instructions. The sun shone bright and the air was actually a bit warm. I noticed a small yellow flower near the ground on the edge of the path among the demo beds as I walked through, breathing in the sunshine. Jessi was already there with Dana, and they both waved as I approached.

"Beautiful day, huh?" Dana greeted me.

I nodded. "I saw a little yellow flower on the path back there," I reported.

"A crocus," Jessi nodded. "I saw it, too.

"The first crocus!" Dana beamed. "Spring is finally here! That seals the deal. I was debating about what to do today, but now I know."

Cleo and Shantel arrived then, arriving together but not speaking to each other.

"Did you see the crocus?" Cleo asked us.

We nodded.

"I missed it!" Shantel exclaimed. "Is that a flower?"

"Uh, *yeah,"* Cleo said with a hint of condescension in her voice. "It was on the path back there, a little yellow one. You'll notice it when you go back."

"Don't worry Shantel," Dana assured her. "It's not going anywhere! Spring has sprung!" So, today I want to open up the farm's beehives and see how they fared during the winter. You have to wait until it's a warm day to open them so they don't get too cold, and this seems like the perfect day to do so!"

Dana went on, "Shantel, since you're allergic to bees, I'll have you seed with Craig in the greenhouse—"

My heart sank.

"—that way, you'll get experience with that aspect of our production system. Go on inside and Craig will you set up."

Shantel looked delighted, bounding off toward the door of the greenhouse, where I could see Craig's blurry figure moving around.

"The rest of you ladies follow me, and we'll get suited up to work the hives."

"This is great, Dana," Jessi started. "I've wanted to work with bees for years!"

"How about you, Kelsie?" Dana asked. "Do you have an interest in bees?"

"Yeah, I guess you could say that." I began, trying to hide my disappointment about Shantel going into the greenhouse. "When I worked at a soda cart during the fair, there was a hive of bees in the tree above us, and they, of course, wanted the soda. All weekend we dealt with hundreds of them all over the cart, flying up into the fountainheads and going for any little drop that spilled on the counter. I was amazed at how well I could move among them, and how slow and deliberate they made my movements. I've thought about them ever since, though not in a beekeeping sense." I pulled at the neck of my shirt, which felt suddenly tight, my eyes darting over toward the greenhouse where Shantel was now talking with Craig. "I didn't get stung once all weekend," I concluded.

"Excellent," she responded with a smile. "Maybe you'll find your calling as a 'bee whisperer.' Cleo, will you light the smoker while I get these gals suited up?" she asked as we approached the barn.

Cleo nodded, grabbing a white suit and netted hat off the shelf, along with a small canister that looked like a lantern with an accordion attached to the back. "I'll meet you outside."

"You'll need a veil at least, and I'll put you both in a full suit your first time, so you feel very comfortable around the bees. She handed us each a pair of white coveralls covered with honey-colored splotches, a netted hood, and a pair of long, white leather gloves.

"Beekeepers wear light-colored clothing so they don't seem like bears or other dark-colored animals that might want the honey," she told us.

We suited up and approached the stacks of white boxes as the sun crept upward in the sky. I counted 15 stacks in all.

"We'll start at one end and move down the row, opening each hive and examining their food supply, the state of their queen, and any other details. This is a superb way to be introduced to beekeeping. You'll get exposure to all sorts of scenarios. You never know how a hive will overwinter, no matter how strong they were going into it."

I looked over toward the greenhouse for some sign of what was going on inside, but I couldn't really see anything. *What if he's already got her shirt off and she's standing there looking all sexy in that red lacy bra...he'll never want me to help him again...and that girl knows how to work what she's got. She will have him right where she wants him in no time, I bet!*

"Kelsie?" Dana was looking at me.

"Oh, sorry. What?"

"Would you mind recording what we see in this notebook?

Flustered, I grabbed it from her. "Uh, sure. Sorry."

"Don't worry," she smiled. "I'll tell you what to write down."

Dana took hold of the smoker that Cleo had lit and cautioned us to put down our veils as we approached the first hive. I could see bees flying in and out of the bottom box, landing on a little lip just outside it as they came back from wherever they were off exploring.

"They're out looking for food," Dana told us. "They've been living off stored honey and pollen all winter and, on warmer days, some valiant scouts venture out to look for early blooming flowers to gather nectar and pollen. They must be careful to return before it gets too chilly again, as bees cannot really fly when temperatures get too low. The poor scouts could get stuck far away from the hive if the temperature dropped, unable to return, and they would surely die."

"It also might interest you to know," she added, "that all the worker bees are female. The females essentially run the hive, doing all the gathering, processing, storing, cleaning, building, guarding, and attending to the queen. The males are only around for the chance to mate with a queen."

Dana lifted the lid on the closest hive, glancing at each of us to make sure our veil was in place. An ominous buzz emanated from the hive, alive with unmistakable electricity, as Dana lifted the second cover. Several bees took flight, many in our general direction, moving clumsily as though their wings or legs were asleep. Below them, hundreds of bees poured over and under each other as they moved in a mass on the top of a row of narrow, wooden slats. Each worked diligently, yet together they appeared as more of an organic unit, like taffy oozing over the surface and into and out of the cracks. They seemed held together by glue, so familiar with each other that it seemed they could not identify themselves as separate from their sisters next to them.

"They're really all females?" I asked.

"Yup, every one of them you see here," Dana replied. "There are probably some males down inside, but they raise very few at this time of year. In a few weeks, we'll start to see more drones."

"Drones?" Jessi asked. "The males are called drones?"

Dana smiled and winked at us. "The males in the world of *Apis mellifera* are good for one thing and one thing only."

She pried a frame loose from the top and lifted it up to examine it. She did not wear gloves, and the bees crawled over her fingers and hands as she worked. She held it up for us to see. Intricate, delicate hexagons covered the entire thing, from edge to edge. Some were built like a sandcastle on the top side of the frame.

"Still plenty of honey in here," Dana noted, pointing out the wax-capped cells still sealed shut.

"Try some," she motioned to us.

Cleo reached out her bare hand and pushed gently on a spot in the top corner. The thin wax broke and golden honey oozed from the indentation of her finger. She brought it to her lips and sucked it gently off her finger, closing her dark eyes in sheer ecstasy.

"Mmm, thank you ladies," she said.

Jessi reached down with her gloved hand, but Dana stopped her.

"They're very calm today, so why don't you remove your gloves. It's best to get used to working without them, if you can."

Jessi obliged, poking at a spot next to where Cleo had ruptured their paper-thin fortress. "I feel bad at wrecking what they obviously worked hard to create."

"Don't worry," Dana said. "They'll have it repaired almost before we're out of the hive. Your turn, Kelsie," she smiled at me.

I removed my glove and reached down into the mass of bees that swarmed the surface of the frame frantically collecting the few drops of honey that spilled out from the intruding finger's invasion. The smooth wax gave way easily as I punctured their stores again. A gentle breeze waved across my finger, caused by the buzzing of hundreds of tiny wings. Almost before I removed my fingertip of honey, bees swarmed over the dent I had created, patching up their perfectly symmetrical storage containers.

"They're so orderly," I breathed.

"Neat and tidy and orderly. That is the way of honeybees." Dana agreed. "Every bee has a job to do, every bee knows her job, and every bee does her job. Nobody is left out of the work of the hive."

Dana leaned the frame beside the hive gently, allowing the bees spilling over the bottom of it to move out of the way before they're squished. She moved very slowly, very deliberately, picking up frame after frame and examining it. In the center of the box, she pulled out a frame whose hexagonal cells had a lumpier, browner covering. "Capped brood," Dana said under her breath. She held it out for us to see.

"The queen has started laying already here," she told us. "Inside these cells lie little bee larva, spinning themselves into cocoons to emerge as adult bees. This is a healthy hive." We'll give them a little supplemental food to hold them over until the nectar flows."

She placed the frame gently back into the hive and picked up a filled glass jug, walking a few steps away from the hive to shake it vigorously. "Sugar water," she said matter-of-factly as she filled a mason jar with the thick, clear liquid. She placed the overturned jar on a little tray and slid it against the entrance of the hive. One by one, she loaded all the frames back into the top box, gently brushing dozens and dozens of bees aside as she worked. Once it was all put back together, she replaced the two covers and we moved onto the next box.

"Kelsie, record that hive number 1 has a healthy queen and a good amount of food stores left. In all, it's a very healthy hive."

A loud crash came from the greenhouse just then. Dana glanced over with a mild curiosity, but quickly moved along to the next hive. What was that? My sweaty palms struggled to grip the pen as my mind raced out of my control. *Are they doing it in there? Did she just drop something? What will he do to her then?*

"Kelsie!" Dana snapped.

"Huh?"

"Are you able to do this job or not?"

"Oh. Yeah. I'm sorry, Dana. I—I—just thought I heard something in the greenhouse, that's all. I hope everything is all right in there," I added quickly.

"You can go check if it's really a concern to you," she offered, eyebrows raised.

Was she seeing through me? The thoughts of what I might walk in on were too much, even though I was dying to know. "No, that's okay," I stammered quickly. "I wouldn't know what to do to help anyway—I mean, if something had fallen or something."

She nodded. "Craig can handle it. In fact, he prefers to handle things himself." With a cautionary look directly into my eyes, she added, "I think your best education will come out here today."

I nodded, swallowing hard. I did not want Dana to be disappointed in me. I vowed to ignore whatever they were or were not doing in the greenhouse, and really focus on what Dana was showing us.

I think she sensed it, because she gave me a small smile before turning her attention back to the whole group.

"Jessi, why don't you open up the next hive?"

Jessi nodded, stepping forward with a hint of nervousness.

"Just take the lid off and set it beside the hive," Dana coaxed her gently.

She removed the top lid, but I could tell as she pried open the inner one that it was a lot quieter inside.

Only a few live bees were wandering around on the surface, amid the carcasses of hundreds of others. It looked like a war zone, where a whole city had been wiped out. We gasped.

"I feared that may be the case," Dana said, lifting the entire top box off the bottom one. More dead bees filled the bottom. "Could have been mites," she said. "Their mite counts were a little higher in this hive last year." Looking around at each of us, she added, "That's a part of it. Some hives do not make it through the winter. We'll save the box for later and see if we can catch a swarm in it."

I pictured Dana on a horse with a lasso around a giant balloon cloud of bees, galloping across the countryside.

"Cleo's helped me do that before, right Cleo?" she asked.

"Yeah, it's really cool," she said to Jessi. I could tell she felt proud of knowing how to do something Jessi did not. "They're actually pretty calm when they're swarming, so it's a lot less scary than it seems like it would be—Oh, Hey! Look who's coming!" she interrupted herself, pointing behind Dana's shoulder.

Dana turned to look, a light smile spreading across her face. She set the big box in her arms down and waved, calling out to the man coming toward us.

"Hey, Joshua!" she called, pulling off her veil.

The Carhardtt-clad man striding across the field toward us waved back, his large frame illuminated by the bright sun behind him.

"A good time to take a break," she said as we walked a few yards away from the hives and toward him. I took the opportunity to remove my veil, too, and scratch my face, which had been itching since I put it on, and shook my hair out of its too-loose ponytail.

Joshua's heavy work boots thudded the ground as he approached. He wore a cowboy hat pulled down low over his eyes, which he tipped forward as he reached us, sounding out a slow, deliberate "Howdy, Ladies."

He brought his hat and his gaze back up to meet Dana's. His warm, blue eyes sparkled like a sunny lake on his rugged, handsome face, his sand-colored curls spreading just below the brim of his cowboy hat. "Miss Dana," he said to her, his strong jaw broadening into a gorgeous smile, "Workin' the bees today?"

"Yup, first checkup of the year. You're just in time to meet some of our interns," she replied, brushing a strand of dark hair out of her eyes.

"I'd be much obliged," he said, grinning. He spotted Cleo and reached out to squeeze her on the shoulder. "Couldn't stay away, Cleo?" he teased.

"What can I say, I'm addicted to manual labor," she joked back. "It's good to see you," she said, tugging at something in her curls. He was probably twice her size. "How are the goats?"

"Joshua works the ground next to ours, to the east," Dana told Jessi and me, pointing toward where Joshua had emerged from the swath of forest that defined the property line. "He runs a small goat dairy there, milking 20 a day by hand!"

I gathered that was impressive, though I really didn't know what it meant. What I was certain was impressive, though, was this man's broad shoulders. They looked like they could swallow a woman whole. He looked younger than Dana, maybe my age, but he carried that same undeniable capability.

"The goats are being goats," Joshua said. "That's why I'm here, actually. They've destroyed a section of their pasture fence, and with planting time upon us, the last thing anyone around here wants is a runaway goat helping herself to your freshly-seeded salad mix."

"But they'd look so *cute* while they were doing it!" Cleo squealed.

"I'm sure Dana would disagree with you there, huh?" he asked, giving her a little wink. "Anyway, Dad's got my post pounder down at his place, and I figured it would be faster to come borrow yours. That is, if you're not using it."

"We're not, and you're welcome to it. It's in the barn with the other hand tools. Help yourself to anything you need." She turned to Jessi and me. "Before you go, though, let me introduce you to our interns."

"This is Jessi Ramone," she said, putting a hand on Jessi's back. "She came all the way out here from the east coast, where she's already done quite a bit of farming."

"Great," Joshua said, giving her hand a firm shake. "Pleasure to meet you."

"And this is Kelsie Thompson. She's from Salem, a bit closer to home." Dana gave me a small push forward, toward Joshua. I stumbled over the bottoms of my too-long bee overalls, reaching out to take his big hand. It was rough, but he didn't grip too hard. I imagined there wasn't a whole lot he couldn't do with those hands. Or with the rest of his broad strong body, for that matter.

I swallowed and looked up into his eyes, catching my breath before falling right in. "I'm a total greenhorn," I blurted out. *Excellent, Kelsie. Nice.*

He laughed, a deep laugh from his belly, still holding onto my hand. "That's the best kind, right, Dana?" he drawled out slowly, keeping his eyes locked with mine. A shiver worked its way from my hand up through my pounding heart and down toward my toes. For all his masculine confidence, there was tenderness in his eyes, an earnestness that made me want to wiggle right out of my skin and run back to the safety of my trailer. This man was looking for something, for someone. And he was not letting go of my hand.

5

He gave it a soft squeeze before releasing me. "Pleasure to meet you," he said, dipping his head ever so slightly toward me.

"Likewise," I stammered, catching my breath.

"Okay, then. I'll leave you ladies to your afternoon of bees. You're braver than I am, working with them like that. I've always admired that about you, Dana."

"Like I keep telling you, I think you'd really enjoy it if you gave it half a chance," she assured him.

"I've got too many animals to take care of already," he smiled, "without adding 100,000 bees to the list."

"Suit yourself," she said. "It's better that way, anyway. You still get honey and we get goat milk!"

"An excellent trade," he agreed. "Speaking of which, you're probably in need of some about now."

Dana nodded.

"I'll bring y'all a gallon when I'm finished building this fence."

With that, he turned to leave, his broad shoulders leading the way as he ambled toward the barn. I watched him saunter away, my mouth hanging open just enough to feel the breeze through my parted lips. Grabbing my water bottle, I threw back my neck and downed half of it, and when I looked up, Joshua had disappeared into the barn. Whew!

Dana relit the smoker and we settled back into our work. The next hive was more irritable than the rest. A cloud of bees rose up and out with fervor when she removed the lid. She puffed a bit of smoke onto the top of the hive, and they quieted down a bit.

"What does the smoke do, get them high?" I asked. Cleo chuckled.

"Not exactly," Dana explained, smiling at me. "Bee scientists aren't completely certain, but they believe the smoke leads the bees to believe their hive is on fire, so they return to the cells to gorge themselves with honey in preparation for abandoning the hive, which then makes them lethargic."

"Sounds brutal," I said.

"I think so too," she replied. "That's why I try only to use it when a hive is particularly aggressive."

"What makes one hive more aggressive than another?" Jessi asked.

"It all has to do with the queen," Dana answered. "Each queen has her own personality, and since she lays all the eggs in a colony, the offspring in that colony will often share similar traits. Also, she emits many different pheromones to communicate with all the other bees in the hive, and through them, she can communicate everything from how aggressive to be with an intruder to how much food to feed the worker bee larvae. If she is a crotchety queen, she will raise crotchety bees. "

Between keeping a lookout for Joshua coming out of the barn and keeping an ear open for Craig and Shantel in the greenhouse, my mind was on anything but the bees, but I had to concentrate so as not to let Dana down. I did notice Joshua making his was back across the field to his property a few minutes later, but kept my eyes glued to Dana, trying to focus on what she was teaching.

Somehow, I made it through the rest of the day, though by the time we were done, I still hadn't seen Shantel come out of the greenhouse. I tried to think about the bees, their amazing lives and organization, or even Joshua's gorgeous eyes and broad body, but a detailed play-by-play of what I imagined was happening in the greenhouse kept interrupting my thoughts. Finally, as I was heating up some leftover soup I had made with Cleo for an early dinner, I saw the light go on in Shantel's trailer. She was back inside, finally. *Damn you, Craig. You and your precious Brassicas can go fuck yourselves.*

I decided I needed to call Caroline. Cell phones didn't work out here, but there was a public phone in the barn that Dana told me we could use if we wanted to, provided we did not abuse the privilege. After I finished my soup, I threw on my jacket and trekked through the demo beds and into the dark, chilly barn. It was creepier in there all by myself, but I grabbed the phone and dialed Caroline's number.

"Hello?" her voice answered.

"Caroline, it's Kelsie! How's it goin'?"

"Kels! Are you on the farm? What's going on? I thought you didn't have a phone!"

"Mine doesn't work out here, but there's a farm one we can all use."

"Great! So, what's going on out there? Are you learning a lot?"

"Definitely, about all sorts of different stuff." I paused. "More than I ever knew I didn't know, for sure."

"Quit being so cryptic!" she snapped. "What the hell is going on?"

"Well, Dana is amazing," I began. "I went to a workshop she held at the farm last night and we collected pumpkin seeds..." I paused again, "...in our underwear."

"WHAT?"

"Seriously. I swear I've been unclothed more than I've been clothed here."

"Are you kidding? What else is going on? With the hot farmer dude? Kelsie! WHAT?"

"Let me talk and you'll hear!"

"Sorry."

"So, let's see...Craig is pretty picky, the pickiest boss I have ever had... The way he punishes you for messing up," I paused, "is by making you take off your clothes." I finished quickly.

"Wow." She started giggling. "Holy shit!"

"I KNOW!" I wailed back.

"That's pretty hot, and pretty effed up, too," she replied.

"Exactly! I don't even know how I'm supposed to feel about it. It totally turns me on, but I think that's probably wrong."

"By whose standards?"

"I don't know..."

"Kelsie, I'll tell you what. If some buff, hot farmer guy wanted to see me naked, I think I would let him. Besides that, there is something sexy about a dude telling you what to do. It's not as if he is being abusive, right? Right?"

"No, no," I answered quickly. "I think he just gets off seeing what he can get a girl to do for him."

I looked behind me, suddenly remembering I was not in a private place. I didn't see any sign of anyone. The evening was quiet, as the clouds had rolled back in again, muffling the universe's noise.

"Well, I don't know about you," Caroline began, "but I love it when a man takes control."

"I guess I do, too, I'm finding out." I thought about it. "That was the problem with Jeff. He was all worried about *'oppressing'* me, and as a result, our sex kind of sucked!"

"Exactly!" Caroline agreed. "These new-age emo dudes need to pull their heads out of their asses!"

"I'm not totally sure I agree with that," I told her, "but I do know it completely turns me on wondering what Craig will ask me to do." I paused. "Except..."

"What now? Except WHAT?" Caroline yelled into the phone. I pulled it back from my ear.

"There's this other girl here, another intern...I'm pretty sure he's doing it to her, too."

"Sounds right. If he does it to you, why wouldn't he do it to the other interns, too?"

"I don't know...I guess I just thought...I just want it..."

"You just want him to only power trip on you?"

"Well, to only want me, I guess." Listening to myself, I continued, "which I guess is pretty stupid, really, since I barely know him and that's probably what he's done with every intern he's ever had."

"Sounds like he's really mind-fucking you," Caroline said plainly.

It was just what I did not want to hear. I glanced around again to make sure no one was listening.

"I know!" I started in again. "I'm thinking about it entirely too much."

"Maybe you could look at it as an exercise in eroticism," Caroline suggested. "Just be turned on by it without wanting to possess it."

"That's pretty *Zen* of you, Caroline." I retorted.

"Yeah, well, I'm not saying *I* could look at it like that," she laughed. "But you've got to do something to keep it from eating away at you, and that seems like a good start. Or you could just leave," she offered.

"No!" I answered quickly. "No way!"

"So, tell me more about it," she changed the subject. "What else are you doing besides taking your clothes off there?"

I laughed. "Well, we worked with the bees today,"

"Bees? Like, bees in hives that make honey?" she asked.

"Uh-huh."

"Cool."

"Yeah, it was cool. But stupid me couldn't stop thinking about what Craig and Shantel were doing in the greenhouse the whole time."

"In a greenhouse? Hot!" Caroline giggled. "Ok, sorry."

"Me, too...let's see...I collect the eggs from the chickens every afternoon. That's one of my jobs."

"Mmm-hmm."

"We've been seeding a lot of stuff in the greenhouse, and Dana mentioned that we'd be starting to *direct seed*—to plant seeds directly into the ground outside—tomorrow. She said it will get pretty hectic now that it's starting to warm up."

"How crazy, Kels." Caroline said. "Who ever thought you'd be learning all this stuff?"

"I know."

"It sounds like you're really enjoying it."

"I am!" I said, feeling somewhat proud of myself. "I really am. If I can keep my mind off stupid Craig and his stupid hot body, I'll be all set!"

"Yeah, except when you're around him. Then you can make him keep his mind *on* you and *your* stupid hot body."

I laughed.

"Well, I guess I should probably get off the phone. It's good to talk to you, Caroline. Thanks."

"Of course! It beats the hell out of my boring life."

"Yeah, what's going on with you? I'm sorry I didn't even ask."

"Yeah, what kind of a friend are you?" she teased. "Seriously, nothing is going on. I'll be sure to let you know if I run into any hot dudes who order me to take my clothes off."

I love you, Caroline.

"And remember, Kelsie," she added. "You're not so bad yourself, so don't get all intimidated by some other girl. You've got your goods, too."

"Thanks, Caroline."

"I mean it. Call again soon!"

"I will. Good bye."

"Bye."

I hung up and looked at the phone for a moment before turning to head out of the barn and into the cloudy night. A friend who knows you well is priceless, I thought, rounding the corner. I noticed a different pickup truck parked outside the farmhouse. I wondered if it was one of Dana's lovers, and I envied her for escaping Craig's spell.

Back in my own trailer, I thought about what Caroline said about enjoying the attention from Craig without wanting to possess it. That seemed easier said than done, but there probably was some truth to it. I brushed my teeth and debated not making the trek to the outhouse before going to bed. Reasoning that I would regret the decision later on in the night, I put my boots back on and headed out again. As I walked by, I could not help but notice that Cleo was not alone in her trailer. Jessi was in there with her.

***

The next day we began what Craig referred to as The Rat Race. All six of us gathered at the edge of the closest field under a balmy sky. This was the season, he said, where the garden demands so much of the farmers that they run around in a frenzy trying to take care of it all. He surveyed each of us as he spoke, and my heart pounded every time his gaze fell on me. I glanced sideways at Shantel, who was very obviously courting his attention, sticking out her chest and assuming the same supermodel stance she had practiced on us in the bathhouse earlier. Her eyes never left Craig, following him earnestly as he paced back and forth in front of us. "In a few months time, we will plant all these acres with dozens of different crops," he said, like a military general preparing his troops for battle, "and each crop we plant has its own needs, its own likes and dislikes. And we try never to plant crops from the same family in the same bed two years in a row, which further complicates things."

"For now," Dana interrupted him, looking at Shantel and me, "don't worry about the bigger picture, of what goes where and how we figure it out. It took us years to get our rotations down, and every year we still struggle with planning a few beds. You'll start simply, learning the techniques for planting the different crops, and after you have a bit more experience, we'll start exploring how we decide what goes where."

She glanced over at Jessi. "And for you, Jessi, feel free to ask questions if you notice something you haven't seen before. We do have a couple of unorthodox rotations. We can show you our maps sometime, too, if you're interested."

"I would be," she said. "Thanks."

"Today we'll be seeding our first salad greens and radishes," Dana explained, "which will hopefully be ready for the opening day of the farmer's market."

"And if we have time, we'll also be transplanting some *Brassica* starts, mostly kale and collard greens, finishing up the rest of the B*rassicas* throughout the week," Craig added.

"I'll get Cleo and Jessi started on the Earthways with the radishes over there," Dana said to him, "if you want to show Kelsie and Shantel how to do salad greens."

"Perfect," Craig said, giving us a wink. Shantel flashed him an innocent smile. My stomach turned itself upside down and my own knees knocked together a bit. I swallowed and nodded.

After the others went off, Craig poked into the large tote of seed packets on the ground next to us, emerging with a bundle of packets.

"We hand-seed our salad greens thickly over the entire bed, so we can fit more into a small space. It takes a bit of practice to get the correct amount of seed laid down, but I'm sure you'll both get it in just a few tries." He looked into each of our eyes with a mock sternness. "I'll be watching you very closely, and correcting any mistakes you might make until you get it right."

I throbbed with anticipation. *Why did this turn me on so much?* Shantel let out a little giggle. *Damn! I knew it! She has totally been inducted into his little club.*

"These beds are 100 feet long. We'll be seeding roughly half a bed with each of the salad greens in this stack," he said, motioning to them, "and a whole bed of these others."

"After we're done, we'll hand-transplant the lettuces from the greenhouse," he concluded.

"Lettuces? Are those the ones we seeded yesterday?" Shantel asked him sweetly. I visualized her being pecked by a chicken.

"Uh, no, Shantel," Craig said, obviously disappointed. "Since we just seeded those lettuces *yesterday*, they're not ready to be transplanted *today.*"

"Oh, right," Shantel blushed. I stifled a snicker.

"The lettuces we'll be transplanting are some that have been in the greenhouse for three weeks now. Every week from now until the fall, we'll be starting 50 trays of lettuces a week inside, and transplanting those that are ready on a weekly basis."

"So, to get started," he began, picking up a packet of seed. "In time, you'll learn to shake the correct amount out of the packet to achieve a thin covering of the bed, where the plants will be spaced about ½ to 1-inch apart." He stood in the path between two long, brown beds of dirt and started walking slowly, shaking the packet so the seeds fell out onto the beds as he moved forward.

"You don't want to move too fast," he cautioned, "or the seeds will be too far apart. You do not want to dump the seeds out too fast, either, because then they will be too close together. Just a nice, slow walk with a slow, steady stream of seed falling from the packet is what you're after," he coached, his steps short and deliberate, moving the packet back and forth across the bed to cover the entire thing from side to side.

When he reached the middle of the bed, he stopped pouring seeds and turned back toward us, marking the place he stopped with a stick. He handed each of us a packet of seed. "Red Giant West Indian Mustard Green," mine said. Shantel had "Mizuna." I had never heard of either.

"Why don't you go one at a time, and I'll watch and correct you," he said.

Shantel turned to me. "I'll go first if you want me to, Kelsie," she said. I felt bad about the chicken pecking fantasy. I nodded, relieved.

"We'll finish the row I started," Craig said, pointing. They walked out to where he left off, and I watched from a distance.

Shantel opened the lip on her seed packet, starting to shake it into the bed. Craig took up position directly behind her, watching the seeds fall. "Too much!" I heard him say. I saw her jump a bit, pulling up on the seed packet. She began again, walking slowly. They were pretty far away now, but I could see him reaching around her. I could not see what he was doing. I craned my neck, my heart pounding. She stopped again, and then began moving after a second. When they reached the far end of the row, they turned around and walked back toward me, Craig in front of Shantel. As he approached me, he flashed me a big smile. "Your turn, Kelsie," he said, stepping out of the row. Shantel followed his last few steps with her head down and an unmistakably bright red face. She would not look me in the eye, instead surveying the ground as though she was looking for something.

My hands were shaking. *What was he going to do to me?*

"Are you ready?" he asked.

I gulped and nodded.

"We'll begin in this next bed here," he said, pointing.

I stepped into the path, and Craig stepped in right behind me. He was so close I could feel his breath on my neck. My hand trembled as I held out the seed packet. I shook out a few seeds and took a step forward. "More," he said in my ear, stepping in rhythm with me.

I shook the packet a bit harder and a cascade of seeds slipped over the edge. Craig's hand pinched down hard on the right side of my ass. "Too much!" he said quickly. I jumped, my heart pounding. I couldn't think straight. I started shaking the packet again as I took a step, realizing with a start that my ass was wiggling a bit as I shook the packet. Craig loosened his grip, but kept his hand on it as I moved forward. I was trembling all over now. My pace quickened a bit and he reached around me, grabbed my left breast in his hand firmly, and pulled me back with it. I stopped. "Too fast!" he said, squeezing it. I let out a little whimper. My swollen clit rubbed against the seam of my jeans and I waggled a little bit to ease the sensation, which just turned Craig on even more.

"I've wanted to do this since the first time I laid eyes on you," he whispered in my ear. A moan escaped my throat. "Now walk," he ordered. I started in again, walking and shaking the packet. Every few steps his hand tightened hard on my ass, signaling me to ease up on the amount of seeds I was spilling out of the packet, or it squeezed and pulled back on my breast, to slow me down. One overcorrection seemed to propel me into the other, and I finished out my half of the row with an ache in both my breast and my bottom. I could barely walk back to the end of the bed, and I definitely avoided Shantel's eyes this time, too.

"You both did pretty well, for your first time," he said, grinning at each of us. There was a noticeable bulge in his pants. "I think I'll watch you each once more, and then you should be ready to seed on your own."

"Shantel, are you ready?" he turned to her. She nodded weakly. He handed her another packet of seeds. "You'll finish off where Kelsie started." He stepped into place behind her. "Walk."

I could see Dana with Cleo and Jessi in the distance. They were walking behind a little one-wheeled machine, lost in conversation. I wondered if they could see what our subgroup was doing. I sincerely hoped not. Shantel was reaching the end of her row. I steadied myself, straightening my bra. As a second thought, I pulled my left breast out of it, letting it rest on top of the elastic and fabric. My nipples were hard as rocks, and it was extremely noticeable through the fabric of my shirt.

"Kelsie, I think you're ready for a full row," he said as he crossed the field again toward me, Shantel trailing along behind him. She had a detectable wobble to her step.

"A whole row?" I asked. He smiled and nodded, handing me a packet of "Arugula." I thought I had heard of that before. The little brown seeds didn't look that different from the last pack I seeded. My heart beating, I stepped into the row and he immediately stepped in behind me. I shook the packet across the bed, stepping forward. He grabbed my ass hard.

"Ow!" I said aloud.

"Shh," he said, still pinching firmly just at the top of my leg. "Not so much!" I wriggled around, trying to free myself from his grip, but he held tight. I jerked against him, rubbing against his hard erection. "Just walk and I'll let go," he reminded me.

I took a shaky step forward, letting the seeds fall again. His grip loosened and I continued walking as he cupped me still in his hand. A finger slid in between my legs, just for a second, and I gasped, lurching forward. He reached around and grabbed my breast, slamming me backward into him. Surprised at what he found there, he fondled me a little.

"Very nice, Kelsie," He whispered, rubbing up against me. "Very good." He pinched my throbbing nipple and I jerked back toward him, where his hand tightened again on my ass.

"That was very good," he breathed again into my ear. "Very good. Now walk."

I could smell my own wetness as it oozed out of me. I started shaking the packet again, my breasts and ass jiggling against Craig's hands. I stepped forward repeatedly as he held solidly from the front and the back. God I wanted him to bend me over right there. I didn't care who was watching. I arched my back a bit, trying to rub against him.

He grabbed me hard. "Stay focused on the work," he warned. "That's what you're here for."

I took the last several steps to the end of the row and he gave my butt a little slap as he let me go.

"I think you've got it now," he said, turning away from me. I followed him back down the row, watching the muscles in his back through his shirt, his dark hair a bit disheveled and an obvious bounce to his step.

Shantel and I avoided looking at each other the rest of the morning, seeding bed after bed, and raking them in gently. Afterward, we transplanted 20 flats of lettuce, which got tedious. I would have liked to talk to her, or to anyone, while we were doing it, but we didn't have the slightest idea what to say to each other. Besides, Craig was there working alongside us, and there was no way she was not also thinking about what I was thinking. Her faraway look and wet, parted lips made it certain. He had us both where he wanted us, and we both wanted to be right where we were, though maybe without the other one around.

That night in my trailer, I opened the book Cleo loaned me, deciding that there wasn't much I could read in there that would embarrass me more than what I had lived through that day. I felt a little guilty, and a little nervous, too, as I opened the cover and turned to the first short story. It was about a woman having sex with a plant, its long tendrils growing around her, up inside her, holding her up off the ground, turning her around and around, entering her from all directions. Yet again, a sexual scenario I had no idea would turn me on until I read it, finding myself again reaching under the covers to attend to my own pleasure.

As I finished the story, all I had been holding inside all day released, flooding out of me with a warm wave of relief. I had not actually had intercourse since I had been there, but already my sex life was ten times more satisfying than it had been with Jeff. *Good riddance.*

***

The newbie crew got our first real taste of farming, planting all week long, working long days and stopping only briefly to enjoy Cleo's delicious lunches. We took Sunday off, but I slept through most of it, rising on Monday morning and starting in again. Sometimes it rained, soaking us as we kept on transplanting and seeding, day after day. Dana and Craig both viewed the rain as a good sign, but I found it annoying. I was wet from morning to night, my feet pink, wrinkly prunes when I removed my boots and socks and collapsed on my bed at the end of the day. Some nights I didn't even eat dinner, I was so tired. On Saturday, I slept through my alarm, and awoke to a knock on my trailer window from Cleo, who had climbed up on the tire and was peering at me through the window above my head. She scared the crap out of me.

"Wakey wakey, Kelsie Welsie," she giggled, tapping on the window.

I shot up, smacking my head on the cabinet above.

Cleo waved, laughing. I flipped her my best morning bird, struggling to my feet and pulling on my dirty jeans, which by now were practically standing upright during the night while I slept, held up by a thick caking of mud.

Jessi was missing when I showed up for work.

"Jessi had to go home for a few days," Dana told Cleo and me when we asked her. "Her grandma died. It sounds like it wasn't unexpected, but still, it's important to be around family during those times. She'll be back soon," she assured us. "It does put a bit of a strain on us to get everything done without her here. She's so fast!" Dana added.

"Yeah, and don't forget about my dad's birthday thing this afternoon," Cleo reminded her.

"Oh, Crap," Dana huffed. I giggled a bit. It wasn't often she got flustered, and it was endearing. "I told him that some of us have to *work* on Saturdays, unlike him and his nine-to-fiver, but does he care? I swear, he's been ordering me around since we were kids!" She smiled. "It's not the end of the world. The alliums will find their way into the ground somehow, if not this week then next week. We have to live our lives. Here," she said, handing us each a flat of lettuce. "You two know what to do with this. Put it in that bed over there, next to the arugula. And when you're done with those, there's more in the greenhouse, labeled for planting this week."

The bed I had seeded with Craig's supervision now wore a patchy, deep green blanket. Thousands of tiny plants huddled together about an inch off the ground, forming a carpet that stretched from end to end down the bed. I could see where I hadn't put enough seed down; the blanket had holes there. It was amazing—I hadn't noticed anything growing there before. It must have sprung up overnight. In fact, many of the beds we had seeded on that first day now wore thick mats of tiny plants in various shades of green, red, and purple. The farm was coming to life.

"It's beautiful," I breathed to Cleo, looking out at the patchwork of colors stretching toward the horizon.

"Yeah it is," she agreed. "Beautiful and delectable."

We set our flats down at the end of the row and together rolled the heavy marker down the bed. The homemade contraption had pegs that stuck out six inches apart and made indentations in a triangular pattern over the bed as it rolled, marking the spot for each little lettuce start. Craig had also made another tool for this task—a board of nails that helped release the starts from their cell trays. You just pushed your flat down on top of the board, lining up the cells with the nails that pushed each start out in unison. That made them easy to get a hold of and pull the rest of the way as you planted.

We chose to work together on each flat, Cleo planting on one side of the bed and me planting on the other, moving down the bed together, flat by flat.

"So it's your dad's birthday today?" I asked her.

"Yup. It's like his 45th or so, I think."

"So he's older than Dana, then?"

"Yeah, by a lot. Nine years or something."

"What about you?" I asked her, jabbing seedling after seedling into the moist ground. "Do you have brothers or sisters?"

"One of each," she replied. "I'm in the middle. I have an older brother and a younger sister. You?"

"I have an older sister. She's two years older than I am. She's about to graduate from law school."

"Oh," Cleo said, looking up at me. "Your parents probably fawn all over her, eh?"

"Totally," I replied. "She's God's gift to the Thompsons, for sure."

"What about you? Are they disappointed in how you turned out?"

"Pretty much. You sound like you may have some experience with that dynamic."

"My brother's in his residency to become a P.A." Cleo confirmed. "Before that he played professional baseball for the Mariners for a couple of years. And he's only 25."

"Wow. Talk about an overachiever."

"Tell me about it," she said, shoving a lettuce seedling into the ground. "And I can barely hold down a job." She looked up at me with a smirk. "That's because I'm really the smart one. My brother and sister are fully in it, cogs in the wheel of the machine. My sister's married with two kids, and she's only 21! My brother's got all these bills—new house, new car, four wheelers—and he works all the time, so he barely has time to use any of it! I might be drifting, but at least I got my eyes open."

That was a good way to put it. "That's how I feel, too, I guess," I told her. "I may not know what I want to do, but I know I don't want to spend my life like a drone."

"And not in the bee sense, I gather," Cleo joked.

"And not in the bee sense." I agreed.

We started a new flat. I was so glad to be working with her, instead of Shantel. There was still this giant, awkward elephant of a subject between Shantel and me that neither of us tried to breech. I could see her working with Dana across the field. It looked like they were seeding something.

"Dang it!" Cleo said, with a tiny, broken lettuce plant in her hand. "I snapped it. Hate when that happens."

I nodded. Even with thousands of the things, it's still sad to be the person who kills one.

"R.I.P., little lettuce," she said, tossing the broken plant and its little plug of soil behind her and grabbing another one.

We finished a whole row and then Cleo headed to the kitchen to make lunch while I started another one. When she yelled, we gathered around the table to a feast of spring greens with hard-boiled eggs and fresh goat cheese with Cleo's homemade sauerkraut crackers. Cleo had a little salad garden in one of the greenhouses, and we'd been eating fresh salads for a week, even though the greens in the field were still too small to eat. Craig slid in next to Shantel, who coyly tossed her hair over her shoulder with a giggle and a smile. I stabbed my defenseless arugula, shoving a bite into my mouth. Its nutty spice filled my nose and I remembered Caroline's advice about not needing to possess him for myself.

"This afternoon Cleo and I have to go to Danny's birthday party," Dana reminded us with a groan. "So Craig will line you two out thinning radishes," she said, nodding to Shantel and me.

"Lord, Dana, it's a party," Craig told her with a big grin. "Your brother's party, no less. Enjoy it!" He winked at me. "We'll be just fine here without you." I saw Shantel jump a bit and wondered what part of her he had just grabbed.

6

I heard the truck pull out of the drive as I carried two empty buckets, per Craig's request, out to the radish rows. Craig and Shantel were already there. As I approached, I could see them pushing a little at each other, flirting like teenagers. I groaned and stomped up next to them, slamming the buckets down a little too hard.

"Oh hi, Kelsie," Shantel giggled, flashing me a flushed smile. Craig ignored her, turning his attention to me.

"I was just explaining to Shantel how important thinning is to the development of root crops," he said.

Yeah right.

He went on, "Root crops like radishes need ample space to develop properly in the ground. Without enough space between them, they'll just grow leafy tops, with only a tiny, withered radish underground."

Like Shantel. All pretty on top and nothing underneath.

"So, we have to be very careful as we thin, to ensure each plant has enough space."

"I got it," I said, a bit annoyed at his redundancy.

"We'll see about that," he replied, raising his eyebrows. "I'll have each of you take a bed, where you'll thin 3 rows of radishes. After each row, I'll check your work and, remove any seedlings you may have missed."

Knowing him, there was a caveat to his "checking," but I wasn't sure what it was. I guess I was about to find out. Despite myself, I started to pulse just thinking about what might be coming.

He knelt down in the first bed, motioning us toward him. 'These are the radish starts, he said, pointing to the line of thin, green plants that stretched all the way to the other end of the bed. "I cultivated these beds this morning so it would be easier for you to tell which ones are the plants. In the future, you'll hoe before thinning."

I crouched next to him, looking down the line at the thousands of tiny plants.

"Each radish needs about three inches all around it to thrive." He began ripping seedlings out of the ground, his fingers flying down the row at an incredible pace. "Some people do this with scissors, but we find a swift pluck works just as well and decreases the possibility of snipping more than one at a time. Pick a healthy-looking one and remove all the others around it." The foot of bed he had just thinned looked practically empty. He gently patted the ground he had just moved over, firming the soil around the remaining seedlings.

"We have to rip out all of those plants?" Shantel asked, eyes wide. "There's nothing left!"

"Like I said," Craig told her, "if you don't give them space, they won't develop."

"Now you two try it," he urged.

I picked a plant and pulled out the ones around it. Then, I picked another and removed several more. "Not enough space," Craig said sternly, measuring the gap with his thumb and forefinger. "You need another inch between them."

Shantel's full lips slipped into a pout. "It's so sad to take them all out!" she exclaimed. "Can we move them somewhere else?"

Craig playfully rolled his eyes. "When you have your own farm, Shantel, you can waste as many hours as you like saving every tiny little seedling the earth spits up. But on this farm, while you're working for us, you'll do it the efficient way."

Taking pity on her, he added, "The seedlings you pull out aren't wasted. They'll go to feed the chickens, who will be very grateful for your ruthlessness."

I pulled out several more plants, getting into a rhythm as I moved down the bed, inch by inch, like a crazed God on high, purifying the gene pool. You stay, you go, you stay, you go, on and on.

"What if the one I pick to stay doesn't end up being very good?" Shantel wondered aloud.

Exasperated, Craig reassured her, "Shantel, they're going to be fine. It's *fine*." I could see her reluctance was eating into his enjoyment of his grander scheme for the afternoon. As for me, I had found something I was sure I could handle. As I moved down the row, a pattern emerged and I gained speed and confidence as I went, leaving Shantel behind to wallow in her own worry about the injustice of it all. As I reached the halfway point, I looked up to survey her progress and saw an unmistakable, burly figure striding toward us. Joshua.

7

My breath caught in my throat. As Joshua approached, I could make out carriers that held glass bottles in each of his hands. He held them away from his body as he walked, which broadened his already wide frame and set off the muscles in his shoulders and biceps. Craig caught sight of him too, and hurried to his feet, shifting his shirt slightly on his chest. Shantel looked up curiously to see what had taken Craig's attention away from her.

"Joshua," Craig said plainly, as he reached the edge of the field. It sounded more like an accusation than a greeting.

"Hi there, Craig," Joshua replied, nodding slightly as he did with Dana and with me before. "I heard Cleo was in need of some extra milk for a special dish she wanted to make." Craig made no move to take the heavy crates from his hands as Joshua looked around for help. "Uh, is Cleo or Miss Dana around?"

"They're out for the afternoon," Craig said, pausing a second. "I'll put this in the fridge for Cleo." Joshua transferred the crate in his right hand to Craig's as Shantel eagerly stood to face Joshua.

"Hi, I'm Shantel Hartwin," she said to him, reaching out her hand daintily. "Who are you?"

Joshua turned to her with a grin, still holding the other milk crate in his left hand. He took her hand. "Joshua Murphy," he said.

"Right," Craig answered. "Sorry about that. Shantel is an intern for the season," he mumbled, his eyes staring at a point just beyond them. "Joshua runs a goat dairy next door."

"That explains the milk!" Shantel smiled confidently, tossing her head so her curls bounced over her shoulders.

Driven by an inexplicable protective instinct, I rose to my feet in the bed, turning toward the three of them on the edge.

"And who's that out there?" Joshua called.

Craig spun around to face me, his eyes lit.

"It's me! Uh, Kelsie," I said, wiping my dirty hands on my jeans and walking toward them.

Joshua's face broke into a huge smile. His beautiful blue eyes followed me all the way to the edge of the bed, where he reached out to take my hand in his again.

"Kelsie from Salem," he said with a nod. "I was wondering when I'd get the pleasure of makin' your acquaintance again." He gave me a wink.

I blushed, taking a step back and nearly toppling into the radishes behind me.

Craig cleared his throat loudly.

"Quite the crew you have this year, Craig," Joshua offered. "Y'all should come over sometime for a farm tour. See how the livestock lives."

"Ooh, I'd love to see your goats!" Shantel chirped, batting her eyelashes at him.

"Well—" Craig began.

Joshua interrupted him and asked, "What about you, Kelsie?" His eyes seemed to reach out and grab me with their sincerity.

I nodded feebly. No words came out my dry mouth, but Joshua beamed with delight. I glanced nervously at Craig, who was glaring at me.

"We'd best be getting back to work," Craig said, grabbing at the crate of glass jugs in Joshua's other hand. "Uh, thanks for stopping by, Joshua. I'll make sure Cleo gets this."

"Right," Joshua said, handing over the milk. "I'd best be gettin' back to work as well. No time for idle chit chat in the spring, eh?" He smiled at Craig, who nodded distractedly.

"Well, hope to see you again soon," he said, staring directly at me.

"Likewise," Shantel replied.

He turned to leave and I let out a massive breath I didn't realize I was holding. Before Craig could say or do anything, I turned quickly and scurried back to my place halfway down the bed. I resumed thinning, keeping my head down and my eyes focused intently on the little radish seedlings. My pulse was strong on the back of my hot neck, but I just kept plucking the radishes as Craig occupied himself with Shantel and her inability to murder a radish.

When I reached the end of my row, I stood up, proud of myself. Shantel was fumbling along, still not halfway down the row and, for once in my life, I felt like I was really good at something.

"Craig, I'm finished," I called to him.

He and Shantel both looked up. He stood and sauntered toward me, surveying the ground as he walked. Three times he stopped, reached down, and pulled up a radish seedling from my row. As he neared, I noticed a flash of something in his eyes that had not been there before. It was wild, angry. When he reached me, he held out his hand to reveal three tiny seedlings.

"You missed three," he stated, looking into my eyes. Desperate anger flickered there in waves between his usual mock-sternness, and it scared me. I thought I had done a good job! Was this about Joshua?

"Kelsie, turn around," he ordered me.

"Craig--Why?" I began, my knees beginning to shake.

"Because I'm your boss, that's why," he said, tossing the three radishes onto the ground.

"Turn around and unbutton your jeans," he said, with more force this time.

I glanced at Shantel, who had stopped working and was watching us wide-eyed from the bed behind Craig. She seemed both terrified and excited.

Quickly I scanned the countryside for any sign of Joshua or anyone else. I saw no one. I did not know which scared me more, doing what Craig said or not doing what he said. I looked into his eyes, and I could see he was battling internally with himself. He gave me a small smile and motioned for me to turn.

Sensing I now held some power over him that I didn't have before, slowly I brought my hands to the button on my jeans while keeping my gaze locked with his. I undid the button and slid the zipper down, pushing the flaps open to reveal a small triangle of black panties underneath. I raised my eyebrows and turned the corners of my mouth up slightly. Excitement flickered in his eyes, and I kept on flirting as I turned slowly around, keeping my eyes locked with his until the last second, when my head snapped around and I was facing away from him.

All my previous confidence dissolved when I lost sight of his eyes. I now looked out past their fields and into the miles of countryside beyond. My backside tingled with anticipation. I wondered what was coming next but deep inside, I already knew.

I felt his hands grab my jeans and pull them down to my knees, exposing my bottom. The late March wind blew on the bare backs of my thighs as I waited for further instructions.

He said, "Spread your legs wide." I brought my legs as wide as the jeans binding me at the knees would allow.

"Now bend forward," he said softly. I could feel Shantel's eyes on us as I brought my hands to my thighs.

"Arch your back," he said louder. "Get that ass as high in the air as you can."

I paused for a second, trying to think rationally, but decided against it as Craig ordered, stronger this time, "Do it."

I arched my back, sending the high cut edges of my panties toward the open sky.

Craig stuck a finger inside my panties and swabbed at my exposed cunt. In spite of myself, I was dripping wet.

"Good girl," he said. "Now for your punishment."

SMACK! His hand came down hard on my bottom. "Aaah!" I

cried out in shock. The sting traveled down the backs of my legs to my feet. I tried to step forward but the jeans around my knees prevented me from getting very far.

SMACK! Again, Craig's hand burst me open. "Ow!" I wailed.

"Hold still, Kelsie," he warned. "And get that ass back in the air."

Shaking, I arched my back again, my ass throbbing in pain, and braced myself.

WHACK! He spanked me again, so hard this time I nearly fell forward. He caught me as I stumbled, grabbing my ass in both hands and massaging it.

"That was three, for the three you missed. Now pull your pants back up and get to work on the next row."

His footsteps faded as I straightened and pulled my pants up and faced the beds again. Shantel's flustered transition from watching us to getting back to work as if she hadn't noticed was lost on no one. Her head bent in mock contemplation, she pretended to be surprised when Craig approached her.

I knelt down in the next bed, working my way with extra care back across it, my sore ass rubbing against my jeans and my mind pounding in time with my heart.

Craig had gone too far this time, I reasoned, trying to keep from thinking about the stinging. He'd hurt me, sort of. He'd hit me hard, harder than I think he meant to. I could see it in his eyes. He didn't want me, or Shantel, for that matter, to have anything to do with Joshua, and he'd let me know that at the same time he'd "punished" me for missing the radishes. I was indignant at his possessiveness, especially since we were here to learn about farming and another farmer had just offered to give us a tour. Plus, there weren't many people out here and it was nice to meet someone new. Especially someone with such an incredible mass...

Yet, I realized, in some ways, our exchange left me inexplicably satiated. I *liked* taking orders from Craig. I liked feeling the strength of his arms and his hands on my exposed skin. I liked feeling dominated by him, made feminine by his masculinity. What would Jeff think about this obvious display of "oppression"? Never mind what he'd think—as the stinging faded, the only thing I really needed to grapple with was the angry look in Craig's eyes when I said I'd like to go see Joshua's farm. I really did want to see Joshua again.

5

Jessi returned three days later, arriving late in the afternoon on a beautiful spring day. We were all working in the field. Dana, Cleo, Shantel and I hoed brassica rows and Craig was off in another field on the tractor. He'd removed his shirt, soaking up the rare sunshine as he drove, although he was too far away to really ogle. This was the second time I'd tried hoeing and I had a hard time getting the hang of it. While Dana and Cleo flew down the rows, expertly weaving in and out of the small plants without hitting them, I moved clunkily, straining to reach across the bed while avoiding the kale plants. It was a good workout, hoeing. I had to use my stomach muscles to have enough strength to get the hoe across the bed, and my triceps burned as well. After so much rain, the sun felt hot.

"Is anyone else sweating?" I asked aloud, looking up to see Jessi striding out to meet us.

"Totally!" Shantel replied. "Isn't it great?"

Dana laughed, looking up and noticing Jessi.

Jessi!" Dana called, waving to her. "Look at that! Just arrived and already ready to get back to work!" Sure enough, Jessi had her jeans and boots on and a hoe in hand. She must have seen what we were doing and grabbed one from the barn on her way out to the beds.

"Welcome back!" Cleo said as she approached. "Sorry to hear about your Grandma."

"Thanks," Jessi replied. "She'd been sick for awhile, so it was sort of a blessing. Surveying the bright patchwork of fields, she switched topics. "Wow! A lot has changed in the last few days! Spring has really sprung! Where do you want me?" she asked Dana.

"We're hoeing the brassicas. Why don't you jump on that red Russian kale row next to Kelsie?"

Nodding, Jessi stepped into the next path over and began hoeing the weed seedlings out of her bed. She was fast, faster than Cleo was and almost faster than Dana, gliding over the row like a dancer on a stage.

"How do you do that?" I asked her.

She laughed. "Trust me, at the end of the season, you'll be this fast," she said. "If there's one thing we get a lot of practice with on a vegetable farm, it's hoeing." She breezed on by me to the end of her row and started on the next one. I gouged at plant after plant, shoving more dirt into my pathway than I left in the bed. I noticed one I missed a few feet back, so I reached around to get it.

"One thing I do that might help you, Kelsie," Jessi offered, "is never go backward. With hoeing, it's best just to keep your head down and move forward through the bed. If you miss a weed, it's okay. You'll have another chance to get it later. Just keep moving on."

"Keep on keepin' on," Cleo called to me, agreeing with Jessi.

"The hoe is all about rhythm," Dana added. "A dance with even steps." She moved in time to an inaudible song playing in her head. "One two three, One two three," she said, sliding down her row with grace.

"I can't dance, Dana." I chuckled to her.

"Sure you can!" she smiled back. If there was one thing Dana didn't abide, it was self-deprecation. "And the hoe will help you."

"The hoe, farm tool and dance workout." Cleo said in a mock commercial announcer's voice. "Pick one up today."

Everyone laughed.

"Get in shape for bikini season," she continued. "In just three weeks, you'll be ready to hit the beach." She paused and rolled up the sleeves of her t-shirt. "You can work on your tan while you're at it."

When the sun dipped toward the tops of the trees, we stopped working and walked our tools back to the barn with a deep sense of satisfaction. The fields behind us looked clean and soft in the fading light. Our bodies held the now-familiar pleasant soreness and tiredness that comes from using them all day.

Cleo invited us all to come to her trailer for a welcome-back dinner for Jessi. Dana thanked her for the offer but said she already had dinner plans.

"You gals have fun tonight and I'll see you tomorrow morning for more farm aerobics!" she said cheerfully, wiping her dirty palms on her long blue jeans. As she walked back into the farmhouse, we trudged back through the demo beds toward our trailers.

Cleo poked me in the ribs on our walk back and pointed toward the farmhouse, where an old truck had just pulled in. A rugged-looking man with his hair in a long, blonde ponytail got out of the truck, carrying a bouquet of flowering branches. He wore a black, dressy Western vest and a worn cowboy hat.

"Ooh la la," Cleo giggled. "Way to go, Aunt Dana."

***

The beginning of April brought Dana's monthly Luscious Earth workshop, and to be frank, I was not exactly looking forward to it. It's not that I didn't learn a lot at the last one. I did not feel like taking my clothes off in front of strangers. I had started bleeding earlier in the day, so my insides pushed at my outsides, making me want to curl up in a ball and hide in my trailer, especially after a long day of work. Jessi convinced me I wouldn't want to miss it—Dana told her earlier in the day that we'd be taking a walk in the woodland next to the farm identifying spring-blooming shrubs and discussing pollination. That didn't sound so bad. Jessi invited us over to her trailer beforehand to drink a little wine, as per Cleo's advice, to get "in the mood" for the workshop.

"Did you notice how perky Aunt Dana was today?" Cleo asked me slyly as I walked into Jessi's trailer. The two of them lounged at Jessi's tiny table with half-empty glasses. I had not been in her trailer. It had the usual small table, bed, and kitchenette, but all in tan instead of the grey of my trailer. She hadn't done much in the way of decorating either, which made me feel better. A slow, mellow female voice drawled out long, twanged melodies from a boom box in the corner.

"Yeah, she was in a great mood!" I said, squeezing in next to them at the table and helping myself to the wine. "I like the music, Jessi. Who is it?"

"Gillian Welch," she replied. "Isn't she great?"

"Yeah, really nice," I said.

"I guess so," Cleo said, "for country."

I laughed. "You only like it if they're screaming their guts out, huh Cleo?"

"Their guts don't literally need to be coming out their mouths," she replied with a grin.

"Where's Shantel?" I asked.

They both shrugged. "Probably off with Craig," Cleo said, rolling her eyes. "I saw them talking after work today."

"Come on, Cleo, she's not that bad," Jessi said, looking to me for backup. I nodded unconvincingly, my mind frantically calculating the last time I saw Shantel and the likelihood of her hanging out with Craig after work hours. "She's trying really hard, and she wants to learn."

I agreed. She had come a long way since the beginning of the season. Just as I had, I guessed. She no longer worried about showing up for work in the morning wearing dirty jeans, and her ruthlessness with thinning and weeding had improved. She could at least identify all the crops we were growing, whereas some were still a little fuzzy for me. Tatsoi and Mizuna, chard and cress, all of it was so foreign to me that I had trouble keeping it all straight. We ate a lot of what Cleo called *braising mix* at lunches, and she would quiz me on the different ingredients as she stabbed them with her fork and brought them to her mouth. I was getting better, but I still missed some.

Although I hadn't had any more one-on-one contact, or even two-on-one contact, with Craig in the past week since our spanking encounter, my heart pounded every time I was around him. The news that he might be off with Shantel when we were not working really bothered me. I was trying hard not to want to "possess" him and to turn the other cheek when he flirted with Shantel. Still, a part of me wanted to be the only object of his desire. Yet another part of me, the part that remembered the ugliness in his eyes as he struggled with his own internal desire for possession, wanted to send him fully into her arms and rid myself of his attention forever.

"You okay, Kelsie?" Jessi asked me, waving a hand playfully in front of my face.

"Oh, sorry," I said, snapping back into the room with blushing cheeks.

"We'd probably best get over to the barn," Cleo said, slugging the last of her wine. "It's almost 6."

We collected jackets, emptied wine glasses, and made our way out the door. I glanced back at Shantel's trailer. It was empty. *Damn it! Where are they?* I scanned the grounds as we walked but saw only the people arriving for the workshop. The *chicas* were out wandering around on their perpetual patrol for tiny specks of food when we reached the barn. With the recent coming of daylight savings time, the light lingered longer in the evening. As we gathered outside the barn, Dana welcomed each guest warmly and made an effort to introduce them to others who were already there. The evening was mild and pleasant, and the sky clear.

"Please stay near the barn here," Dana urged the participants, who milled around checking out the demo beds, the chickens, and looking out to the patchwork fields beyond. "Since we don't have much daylight, we'll want to begin promptly."

Someone put a hand on my back and on Cleo's next to me. We turned around in unison to see Joshua, grinning down at both of us. "Howdy, ladies," he said, and, nodding toward Jessi, "Hi Jessi."

I sucked in a huge gasp of air, looking up at him as he kept his hand just below my shoulders. I managed a smile, hoping he couldn't feel my heart pounding through my jacket.

"Joshua!" Cleo exclaimed. "Here for the workshop?"

He dropped his hands and we turned to face him. "Your aunt asked me to come along on the tour this evening, to add anything extra I know to the discussion." He shook his head at Cleo. "But we both know that isn't necessary. She knows everything there is to know about the plants around here. I'm here to learn, more 'n anything."

"Joshua!" Dana called out to him. "So glad you could make it!" Turning her attention back to the group, she began. "Please gather around, folks. Welcome to the April Luscious Earth workshop. This evening we'll take a walking tour of the woodlands to the west of the fields here and look at the fascinating ways nature works in concert with itself to create beauty and bounty through diversity. We will identify and enjoy many species of early-blooming woodland shrubs and we'll explore the ways the Magic Presence unfolds to link their lives with the lives of those who fertilize them. Incredible as they are, plants have a major flaw when it comes to having sex—they can't move! Whereas animals wander over to the watering hole or the neighborhood bar and survey the selection of potential mates, a plant is forever stuck in one place, resigned to waiting for a sperm to come to it." I was keenly aware of Joshua standing next to me as Dana went on about wandering sperm and plant sex. I wiped my sweating palms on my jeans and cleared my tight throat quietly. Joshua looked over at me with a twinkle in his eye, which I caught in spite of my best effort to pretend I was not looking at him.

"A flower has one job and one job only," she continued. "To attract a pollinator. It pulls out all its tricks in its quest. It adorns itself with gorgeous, silky petals; it emits sweet scents; it does whatever it can do to attract someone to come over and touch it." She smiled. "Ahh, would that we all saw ourselves as the gorgeous flowers we are, just wanting someone to touch us..."

I took a step away from Joshua and bumped into Jessi, who looked at me with alarm. "Are you okay?" she whispered.

I gulped and nodded. I could feel Joshua's eyes on me, but he turned back toward Dana when I glanced over nervously at him. I felt fidgety and wished that Dana would have us start walking soon.

As if reading my mind, she motioned everyone to follow her as she made her way back through the demo beds and toward our trailers. It was odd to have a group of people walking so near to our little cove.

Seeing my trailer from outside eyes embarrassed me a bit. Dana hurried people past and behind the hot tub/sauna to the thicket of forest behind.

"On the edge of most farms around here, you'll find thickets of blackberries. These tasty invaders serve an important function. By colonizing disturbed areas such as the edges of cultivated farmland, they in essence create a fence that protects the more highly-functioning orchestra of the woodland inside."

Joshua leaned over to me. "Which one's your trailer, Kelsie?"

Damn it! "None of your business," I wanted to say to him. Instead, I weakly pointed toward the one on the end, closest to us. He made a low whistle of approval and gave me the a-ok sign with his thumb and fingers, which cracked my nervousness into a smile. That shithead. Relaxed by his easiness, I playfully elbowed him in the side.

"See," Dana went on, motioning out toward the patchwork fields rolling soft through slanted sun lips, "even highly diversified vegetable farms like ours are still simplistic systems compared to the natural world. We humans can't mimic the impeccable interconnectedness that allows a forest to grow and live indefinitely. These fields here," she said, "would all return to woodland if humans stopped cultivating them."

That was quite a thought. I raised my eyes at Cleo and Joshua, imagining a tangle of forest where we worked so hard. How on earth could the pioneers have cleared it all in the first place?

"Must have been tough for the pioneers, huh?" I whispered to them.

Cleo nodded and Joshua grinned broadly at how our interaction was evolving. "Actually," he whispered back, leaning down so he was closer to me, his breath tickling the skin under my nose. I parted my lips slightly to feel it in my mouth. "The Native Americans that lived here before white people came managed these areas with fire so camas root and other native foods didn't get shaded out by trees. The oaks were some of the only trees that could survive their controlled burns." He gave me a small wink and turned his attention back to Dana.

Whew. Could this man be any sexier? Dana led us to a hole in the thicket and motioned us inside the woodland, which covered a few acres between us and the next farm over. I followed Joshua's broad body inside, reasoning that yes, indeed, he could be even sexier with his clothes off. *To hell with Craig and Shantel, doing whatever they were doing.* Entering the woodland less than one hundred yards from where I had been living for over a month, we were transported into another world entirely. How come I never walked back here? Evening light splattered the ground like fallen leaves. Straps and twigs of green pushed their way up through the thick mat of grasses and duff winding, twisting, unfolding toward the sun. The woodland held a stillness and a quiet earthy smell that brought tears to my eyes. I had not been "into" nature before, but, somehow, after working in the dirt for the past month, this place seemed to make sense. Perfect, beautiful sense.

Dana breathed deeply and asked others to do the same. "Places like these are rare near farms," she said. "This one has been left alone for decades. You'll notice more conifers like these Douglas Fir and hemlock." She motioned a long, slender wrist toward a tall, slender tree with soft green needles. "These places connect us deeply to our most sensual selves. They are the essence of sensuality—the raw, luscious business of interactions between parts to form a passionate whole." Joshua's hand brushed mine, as we stood under the thick canopy in the fading light. I wondered if he had done it on purpose. As Dana continued, my fingers tingled with the possibility that he might brush up against them again. I moved them ever so slightly outward, groping the electrified air around in hopes of connecting with them again, but I felt nothing.

Dana's voice rose to a fervor. Her hands flapped wildly like an orchestra conductor calling in the trees, the birds, the flowers, while her bracelets and rings clanged together as she harkened the forest. "Here, the death of one member is life for another, the corpses of rotting logs hauled off by armies of insects to buried treasure chests! Brazen flower seeds snuggle into fallen logs and promiscuously unfold, spilling out over the decaying wooden bodies, unrolling silken leaves and garish petals with a rawness that can make you blush!..."

I didn't know about the flowers, but Dana certainly had a way of making me blush. Joshua also fidgeted a little, but kept his gaze fixed rapturously on her.

"You blush," Dana went on, a twinkle in her deep brown eye, "unless you are one of them." She pleaded to us, moving around the group with a slow, deliberate nod at each participant. "...Opening...unfurling...revealing ever more...blossoming into astonishing nakedness, inexplicable beauty..." When she locked eyes with me, I held her intense gaze for as long as I could before shifting my eyes to the ground in front of me. I had a long way to go before I could blossom like Dana. "Bold, fierce love from the seed of your belly," she finished, nodding with satisfaction while pressing both hands around hers.

"No matter how insignificant we might feel in daily life," she said, looking directly at me, "places like these remind us that we are a part of the wild orchestra, entangled in the middle of it. Every step we take, we add to the symphony. We might crack a tiny twig and lighten the load for an ant who wishes to carry it back to her queen. "

A bird squawked loudly from a high up tree branch, beckoning someone.

"Or," she continued, "we may kill the ant on his journey home with our footstep, creating food for the microscopic insects that will rush in to consume his body, breaking him down into smaller and smaller particles until he is only nutrients that the small sapling sprouting next to his death bed will find, helping it grow taller."

Joshua leaned over to me, grinning. "Makes you not want to move at all, huh?" he whispered. His hand brushed mine again as he stood upright. This time he left it there for a split second before pulling away. My heart sped up, as I looked him in the eye with a nod of agreement. I would not have minded if we stayed stuck in the woodland forever, as long as the twilight stretched long around us, wrapping us together in its blanket. Cleo giggled, and I snapped away from Joshua's eyes to look at her. Looking at us, she blurted out a little too loudly, "Great! Now I'm scared to take a step!" Several people chuckled and Dana broke the spell by walking up to put an arm around Cleo's shoulder, possibly murdering or feeding hundreds of insects in the process.

"Let us not become frozen with the fear that we will do harm by our actions," she offered confidently to the group, squeezing Cleo's shoulder firmly. "The earth needs us to move swiftly with love. We are all flowers, blooming alive upon death. We must unfold, lure love to us, and love fiercely those around us. And after the great love affair of our life, we will return in death to feed new life."

Hearing her say those words under the soft, swaying arms of an army of trees, tears welled up inside me, unexplainable tears. It was as if Dana were unlocking a box in my being that I had not seen before, and I was scared of what would come out. I tried to stop them, but a couple trickled down my cheeks and dripped onto the front of my jacket. Panicked, I turned my back to Joshua, only to be met with more forest, more trees, more flowers dancing in the fading light. My body shook with sobs that begged to be freed but I held my mouth tight. They found their way out my eyes, one by one leaking and plunging downward toward the soft earth. *Why is this happening right now?*

Dana led the group further into the woodland but I stayed with my back to them, listening as they walked away. The forest breathed and swayed slightly, filling me with breathtaking, patient acceptance. It was as if I had come home to myself, finding my little place in the vastness of it all. I brought my sleeve to my mouth and sobbed into it. I felt exhausted, embarrassed. What would Joshua think? Why was I crying? Maybe I could sneak off to my trailer and hide. Or should I go back and join the group? My eyes no doubt would give me away. But I didn't want my time in the woodland to end, my time with Joshua, my time listening to Dana. I decided the hell with it—I would go back to the group, red eyes and all, and finish the Luscious Earth workshop.

Dana was still talking as I quietly approached, trying to blend into the back of the group. Joshua was in front of me and I tried to keep it that way. "...The Douglas Fir also invites other forest species to find a niche," she said, "like this spring-blooming jewel." With her ring-clad hand, she fingered a waist-high shrub adorned with red flowers; her bracelets caught slivers of light as they sliced through the edge of the thicket. "Does anyone know what this is?'

I glanced over at Joshua, who winked at Cleo next to him. He mouthed something to her as several other people in the crowd answered out loud. Dana nodded her approval. "Yes, yes, red-flowering currant. *Ribes sanguineum*. Sanguineum means bloody, and a variety of this plant is commonly called blood currant. How's that for sensual? Just a couple of weeks ago, these twigs were barren, unnoticeable. How incredible it is that a bare twig can become covered, absolutely *covered* in garish, blood red flowers! All to lure the love of a bee that will spread its pollen, fertilize its egg, so it can grow its fruit and make seeds! "

Joshua knew these woods, too. He knew the plants and how they all fit together like Dana did. "Miss Dana," he interrupted, pointing at the ground at her feet. "I think we'd enjoy eating some of that miner's lettuce sproutin' up."

"Great idea, Joshua!" she replied gratefully. Addressing the crowd, she added, "For those of you who don't know him, Joshua Murphy is our neighbor to the east. He's grown up around here, so he knows pretty much everything there is to know about the area. I asked him to come along this evening to share anything extra he thought of, and lucky for you, he did!" She reached down and pinched off a small, spade-shaped leaf off the ground. "Claytonia is a nutritious wild edible green that comes up thickly in these areas in the spring. Sample a sprig, if you like." A few folks stepped forward and pinched off a leaf for themselves. I hung back, feeling shy about returning to Joshua's side after my little episode. The sun was almost down and it was getting harder to see. "I was so focused on the flowers," Dana laughed, "that I forgot about the leaves!"

We walked for a few more minutes, but finally even Dana had to admit it was getting too dark to continue. She thanked us and encouraged us to move swiftly forward into the night with love. I hadn't worked up the guts to rejoin Joshua and Cleo, and thought I had missed my chance. Sadly, I turned and followed the woman in front of me toward the edge of the woodland, exhausted by the events that had just transpired. It was probably good that I had maybe ruined my chances with Joshua by losing it. Craig certainly did not want me to take an interest in Joshua and it could make my work situation very tense if I did. I weaved through the shrubs and grasses, around the trunks of trees, and toward the open fields beyond. At the edge of the woodland, I stopped briefly and stared at the treetops, some with tiny new leaves sprouting. The sky beyond darkened into a deep gray-blue with the faintest outlines of stars. The voices of the group faded as people returned to cars and lives off the farm. I saw Cleo and Jessi lingering on the edge of the thicket looking at something on the ground. I decided to go join them, silently thanking the forest around me as I hurried to catch up. A strong hand grabbed my shoulder, startling me and, even before I turned around to face him, I knew who it was.

9

"Joshua..." I began, turning to look up into his eyes.

He took both my hands in his, and I noticed they were shaking a little. "Wait," he said nervously. He took a breath. "Kelsie, would you like to come have dinner at my place tomorrow night?"

I swallowed hard, trying to think of what to say. The night came quickly and, without the openness of the fields and the forest that felt so nurturing moments before, seemed to trap me. Hadn't I just wished for this to happen? But I did not want to upset Craig. Moreover, I sensed Joshua shared Dana's ability to open the closed box inside me and that really scared me. I racked my brain for an excuse, a way out, but in the end Joshua's tender, pleading eyes won me over.

"Okay," I agreed. "I'd love to."

"Oh good," he breathed. "You had me nervous for a minute there." In the dim light, I could see his big smile flashing. "Come over around 7, and I'll try to cook us up something edible. Just walk through the gate in the fence," he pointed at the other side of the farm "--and come on up to the house."

I swallowed and nodded, my mind racing. He let go of one of my hands, but held on to the other one gently and led me out of the woods. I could see the light on in Cleo's trailer but Jessi's and Shantel's were both dark. Joshua's big, rough hand swallowed mine, dwarfing it, and I thought about how much I had ached to touch it earlier. He walked me to the metal stoop of my trailer and, for a split second, I worried about how we would part ways. Joshua curbed any awkwardness by simply giving my hand a squeeze and letting it go. He brought a hand to his forehead in his characteristic nod and said, "It seems we've arrived at your humble abode. I'll see you tomorrow night." Then he turned and walked off into the night without as much as a glance back over his shoulder.

I watched him walk away until he disappeared into the darkness, then burst into my trailer and flung myself down on the bed, arms stretched out wide. What a night! I had a breakdown in the woods, an incredibly sexy goat farmer asked me out on a date, and I didn't have the slightest idea what to make of any of it. I brought my hand to my face and ran it along my lips, inhaling for a sign of Joshua, but it was just my plain old hand, smelling like my plain old hand. My palm felt rough with all the calluses it now sported, and in the last few weeks, a band of dirt had etched itself into the cracks on the side of my index finger so deeply I couldn't wash it off, even with soap and hot water. I may still have a lot to learn about farming, but physically, I was starting to look the part.

***

"BZZZZZZZZZZZZ!" I groggily reached up and slammed the button on my alarm clock. Out of the fog, my present reality pieced itself together. After the usual few fractured moments of *Where-am-I, What's-for-breakfast, Is-it-raining?*, the nebulous cloud that is a mind as it wakes crashed hard into reality and my eyes flew open with a start. I was having dinner at Joshua's house tonight. And I had all day with Craig and everyone else to fret about it.

After pulling on my mud-caked jeans and a v-neck t-shirt I was pretty sure I'd only worn one day since washing it, I scrambled an egg and wolfed it down along with a piece of toast and 2 cups of coffee. Then I walked outside into a beautiful, sunny morning. Dana asked us to meet her at the barn to round up tools to spend the day working in the demo beds. Jessi and Cleo were already there with her, grabbing hoes, rakes, and shovels off the pegs where they hung.

"Good morning, Kelsie!" Dana called as I approached, collecting trowels and pruners into a pile. She looked radiant and well rested, wearing well-worn jeans with a small hole high up on the thigh of one that gave a glimpse of her long leg underneath. "Beautiful day, huh? Grab a couple of empty buckets over there, will you?"

I hurried to get the buckets and tripped over something on the ground, falling forward with a crash.

Cleo rushed to my side, offering a hand up. "You okay?" she asked with a smile. Had she heard Joshua ask me out? I gave a weak nod, climbing to my feet with a forced laugh.

"Maybe I shouldn't have had that extra cup of coffee this morning," I joked to them. I ripped a small hole in my jeans and scraped the knee underneath a little. Blood appeared in small spots around sand grains stuck to the flesh. "Sheesh," I said out loud. "I've gone and impaled myself on the barn floor."

"The perils of farm life," Cleo boomed in her mock announcer voice. "Tragic tales of heroism in bucket grabbing." I rolled my eyes at her and wiped the blood off my knee with the inside of my jeans, something I wouldn't have dreamed of doing two months ago. Briefly, I thought of Caroline watching with disgust and smiled. I'd have to call her again soon.

"I've been thinking about how to use the demo beds to aid each of you on your own educational path," Dana told us. I grinned at Cleo. Dana was always thinking of us and of ways to teach us better. A surge of gratitude for her overwhelmed me as she continued. "What I'd like to do is divide the demo beds among all of you; each of you will tend your own beds. In your section, you can grow things that interest you. We'll tie the beds together with flowers and other design elements, so they're visually cohesive and pleasing. It's like having your own garden," she finished.

Just then, Shantel emerged from the hedge between the trailers and the demo beds. It all came rushing back to me the second I laid eyes on her. Where had she been last night? Was she with Craig? I glared at her as she approached, studying her body language for clues. Her blonde curls bounced in the sunlight as she came toward us. She carefully avoided my gaze, which I found suspicious.

"Shantel!" Dana said. "We missed you last night!" She blushed a bit, mumbling something about how she was sorry to miss the workshop, proving her guilt in my mind. When I watched her and Craig's interactions when we stopped for lunch, I was sure they had sealed the deal. They both avoided eye contact with each other, and Craig seemed especially intent on drawing me back in. I met his flirtatious comments and haphazard touches with a rock hard coldness, making sure he knew that *I* knew exactly what was going on. The more cold and distant I got, the harder he tried, and for once I was eager for Cleo's delicious meal to be over so we could go back to work in the demo beds and he could go fuck himself. Besides, I had my own extracurricular activities to focus on. In a few hours, I would be going on my own date with my own hot farmer. *Eat your heart out, Craig, you bastard.*

I took a quick bath at the end of the day, having warmed up the tub during the last hours of my work, and returned to my trailer to decide what to wear. It had been a long time since I'd been out on a date. It was the first time a man asked me over to his house so he could cook me dinner on a first date. I fumbled through the tub full of clothes in my tiny bathroom when a knock came at my door.

"Who is it?" I called out, my head buried in the shower curtain.

"Cleo!" I heard the reply.

"Come in!" I closed the door on the pile of clothes and came to greet her.

"Whatcha doin'?" she asked casually as she entered, looking around the trailer. She had on an outrageous pair of tight black jeans that were completely covered in zippers of all shapes and sizes, and a pair of black Chuck Taylors. Her hair looked like she'd slept on one side of her head and not the other.

Should I tell her? Would it be weird? "Just getting ready to cook some dinner," I lied.

She raised her eyes at me. "You fired up the tub in the middle of the afternoon so you could clean up to cook yourself dinner?" she asked.

Damn it! I've always been a horrible liar. "No..." I began, unsure of how to say it.

"Are you going to see Joshua or what?" she exploded.

I nodded sheepishly, my mouth breaking into a grin.

"I *knew* it!" she roared back, slapping me on the leg. "I saw how he was looking at you last night. I was worried he wouldn't work up the guts to ask you. He's so shy," she added.

My eyes widened. "You did?"

She nodded, laughing. "Yeah, he was practically falling all over himself trying to pretend he wasn't watching you while Dana was talking."

"Really? I've been wondering if he was interested, but then when he asked last night, I didn't know if I should say yes or not."

"You like him, right?" she asked.

"Yeah, but..." I paused, uncertain of how much to reveal.

"But you're worried about Craig?" she interrupted.

Whoa. Cleo wasn't stupid. Of course, she'd been noticing all that was going on. Plus, she'd seen Craig with countless other interns for years before me.

I nodded again, breathing a sigh of relief at finally being able to process the whole mess with someone.

"Fuck Craig and his fucking head games," she said. "You deserve better than that."

That was nice of her to say, though I wasn't so sure of that myself. I shrugged in reply.

"Kelsie, I love Craig, but he's got a bad case of rooster fever."

I laughed. "He does like to keep the hens in line," I said. Looking at Cleo, I added, "Ever since Shantel showed up, I've felt like we've been in competition for his attention. Last night when she didn't show up for the workshop, I figured she'd won it. Then Joshua was there and I'd really like to get to know him, but I don't want to make things weird with Craig...he seems like he really doesn't like Joshua."

"Of COURSE he doesn't like him!" Cleo bellowed. "Joshua's the only other single man around for miles, the only threat to Craig's White Oak Empire! And he's an amazing man at that! Nothing worse for a ruler of the roost than another rooster strutting his stuff in front of the hens, especially one that can catch their attention." Cleo's eyes hinted at something else she wasn't saying.

"What are you implying, Cleo?" I asked her. Now the tables were turned. She wasn't telling the whole truth, and I could see she wasn't sure if she should.

"Well," she said, leaning in closer. "Don't tell anyone else this, but I'm pretty sure Joshua is what finally broke Dana and Craig apart."

10

That *was* a surprising secret. "What do you mean?" I asked. "Did Dana sleep with him?"

Cleo nodded. "When they first came here, Joshua helped them get the place set up to farm. He was really young then, pretty inexperienced, and I think Aunt Dana, uh, *enlightened* him a little."

Wow. I snickered a little. "Really? Holy *shit* this place is small!"

"Totally," she agreed. "That's why I couldn't live out here permanently. Too incestuous."

I laughed harder. "So Dana slept with Joshua when he was young. Huh. No wonder he stares at her like she's a goddess."

"Don't we all?" Cleo asked. "She *is* a goddess! Anyway, Joshua couldn't handle her. Dana's probably the only person he's ever met that wants multiple partners. He's old fashioned." Cleo winked at me. "He's a one-woman kind of guy." Something about her saying that made me feel both safe and terrified at what was ahead for me that night. I tried to push those thoughts from my mind and focus on Cleo's story.

"She said it was the last straw for her and Craig. He got so angry after she did it that she told him she couldn't date him anymore. She had been honest about her polyamory from the beginning, but he never was okay with it. Like I said before, he wants all the hens for himself."

"He's going to have a hard time with that, huh?" I said, picking at the fuzz on the cushion of the couch-bed, mocking my best impression of Craig, "'I can hook up with whomever I want, but everyone else can only be with me.' Quite the tall order," I finished.

"That's why Dana won't date him anymore," Cleo said. "And that's why you should stop chasing him too, and go for Joshua!" She paused, then quickly added, "Not that it's any of my business."

I reached out and patted her on the shoulder. "I appreciate your advice, Cleo. I'm glad you came over here tonight. I've been stewing about all this for weeks and haven't felt comfortable talking with anyone about it!"

"Yeah, I know what you mean," she said.

I raised my eyebrows again at her, and took the same stab she'd hit me with earlier. "So, what's up with you and Jessi," I asked with a twinkle.

"Aaaaarrrrgghhhh!!!" she half-screamed, burying her head in the sofa cushion. "She's so CUTE!!!"

I laughed as she extracted her melon hair, standing on end with the static from the cushion. Cleo was hilarious.

"So, are you 'day-ting'?" I asked, drawing quotation marks in the air with my fingers.

"I don't *know!*" Cleo wailed. "She's so focused on farming that everything else gets lost." She caught my eye and winked. "We have been hanging out a lot."

"Ooh la la," I teased back.

Cleo scuffed her foot along the threaded carpet on the floor of the trailer. "I really like her. She's not like my friends back in Portland." She paused, looking off into space, then continued, "She's healthy. She's driven. She has a goal and she's going for it instead of just sitting around talking about it. And she's really pretty," she added with a smile.

"Yeah, she's great," I agreed. "Really smart, and a really hard worker. I think you two would make a good pair!"

"Not as good as you and Joshua," Cleo teased back. "When are you supposed to be there?"

"7," I said, looking at the clock. "6:30—Shit! I'd better get ready!"

"What are you gonna wear on your big date?" she asked me.

"Cleo, I don't know. I'm horrible at this stuff. My friend Caroline usually gave me fashion advice for important stuff." I laughed, thinking of Caroline and how excited she would be for me to be going on a date. "She dressed me for my interview here," I told Cleo.

"Well, I think Joshua would like you even if you showed up in a paper bag," Cleo said.

"I don't get it," I told her. "He's been staring at me with this crazy intense stare ever since the first time I met him. He doesn't even know me! How can he think he likes me when he doesn't even know me?"

"You know you like him, right?" she asked.

I nodded. "I know I'd like to *get* to know him."

"Kelsie, you remember what I told you the first day we met?" she asked.

I did remember. "You said I was ripe."

"Exactly. You may not be able to see it in yourself, but it's obvious on the outside. You are a balloon that's swelled to the point of bursting and, any day now, you're going to explode and shower this world with your incredible talents. Joshua can see that."

"Incredible talents? Cleo, I don't mean to disillusion you, but I've never been particularly talented at anything."

"You're a natural on the farm," she said. "Don't fool yourself. You're considerate and caring, and you have a real desire to do something meaningful with your life. That's a rarity."

"Thanks, Cleo," I said, burying my head again in the clothes-filled shower. I emerged with an emerald green top that I didn't remember wearing yet on the farm. It smelled relatively clean, which at this point was the best I could do. "How's this?" I asked Cleo.

"Not exactly my style," she said, zipping and unzipping one of the many zippers on her jeans, "but on you I think it'll look great."

"Yeah, those pants are really something," I told her. She nodded, laughing at herself.

I had brought what Caroline called my booty jeans. "Everyone needs a pair of these," she'd said. I promised myself I'd never wear them to work, so I had something nice in case an occasion arose. I slid them on over a plain white pair of panties. I didn't figure Joshua and I would be progressing to a point where he'd be seeing my underwear, which suited me just fine. I wasn't ready to go jumping in.

I looked myself over in the full-length mirror on the bathroom door while Cleo made low whistling sounds. "You look great," she said. "And don't forget it!" She pulled a bottle of wine out from under her hoodie and handed it to me as she gave me a good-bye hug and thanked me for talking with her about Jessi. "I didn't want to be presumptuous about your evening plans, but I brought this along just in case you *were* doing something where this *might* come in handy."

"Thanks, Cleo." I followed her out the door on my way to Joshua's house.

I snuck around behind the greenhouses and past the bee boxes to the gate Joshua had told me about, trying to avoid being seen from the farmhouse. The last thing I needed was Craig seeing me and coming out to find out what I was up to. Finding the gate was easy. I stepped through it onto Joshua's land, snagging my shirt on a blackberry bramble that reached through the gate as if waiting for just such an opportunity. *Damn it!* I said out loud, pausing to remove its thorned tentacle from the fabric. The damn thing had ripped a small hole in the side of my shirt. I could see lights on in the house in front of a high-roofed, red barn. Looking out beyond the barn, Joshua's land looked completely different from Dana's and Craig's. Instead of rows of patchwork vegetables, fences sectioned the pastures into small paddocks in a complicated grid that stretched back as far as I could see.

My heart caught in my throat as I passed by the barn and found a well-worn path that led to the back door of the house. Large boot-prints punctured the muddy trail, and I fit my own smaller boot neatly inside one of them, satisfied at how tiny it seemed. Everything about this man made me feel small, a feeling I had not experienced in my previous dating life. For whatever reason, all the men I wound up with to this point were impossibly skinny, and our lovemaking always made me, with my ample breasts and hips, feel oversized. A tremble streaked between my legs as an image of making love with Joshua flashed through my mind. I was positive there wasn't a small thing about him. Stuffing that image away, I climbed the few steps to his back door and knocked timidly.

In seconds it opened, and there stood Joshua, spatula in hand, rumpled blonde hair curling gently over the tops of his ears, wearing a large flannel shirt and a gorgeous smile that set off his strong jaw. His eyes looked excited and a bit nervous as he welcomed me inside.

It did not occur to me before, but it had been over a month since I had set foot inside an actual house. It felt so cozy and, though small, it was roomy as a mansion compared to my trailer. I smiled back at him and offered the bottle of wine Cleo had brought me. "I didn't know if you would want this..." I began, talking a little too quickly. "I forgot to ask yesterday if I should bring anything." It smelled good in his house, a mix of wood smoke and basil.

He tipped his head in gratitude, taking the bottle from me, pausing for a minute when our fingers touched before pulling it away, sending a chill down my entire body. His eyes didn't leave mine.

"It smells really *good* in here!" I blurted out, too loudly. Joshua grinned. "You want to take off your boots and I'll give you the grand tour? I try to keep the mud on the outside as much as possible.."

"Oh sure," I stumbled a bit as I bent down to untie my laces. *Why did I always feel so awkward in situations like this?*

Joshua proceeded to give me a tour of his house, living room, kitchen with dining table, spare room, bathroom, bedroom, which I quickly hurried past. It was simple, not cluttered and not fancy, clean but not too clean. A single man's house, I reasoned. A single goat farmer's house.

"What are we having?" I asked as we returned to the kitchen.

"It's an *Italian* theme," he said in his best aristocratic accent. "Tortellini with goat cheese, pesto, and walnuts. Should go good with this here bottle of wine, huh?" He uncorked the bottle. In his large hand, the oversized bottle looked like a beer bottle or something--the perfect sized vessel for him to drink from, which made me smile.

"What?" he asked, grinning back at me.

"Oh, nothing," I responded quickly. "It's just that that bottle looks small in your hand."

"Yeah, pretty much how it is. You should see me milking the goats!" He laughed out loud, a great, hearty, sparkling laugh. "I'll have to introduce you to the girls. You'll fall in love in no time!" His easiness was beginning to rub off, especially once I got a glass of wine in my hand.

"You and Dana, both with your flock of girls," I teased him. "Only hers apparently speak Spanish."

Joshua chuckled again. "I've always found that interesting too. My girls are unfortunately monolingual, just like me." He took two plates out of a wooden cupboard and rummaged in a drawer for some silverware. "What about you?" he asked nonchalantly. "Do you speak anything other than English?"

I shook my head. "I took a semester of French in high school, but I don't remember any of it."

He offered me a plate. "Do you want me to dish you up, or do you prefer to serve yourself?"

I appreciated his consideration. "*Merci*," I smiled, taking the plate.

We brought our plates and our wine glasses over to his small table and sat across from each other. The sun was barely detectible outside the window, which made it feel cozier inside. He held his glass up and clanked it with mine. "To our first dinner together," he said.

Our first *dinner together?* That seemed a bit presumptuous to me. I raised my eyebrows at him, but he just grinned confidently back at me with his warm, blue eyes.

The dinner was delicious and the conversation flowed easier and easier. Between bites of scrumptious pasta, made with frozen pesto Cleo had given him from last season and delectable cheese he'd made from his girls' milk, we shared stories, filled in the blocky outlines of our lives up to this point. I told him about my family, my sister the soon-to-be lawyer, and how I never felt like I fit. Joshua told me about his family, how they had all grown up around here, and how he was farming this land that belonged to a family friend because his own dad was still farming his family's land just a couple miles away. He was saving to buy his own place soon. "How about you?" he asked. "Do you think you want to make a career of farming?"

I hadn't decided I *didn't* want to do that, but I obviously still had a lot to learn. "It's the first thing I've really ever felt passionate about," I told him. "Jessi was saying the other day what she loves about farming is that you can spend your whole life doing it and just keep learning more and more, getting better and better at it."

"Like Wendell Berry," Joshua offered.

"Who?"

"Oh, he's a great writer-philosopher-farmer. He says that people want to travel all over the world to better understand it, but that the best way to understand the world is to settle into one piece of land and study it for a lifetime. He says that after a lifetime of studying it, you'll realize it will consistently surprise you, proving that we never really can understand the whole world."

I liked that. Joshua poured me another glass of wine and asked if I'd like to go meet his goats, which, of course, I did. We strapped on boots at his back door and he offered me a flannel shirt for some extra warmth, as it had gotten a bit cooler since I arrived. He held it while I slid my arms in and we both began laughing when my hands couldn't reach the ends of the sleeves. "I feel like I'm wearing a blanket!" I told him. He pushed the ends of the sleeves up over my hands like a dad dressing a little kid. When he had excavated my second arm from the fabric, he took my hand and led me through his open back door. I cherished how he held my small hand in his big one. I leaned casually against him as we walked the well-worn path out to his barn in the dark. The goats were asleep inside but they stirred as we entered, their bodies softly lit by the moonlight shining in through the barn door. I saw two or three babies curled up next to larger mamas on the straw floor. Some lay in groups, some lay by themselves, all of them watching us with mild curiosity.

"Here," Joshua said quietly, leading me by the hand to one of the smaller goats curled up in the straw near us. "This is Chestnut."

Joshua knelt down beside her and scratched her head and she rose to meet his fingers, bleating softly. "She loves this," he said to me with an enchanted, sideways smile.

And so it happened. Kneeling on the straw-covered floor of his barn in the moonlight, I fell head over heels in love with Joshua Murphy.

Of course, I would not admit this to myself yet, but witnessing this giant man so openly and tenderly loving a small animal, and seeing him share that intimate part of himself so freely with me, touched my heart in a way it had never been touched before. I watched his profile, lit from the side, and his big, strong arm so gentle on Chestnut's wiry hair. He brought my hand to her body, and her skin tensed slightly at my touch. "Don't be nervous," he whispered to me. "She'll love you forever if you scratch her right here by her shoulder." I did as he suggested, and she turned her face toward me, staring a hole through me with her odd eyes with slits that ran the wrong way. "Her eyes are kinda weird," I said, embarrassed.

He chuckled. "Yeah, they take some getting used to. It's like they can see into your *soul*," he said, over-dramatically. I smacked him playfully on the arm.

"Well, Chess, we'll leave you to sleep," he said to her, giving her a few strong pats on the belly before rising to his feet and pulling me up with him. He followed me back out the door and closed it behind us.

We found our full wine glasses when we got inside, and Joshua led me to the sofa with them. Looking at him was almost too much for me to bear at this point; this ache that had swelled in the barn was painful. I yearned, a tragic feeling, like when you're next in line to get on a huge rollercoaster. You're putting yourself into a situation where you'll be flung here and there, dropped and lifted up, your heart and your stomach will do flips, and it will be exhilarating, liberating, terrifying. It most certainly will end sooner or later. You know all of this will happen before you even step into the line, but you do it anyway. *And you'll do it anyway*, I frowned into my wine glass, my hair falling over one shoulder.

"Kelsie from Salem, you are absolutely beautiful," Joshua said, his voice slow and confident. My stomach tightened and I gasped a small breath, then turned accusatorily to meet his intense stare as he sat casually on the sofa, one leg propped up on it so he could turn and face me. I didn't know what to say. To my memory, no man had ever called me beautiful before, at least not outright like that. "How do you know?" I asked him, shooting back. "You hardly know me!"

"I know you well enough to know that."

He was cocky then. He took a reckless swig of wine and set his glass down on the table. Then he grabbed my arms and pulled me easily to him. Before I could even calculate what was happening, he wrapped his arms around my waist, leaned in, and brought his lips down on mine. He smelled and tasted incredible—wholesome, manly. His hands pressed against the small of my back, drawing me in further, and then he lay back on the sofa, pulling me down on top of him. He held me there firmly, my thigh rubbing against him as he swelled. I brought my mouth down on his then, drinking him in to avoid dying of thirst. My breath got heavy, he gave small moans of pleasure as I stretched myself out along the full length of him, rubbing, tasting his open mouth.

Suddenly, he lifted me up off him, and quickly flipped himself on top of me, pinning my hands down over my head with his own. He stared down at me as I lay there, calculating what he wanted to do next. My hair splayed out over the cushions, I could feel air on my belly where my shirt had slid up toward my breasts, which heaved with each short gasp I took. Joshua's eyes were hungry, passionate, his mouth wide with a grin at what he had caught. Like a trapped deer, I writhed below him in anticipation, my body frantic, desperate.

His eyes twinkling, he brought his lips down to mine but as I opened to drink him in again, he brushed over them, drawing his head down to my neck, still holding my hands above my head. He teased the vulnerable skin under my chin with his mouth, softly at first, then sucking harder as I wriggled to get free of his hands. I moaned out loud with pleasure, in agony, and finally he let go, bringing one of his hands to my bare stomach, keeping the other one pinned over my head. He cupped my whole belly in it, rubbing the smooth skin as he kissed at my neck gently, teasing me. "You feel so good," he whispered in my ear, sliding his hand up under my shirt, under my bra. My heart pounded harder as he found my breast and took it easily into his hand. Finally, a man whose hands fit me! He let out a low moan. His kisses grew harder on my neck as he squeezed me, filled his hand with me, and then gave my nipple a little pinch as he bit my neck playfully. I gasped, arching my back into him, which turned him on even more. He rubbed against my leg, biting, pinching. I brought my hand under the back of his shirt and scratched at his strong back, my swollen clit tickling his swollen penis through our jeans.

He brought his other hand behind my back now, lifting me up off the sofa and sliding my shirt up over my head. I raised my arms and he pulled it over my head. As he struggled to unhook my bra, I started to unbutton the buttons on his flannel shirt, revealing his white t-shirt. He left my uncooperative bra and rose instead to remove the flannel first, exposing his broad chest, biceps bulging at the soft t-shirt fabric underneath, and then the t-shirt, uncovering his wide stomach and his strong, barreled chest covered in a mat of blonde curls. I think my mouth dropped open a bit then, but he pretended not to notice. Instead, he grinned cockeyed at me and said, “Your turn.”

I reached behind my back and undid my black bra, freeing my breasts and sliding the fabric off my arm and onto the floor. Joshua smiled hungrily, and brought himself down again on top of me, his mouth and his hands moving all over my belly, my breasts, my neck, my lips. I reached as far as I could around his back, tracing the lines and valleys with my fingers, pressing into him as he pressed into me. I ran them up into his blonde curls and over the curve of his neck. I wanted to consume him wholly, right there, to have him consume me too. I dipped my fingers down his back and under the elastic of his briefs and he pushed harder into me, his weight heavy on my legs, on my cunt. I slid them around to his stomach and teased at the area around the button of his Carhardtts, but to my dismay, he pushed my hands away.

While he continued to kiss me, I tried again, and again, he pushed my hand away. I gave a small whimper, but he just brought his lips to mine again. I felt dangerous now, unbridled. Why was he holding back? I thrashed against him, rubbing his rock hard penis with my legs. He was obviously ready. “Joshua?” I breathed, half pleading, half whining.

He stopped and pushed himself off of me, panting. He fixed his blue, blue eyes on mine and said, his voice shaking, "Kelsie, I want you. I want you so badly right now." His lips hung slightly open, his hair wild from my hands in it. "But I really like you, and I don't want to rush this and mess it up."

He cupped his hand gently on the curve of my cheek and leaned down, kissing me long and soft on my lips, and I kissed him back, just as soft. Tears rose gently to my eyes as I realized that he truly did. He pulled himself up and studied my eyes again while I blinked in panic to hide them, but he just smiled a warm, deep knowing, and wiped the one tear that had managed to leak out onto my cheek.

"How about this?" Joshua offered. "If you wake up in your trailer tomorrow and you still think you would have rather stayed here tonight, I'll be happy to oblige you next time. Just as soon as you ask me out again," he added quickly, grinning at me, and, despite myself, my mouth broke into a smile. I grabbed him around his neck and pulled him down on top of me again, and kissed him all over his face. He walked me back to my trailer later, and I stepped up onto the stoop so we were at eye level. There, he gave me the longest, sweetest goodnight kiss I'd ever received.

11

Getting out of bed the next morning was pure torture. I lay huddled with the sheets wrapped around me, hands moving frantically over my skin as I struggled to remember every second of my evening with Joshua. I stared at the cardboard ceiling that shielded me from the rain pelting the tin roof and pictured him on top of me, his hair rumpled and his beautiful blue eyes beaming down at me while he moved my body like taffy with his strong hands. How was I going to make it through the day? I wondered, wanting to remain in my reverie all morning. Instead, I did what all farmers do—I got my ass up, made myself some coffee, pulled on my rain gear, and got to work. We were to begin harvesting that day for our first farmer's markets. Some of us would go on Saturday to a market in Portland, and others would set up the booth in Salem.

As Dana and Craig rallied the troops for our harvest experience, Cleo stepped close to drill me on the events of the evening. The rain was falling heavily, but at least it was warmer than it had been.

"So?" she whispered, raising her eyes under the hood of her leopard print rain slicker.

I blushed uncontrollably, unable to stammer a word.

"That good, huh?" she smiled.

I raised my eyebrows in agreement, chills running through my entire body. I gave a small shiver and turned my attention back to Dana, whose stern gaze in our direction left no uncertainty about our need to focus quickly on the day.

"Harvest is a whole other animal," Dana said, sounding more like Craig than her own laid-back, confident self. "It can be grueling and tedious, especially in the rain, and it will take some time for everyone to get on the same page about the techniques for the different crops. Every farm has different standards for harvest. On this one, we have different standards for the different markets we service—farmer's market in Portland is more competitive, so we take the nicest selection there. Farmer's market in Salem is a little less so, but things still have to look gorgeous for people to stop at our booth and buy them. When we start CSA next month, we can give our members some things we can't sell at markets, because we have more personalized interactions with them." Looking at us growing soggier by the minute, she ushered us over under the roof of the wash station to continue the pep talk.

I glanced over at Craig as we stepped under the tin roof. He didn't seem particularly interested in me, which I took as a great sign that he didn't see me going over to Joshua's last night. The thighs and knees of my jeans were already wet, but my torso stayed dry and warm under my rain jacket.

Dana continued. "I will be organizing the harvest in the field while Craig organizes the activity in the wash station. You'll get a chance to try harvesting, washing, and packing the produce today, and you'll become more proficient than you'd probably like to be at all of it by the end of the season." She smiled her warm smile. Jessi and Cleo laughed, which I guess meant they knew what she meant by that and apparently agreed. I politely laughed with them, though I was sure I'd love the harvest. It was the culmination of all our work. What wouldn't we love about it?

Shantel echoed my thoughts, in her own cheerleader way, which was growing more annoying to me by the minute. "Oh, I doubt that! I'm so excited to start harvesting!" She smiled at Craig, who immediately threw an *"I want you, too"* look toward me. The curls that hung out from under the hood of her floral-print slicker had turned to blonde strings, with droplets of water sliding off each one. Seeing Craig's too-obvious glance in my direction, she shot me her own haughty but panicked glare. Maybe it wasn't going to be smooth sailing today after all. I slunk my head back into my hood and took a deep breath. I could still feel Joshua's lips on my neck.

"...braising mix, the mild and the spicy salad mixes will all be harvested the same way." Shit! What was Dana saying? What did I miss? She was pointing to a large white board hung on the wall that had all sorts of crops and numbers listed on it. "Jessi, I want you and Cleo in the field with me to begin. Once we get a few things finished, one of you can head back into the wash station and plug in there. Kelsie and Shantel, since you'll need a lot of instruction this first time, I'd like to split you up, taking one of you with me and leaving one of you with Craig in the wash station. I don't care who."

Shantel looked nervously at me. I know she thought we'd both want to be with Craig, but at this exact moment, I wanted to be as far away from him as possible. As I opened my mouth to say I'd go with Dana, she and Craig spoke in unison.

"Kelsie, why don't you start with me?" he said, just as Shantel blurted out, "I'd like to start in the wash station." She glared at Craig and folded her arms across her chest. I couldn't believe how blatant she was.

Aah! My palms clammed up and I swallowed hard. Luckily, Dana came to my rescue. "Kelsie will start in the field, and Shantel will start in the wash station." I gave her a grateful smile and took a step toward her like a little kid who was thankfully chosen by the team leader to be on her red rover team. It caused Cleo to snicker a little, and I shot her a panicked, haughty look of my own. God it was going to be a long day.

We left Craig and Shantel in the wash station and headed out into the rain with garden carts packed with giant plastic tubs, knives, and scissors. Dana demonstrated her desired cutting technique on the bed of Mizuna that Shantel had seeded our first day out in the field with Craig. The memory of it flooded my mind and I remembered how turned on I had been by him, how eager I was to please him, how confidently he'd grabbed my behind and my breast as though they were rightfully his. What would I do if he did those things today? I certainly still found him attractive, but after last night with Joshua, I'd feel guilty letting him touch me again. Plus, he'd gone and hooked up with Shantel outside of the workday. Even without Joshua in the picture, I was growing weary of competing with her for his attention. But how could I change our relationship now? How could I explain that I wanted him to treat me more like he treated Cleo and Jessi now? Would he make me leave the farm if I did? What if I told him about Joshua?

"Kelsie!" Dana snapped. "Are you getting this?"

Oh, crap. "I'm sorry Dana. I'm having trouble concentrating this morning. I promise I'll do better." I knelt down to watch as she expertly sliced through large chunks of mizuna and threw handful after handful into the bucket. "We'll fill four totes with this mizuna," she said, "less than we usually would. The first market in Salem is generally slow, especially if it's raining like this tomorrow, and it will take us a few weeks to re-establish ourselves in Portland. You stop coming for a couple months and people forget who you are."

She continued, still chopping away even as she turned the bed over to Cleo. "Cleo, why don't you finish up here with the mizuna, and Jessi, now that you've seen our technique, go ahead and do the same with the red giant—just two of those. Take the totes to the wash station after you've filled them. Kelsie," she said, taking me gently by the arm, "you and I will go over to the arugula bed so you can get some practice."

I nodded and scurried after her, feeling less like the kid she picked for her team and more like a puppy who was just scolded by its mother.

We knelt in the bed I had seeded with Craig just over a month ago, which now wore a deep green carpet of leaves about six inches tall. I took a hold of a handful of plants as Dana had showed me and sliced through them clumsily with my knife. A pungent, peppery smell wafted from the cut stems of all those leaves. Dana reached down and moved my hand slightly to get a better angle the next time around. I tried again, with more success this time.

"Great," Dana said. "You'll get the hang of this in no time." A second wave of spice met our noses. "I love cutting the arugula," she said. "It's incredible how such an unassuming green leaf holds such potency inside."

I nodded, inhaling the now-familiar scent. I had really grown to love the nutty, spicy taste in our lunchtime salads. "I never thought I'd be eating this kind of stuff," I confessed to her.

She smiled. "I know, it's so invigorating, isn't it?" She joined me on the other side of the bed, slicing off section after section of greens, leaving a little stub poking out of the ground. Of course, she whizzed ahead, stopping to snack on stray leaves every few handfuls. "Now there's food everywhere to eat while we're working!" she cried, stuffing a wad of arugula into her mouth. I helped myself to a few leaves as well, wet with rainwater, right out of the garden, letting their pungent flavor fill my mouth and the sharp aftertaste tickle up into my nose. How amazing! I thought of Joshua's goats out in his pasture, munching away on the grass, but without rain jackets. We grinned at each other as we chomped away. We weren't all that different from the goats right now, except we were using knives instead of our mouths to collect our food.

The stubble of greenish-white stems grew behind us as we moved down the bed, a desolate-looking massacre. "What happens to this bed now?" I called to Dana, who was now well ahead of me in the row.

"We'll take one more cutting off it all but the last little block at the end, which we'll let go to seed. Then the bed will get turned under and planted with something else, probably peppers."

I studied the bare ground lined with tiny plant stems behind me, trying to picture how leaves would grow out of them again, but I couldn't imagine how it could happen. Obviously, Dana wasn't pulling my leg, so I would have to wait and see. I concentrated on my technique, trying to move faster like Dana. She reached the end of her side of the row and started back toward me on mine. Her second tote was already brimming with greens. I looked into mine. Over half-full. It sure took a long time to get a whole tote! She grabbed another one and raced back toward me, slicing and tossing the greens into the tote. Finally, we reached each other. She'd filled up three while I had filled only one. But the bed was finished.

"You did great, for your first harvest!" she assured me as we each packed our totes onto the garden cart at the end of our row. I shrugged, not really agreeing with her. Four totes fit the cart perfectly. Dana wheeled it toward the wash station while I tagged along behind her, glancing back at the barren bed that this morning had been a vibrant plate of dark green leaves.

"Kelsie, you seem distant today," she said. "Are you doing okay?"

I mumbled a feeble "mmm-hmm," guarding all I had bubbling around inside me.

"I have a book I think you might like. How about meeting me for a few minutes after work so I can give it to you, if you're interested."

"Okay," I said cautiously, not sure what exactly she was getting at. For some reason, meeting with Dana after work made me extremely nervous.

"Kelsie, I'm not going to attack you!" she laughed, stopping the cart and reaching over to squeeze me on the shoulder. "I just like to do periodic check-ins with the interns to make sure you're getting the most out of your time here."

We stepped out of the rain and into the wash station, where Craig and Shantel were quickly dumping totes of greens into sinks full of water. Cleo and Jessi had already brought in some of their harvests and were out gathering more.

"Here's the arugula," Dana announced, lining the totes up on the table behind them. "Kelsie, this is where you'll put items from the field that are ready for washing."

Craig turned around and smiled at me. "How'd you do out there?" he asked. Just having him look at me made me lose my breath and I struggled to find my voice to answer. Before I could, Dana butted in for me.

"She did great! A real natural. A couple more weeks and she'll be as fast as Cleo."

Craig grinned at me and I held his gaze for a second before turning away. My face felt hot, even though my body was dripping wet.

"Ready to get back at it?" Dana asked.

I nodded feebly and followed her and the cart back out into the field, after she'd stacked two more totes on.

"We'll be doing kale now, just a couple of totes for a braising mix," she told me. "We'll pick a few leaves from all the different plants so we have a lively and colorful mix. We'll also do this with the chard, later."

Out in the field, she showed me how to break the bottom leaves off the small plants to encourage their other leaves to grow bigger. I remembered doing a similar thing with Cleo to harvest the humongous collard greens in the demo bed, and so I actually got the hang of it quickly. Dana told me we'd be bunching the kale when the leaves got bigger. She beamed at me as we filled our second tote.

"I think you've got this pretty good. I want to show you how to harvest the radishes, and then I'll have you switch with Shantel and get some experience in the wash station."

It had to happen sometime. *Nothing to do but do it. It's just a part of the job.* Dana asked me to wheel the cart with our kale totes to the wash station and grab a couple more while she checked on Cleo and Jessi.

I trudged back through the soggy ground, dragging the cart behind me. As I approached the wash station, I saw Craig leaning into Shantel, possibly kissing her. A wave of jealousy crept over me and I made a loud cough as I reached the threshold.

"Kelsie!" Craig exclaimed. Shantel pulled back abruptly, whipping back around to her sink full of greens. I was furious.

"Craig!" I sarcastically retorted in mock surprise.

"You, uh, coming in here soon?" he asked. Shantel scowled at him.

"Unfortunately, yes," I snapped at him, wiping rainwater off my face. "Though I hate to leave the lovely weather outside." I slammed the totes down, picked up the empty ones, and tromped off into the field again, leaving the two of them to whatever they were just doing.

Why was I so angry anyway? I wondered. It wasn't like I didn't also have a steamy night last night with Joshua. In fact, after my incredible evening with Joshua, I didn't even feel like making out with

Craig. Was I acting like him, like Cleo said he was? Like it was okay for me to do it but not for him? And poor Shantel. He really had her roped in.

I reached the radish rows, covered with the now-familiar white blanket of row cover. I remembered my last day working in it, seeing Craig's anger as I told Joshua I'd love to come see his place. Baring my butt to Craig's punishing hand, all the while dancing the weird dance with Shantel that kept us in competition with each other over a man who wanted to have us both. The whole experience felt distasteful today, after a night of wonderful connection and some truly hot chemistry with Joshua. Not that Craig hadn't made me feel that way on occasion, but there was an openness, a sincerity that I felt with Joshua that was unparalleled by any relationship up to this moment in my life.

Dana interrupted my critical monologue in her cheerful, matter-of-fact way. "Let's see how they're coming along!" she said, reaching down and pulling a round, red radish from the soggy earth.

"Wow!" I exclaimed. "Those were nothing just a couple weeks ago!"

"Not bad, eh? That's the beauty of radishes—a quick crop, and something other than leaves, which is very welcome at this time of year." She pulled another, a bright purple one this time. "Let's put 10 in a bunch," she said to me, plopping the little globes out of the ground at a rapid pace. Pink ones, red ones, white ones, purple ones, all that color hidden below the soil, with only a set of scraggly, poky leaves sticking out.

"I don't think I would have thought to pull one up if I hadn't already learned they were radishes," I told her. "They don't look like anything on the surface."

"Yes, yes, a miracle," she murmured, whipping twist ties around the bunches and putting them into a tote.

I was too cautious. I couldn't tell if they were ready yet, and I skipped over some in the row that looked a bit too small.

"Kelsie, just pull them all out. If they're not big enough to bunch, throw them into the tote loose. We'll sort and bunch what we can later, and give the rest away to Food Not Bombs. If we leave individuals, they'll get lost in weeds before we can get back to them."

"No problem," I said. "What's Food Not Bombs?" I pulled a particularly gigantic bright pink radish out of the ground. "And can I eat some of these?"

Dana laughed, straightening up for a minute. "Of course you can eat them!" she said, wiping the mud from the deep purple radish in her hands on her wet jeans and chomping down on it. I followed suit, splattering a streak of thick mud across the wet thighs of my jeans. I took a tentative bite. An incredible burst of sweet-spicy juice shot into my mouth as I crunched down on the crisp, white flesh. "Wow! These are really GOOD!" I told her.

She laughed again. "You sound shocked, Kelsie! Of *course,* it's delicious. It just sprouted and grew from the goodness of the earth!"

I finished chewing that radish and stifled the urge to stuff another in my mouth. I needed to fill up my bunches, not my belly. I made myself a promise that I'd make three bunches before I ate another.

"Food Not Bombs is an anarchist organization with groups all over the country. They take food wherever they can get it—from dumpsters, farms, donations from grocery stores, wherever—then cook it up and give it to people for free. There's a group in Portland."

"Who are they?" I asked.

"Just people who want to get food to people who need it. How many bunches do you have there?" she asked me.

I looked in my bin. "Twelve," I replied.

"We'll take 100 today. It's hard to say how they'll sell. But they make the booth look lively and attractive, so in that way they're a hit at a spring market." She looked into her own tote. "I'm at 36. Let's keep track now and stop when we reach 100."

After we finished, Dana sent me back to the wash station with the bunches of colorful, mud-caked radishes. I stomped in and loaded the totes onto the long table.

"Your turn with Dana," I said to Shantel's back. I saw her straighten her blouse a little before turning to face me.

"Thank you, Kelsie," she said, too sweetly, pulling on her rain jacket and bounding out into the field. I for one was happy to get mine off, hanging it on a hook near the white board and noticing a thick line of water leading from the v in my grey v-neck down to the button of my jeans. Giving a huge sigh of resignation, I walked up to Craig, where he was spinning what looked like a huge wooden-slatted barrel held on its side by a large metal shaft with a crank.

"Kelsie," he said, giving my wet chest the once-over. I turned away from him and faced the contraption he was spinning.

"It's a salad spinner," he announced proudly. "Built it myself. It mixes all the different greens so we get an even distribution of each as we pack the bags, but it does it more gently than the commercial ones so it doesn't break as many leaves."

I obviously hadn't seen the commercial ones, but this one was impressive. "Cool," I said, temporarily forgetting the awkwardness between us. Greedy womanizer or not, he was a damn good farmer with a lot of creativity and wisdom to share. He opened the door to the barrel and gently removed a handful of leaves. "Mild mesclun mix, ready to go!" he beamed. "We'll bag this and then move on to the braising mix. Grab the bags over there, will you?" he asked, pointing to a roll next to the white board.

I retrieved them and he showed me how to gently bag half-pounds and weigh the bags without breaking too many leaves. We worked together on it and, of course, like Dana, he was a lot quicker than I was. As we bagged, he explained his wash station system, which was very exacting, just like his greenhouse. Certain crops get washed first, certain ones later (namely the dirtier ones), sanitize the totes after use, everything in its place, orderly and tidy. I smiled inwardly at his obsessive nature, and how he'd found the perfect profession to showcase it in an effective and sexy way.

He must have sensed my shift in mood, because the next time I turned to weigh a bag of mesclun mix, he rested his hand on my ass.

I whipped around accusatorily, and he pulled it away with an exaggerated, "Sorry!" He seemed as confused by my change in behavior as I was, and we worked in silence for a while. Every few minutes, he would snap an order at me, a way of doing something different so it was more efficient, but other than that, we didn't speak.

We finished bagging the mild mesclun mix and he led me into the walk-in to show me where to put it. When we entered the cold refrigerator, I saw a shelf of greens already bagged up. "That's the spicy mesclun," he said, pointing to it. "Shantel and I finished it earlier." I winced at her name and, apparently, he sensed it too, because he turned and grabbed me by the arms, pulling me into him.

12

Before I could protest, Craig brought his mouth down hard on mine. I fought to break free even as insatiable lust welled up inside me. I had wanted this for so long, but now here it was, and it wasn't right at all. Craig felt good, smooth, but he didn't feel like Joshua. I finally broke free of his grip and shoved him so hard he almost knocked into the shelf of mesclun mix we'd just filled.

"God Damn it, Craig!' I yelled as he straightened his shirt and sputtered a miffed little "Sheesh!" He really was like a rooster, strutting around grabbing at the hens when he felt the urge, ruffling his feathers at rejection.

He stepped toward me again under the fluorescent light of the walk in. The cold and my rage made my nipples stand on end and I turned to walk out the door before he could notice.

He grabbed me from behind then, sliding his hands around my waist and talking fast in my ear. "I'm sorry, Kelsie," he said. "I'm sorry." I softened a little into his touch. "I just want you so bad. Don't you want me too?" His hands slipped under my shirt and kneaded my belly.

My knees got weak. I could feel his breath on my neck.

"Won't you join me after work, Kelsie?" he whispered, giving my ear a small nibble. "We could take a walk in the woods..." His fingers moved fast over the soft flesh of my front as he pushed hard against me from the back.

"Um, um, I can't," I finally let out, pulling away from him again. I turned to face him. "Dana asked to speak with me after work."

"Oh, I see," he said, composing himself once again. "Maybe another time." He passed me nonchalantly and walked out the door, holding it for me as though nothing had happened. "Let's get back to the braising mix."

Heart pounding, I followed him out into the rainy midday. Two totes of small, white turnips had arrived since we went inside the walk-in.

"SUUUUUUEEEEYY!" Cleo's unmistakable lunch call sounded. Relieved, I threw on my jacket and ran toward the outdoor kitchen without as much as a glance at Craig.

We analyzed the harvest over a delicious mixed green and phyllo pie Cleo had made with Joshua's goat feta, along with a green salad with hard-boiled eggs, toasted hazelnuts and the white turnips Jessi had harvested earlier.

After lunch, first Jessi and then Cleo joined Craig and me in the wash station. I welcomed their presence. Eventually, all six of us packed the little shed, completing our harvest as the sun slanted sideways, breaking through the clouds and shooting powerful beams of light over our fields and the fields beyond.

Craig emerged from the walk-in with a six-pack of Ninkasi, my favorite microbrew from Eugene. "To the first harvest!" he offered, handing each of us a bottle. Cleo grabbed Jessi's and expertly popped the top off it with the cap from her own bottle.

"Wow, Cleo," Jessi teased. "Had a little practice with that?"

"There are a great many survival skills one learns in Portland," she retorted, handing Jessi her open beer.

I laughed hard at that. Even though I grew up an hour outside it, Portland was like another universe, one that intimidated me.

"Drink up and get to bed early," Craig told us. "We'll need you out here by 5:00 a.m. to load up for market."

A collective groan circled the crew and butterflies flapped hard in my stomach.

After we finished our beers, Dana went with me as I headed toward the chicken coop; I needed to collect eggs. The beer relaxed me a bit and I walked easily alongside her long gait.

"What did you think of harvest?" she asked me.

"It was incredible to see all that food piled up after we finished," I told her. "I've never thought about all the work that goes into getting stuff ready to sell like you see in the store."

"Faceless food," she agreed. "It's a tragedy. People would make different choices if they saw the whole process of growing food."

"I never would have understood the process, if I hadn't come here."

"So you're enjoying your time here then? Learning a lot?"

I nodded emphatically. "You have no idea," I said. "I feel like a whole world is opening up to me, and I'm opening up along with it." I glanced shyly at her, though I knew I didn't need to be nervous about admitting that. Dana saw me opening to it the first day she met me. It took me awhile to figure it out.

"What, in particular, interests you?" she asked.

Joshua's blue eyes filled my mind first, but I waited for what came next. "The bees really fascinate me," I told her. "I like their orderliness."

Dana nodded. "I thought so."

We'd reached the chicken pen, and the *chicas* made a veritable stampede toward us when we came into view. Laughing, I continued, "Of course, I'm loving the chickens. And the vegetables are great." Dana let out a laugh, too. "I guess I covered it all," I said.

"Well I'm glad you're enjoying everything," she told me. "Specifically, I've been looking for someone to apprentice with the bees. Since you live not far away, you may be able to continue with the bees after you're done with the internship."

I blinked at her while a black and white *chica* pecked half-heartedly at my shoelace. "So you want me to learn how to care for the bees more?" I asked.

She nodded. "I'd like to teach you everything I know, if you'd like to learn it."

I felt honored. "That would be great!"

"We'll probably have to work with them outside the normal work day, at least until June, when it slows down. Is that okay with you?"

"Sure," I replied. What else did I have to do out here? I could use a little evening distraction from thinking about Joshua.

Dana handed me a book. "This is the book I wanted to share with you," she said. "It's my favorite book about bees and beekeeping. It's what first made me fall in love with them."

A Book of Bees, the cover read. "Sue Hubbell keeps bees in the Ozarks," she said. "I know you'll love it."

I hugged the book to my chest. "Thanks, Dana. I really appreciate it," I said.

"Well, it's not always smooth sailing around here," she said, raising her eyebrows at me, "so I like to do whatever I can to help you all stay focused and positive."

"I'll see you bright and early tomorrow," she said, wrapping me warmly in her long arms before releasing me into the evening.

Since I found out I would be working the market in Salem, I asked Dana for permission to drive myself in so I could have lunch with Caroline after the market was over. Dana agreed, assuring me that I had worked hard enough to deserve a break. Luckily, Caroline had the afternoon off. I couldn't wait to see her and get her perspective on my crazy life. I knew she would be able to guide me. *And I could use some serious guidance. Two hot guys vying for my affection? Definitely a first for me.*

13

4:45 am. Here I was, dressing in the dark for my first farmer's market. I laid out my clothes the night before, choosing my booty jeans and a simple cotton button-down shirt. I was actually going to *be* the person behind the counter who, only months earlier, had intimidated me. When I stumbled out to the packing shed in the dark, Dana and Craig were already there, each loading a pickup truck with coolers, tables, and boxes.

"Good morning, Kelsie!" Dana greeted me cheerfully. "No rain today, thankfully!"

"Kelsie, come help me grab these tables," Craig's muffled voice came from inside the shed by way of a greeting.

"Sure thing!" I called.

We loaded the table into the blue truck, and packed another one toward the red one.

"Bluebell will go with you to Salem," he told me as we crab-walked backward holding the heavy table awkwardly between us. "Big Red is going with us to Portland."

So Craig wasn't going to Salem. Perfect! I wondered who else would be going with us.

Cleo, Jessi, and Shantel arrived within a minute of each other, mumbling drowsy "Mornings."

"I need some help in here!" Craig yelled from the walk-in, and Shantel just about knocked us over to get there first. Cleo shot me a "see what you *don't* want to turn into" look, and followed her in. Craig passed along box after box of greens and veggies, barking "Salem!" or "Portland!" with each to direct us to the right truck.

We were completely loaded by 6, and Dana handed us all ancient plastic gas station mugs, pointing us toward a large thermos of hot coffee.

"Last chance to fill up before we go!" she told us.

This time I scrambled to the front of the line, filling my day-glo orange mug with the ill-fitting lid.

Dana told me to follow her and Jessi into town so she could show me where to park, and together we would set up the booth. I grinned at Jessi, relieved that she would be my market buddy. Then I watched Cleo with pity as Shantel bounded into the Portland truck so she could snuggle up to Craig. Cleo threw her arms up in the air in panicked frustration, and climbed inside the cab as Craig revved the engine a bit too ostentatiously.

Once on the road, I realized it had been awhile since I'd driven. In the dark, the scenery whizzed by fast, faster than I'd noticed before. I guessed I hadn't even *been* in a car in a good six weeks. I don't think I had ever gone that long; during my childhood, we drove somewhere almost every day, even if only to daycare and back.

As the sky began to lighten, the silhouettes of the trees darkened on either side of the road. The moving car punched through the air, but sealed in my little bubble, protected by the windshield, I felt none of it. The world was happening outside; inside I could have been anywhere, locked away in a thin box of metal and plastic.

I was relieved to escape it when we arrived in Salem and drove the familiar tired streets through town and toward the capitol. Salem is unremarkable. As a city, it isn't very nice, but it isn't gritty either—it's too boring for that. It's the sort of place full of people who've either lived there forever or were forced by family members to move there, and no one is overly fond of it. It's the capital of Oregon, but when you're there, you get the feeling they should have given it up and let Corvallis have the honor, as many of the state's early movers and shakers wanted. The capitol building itself is a fitting testament to the town's character--a blocky white marble structure that's trying to be chic and modern but just ends up looking cheap, out of place, and weird. "Nazi architecture," my friend Brandon describes it. To add irony to its oddness, the building announces itself trying waaaaaaay too hard, by sticking a twenty-two-foot tall gilded bronze statue of a pioneer with an axe in his hand smack dab on the top. In high school we called him "Pete the Pioneer," asserting that he was looking toward the freeway onramp, pointing at the way out of this hellhole. In Oregon history class, we learned that Pete was shipped from the artist's studio in New Jersey all the way through the Panama Canal and up the coast to Oregon. I'd argue they should have kept him where he was. When I first met Jeff, he was part of a campaign to remove the slogan etched into one side of the marble face of the building: "Westward the star of empire takes its course." Jeff felt it was a blatant affront to the Native people that lived around here, before Pete the Pioneer crashed onto the scene. As I recall, his ire switched focus to the second war in Iraq not long after that, leaving Pete and his empire to continue to survey the city from on high.

The market parking lot was lively with trucks and trailers unloading, and people greeting friends they hadn't seen all winter. We found our assigned space and joined in as the sun crested the trees to the east. We popped up a dark green awning and organized tables underneath it.

"We like to get as close as possible to the street," Dana explained. "People need to have easy access to your food if they're going to buy it."

Jessi dragged a table to the front of the booth. "Doug and Mary, the farmers I last worked for had the opposite philosophy," she shared with Dana. "They set up their market booth in a U shape, inviting people inside the booth to shop."

"Interesting," Dana mused. "Everyone has their own style. You'll have to tell us which you think works best." She showed us how to construct additional shelves on the tables with overturned buckets and boards, and then covered the whole thing with colorful tablecloths.

"Kelsie, will you arrange these baskets for me?" she asked. "We'll wait until just before the bell to put out the veggies, so they don't wilt."

Summoning lessons from my high school art classes, I grouped the baskets, shifting them to create focal points, varying style and texture.

"Picassa creating her masterpiece," chuckled an unmistakable deep voice behind me.

I whipped around to see Joshua, standing in the bed of an old pale yellow Dodge, hoisting tents and coolers into the booth directly across from ours.

"Lookin' good over there, ladies!" he called to us, and then shot a very conspicuous wink in my direction.

Dana motioned us across the aisle to help him unload his truck.

"Miss Dana, I am capable of moving these tables myself," he told her playfully as she swooped in and grabbed the end of a table.

"Of course you are, but we're pretty much done over there, thanks to these two—" she pointed toward Jessi and me. "Let us give you a hand!"

Joshua handed Jessi a cooler and then slid one toward me. When I grabbed the handle, he brought his hand down over mine and squeezed it gently. He looked into my eyes and smiled his deep smile. I held his gaze with a weak smile for just a moment before pulling away. I didn't want Dana or Jessi to know what was going on between us. It was all so complicated. A lot had happened in the day and a half since I had been undressed on his couch. Craig had kissed me and asked me out. Dana had hinted that she could tell something was up. And I was stuck in the middle of it all. Joshua seemed utterly unfazed. All was right with the world in his eyes, I could tell. *Just make it through the morning, and I can unload this mess on Caroline and let her help me clean it up.*

"Kelsie, do you want to have lunch with me after the market is over?" Joshua asked.

Shit! My eyes widened to the point where they could just tumble out of my head and I flung around to look at Dana, at what she was thinking, my mouth hanging open like a fish out of water. Her face was distorted and her body shook. I learned then that Dana couldn't hold in an emotion that her body wants to let out.

14

Dana burst into bright laughter, holding her belly, her eyes gleaming. I stood between her and Joshua like a deer in the headlights. Jessi seemed as confused as I was with the situation.

Why was she laughing? I looked back at Joshua, who smiled at her with mild interest, and then turned his attention back to me and my answer.

"I, um, have to have lunch with my friend Caroline today," I told him.

Disappointment flashed in his eyes, and then something else—nervousness? Hope? I realized he was waiting for me to say more.

"Maybe next week after market?" I asked him. "I mean, if Dana says it's okay..." I trailed off, glancing at her. She'd composed herself, but still looked thoroughly amused.

"Of course," she said. "Who am I to stand in the way of a popular gal's Saturday afternoon dates?"

Joshua beamed at me. "It's a date then. I can bring her home, Miss Dana," he said.

"Of course you can, Joshua," she stammered out, on the verge of losing it again. "Let's get back to work, ladies," she said skipping quickly in front of us back to the booth. When she turned around, she looked at me with what can only be described as sheer hilarity. I had no idea what she thought was so funny, and I frankly didn't want to find out. Given all that I knew about her history, and Joshua's, and Craig's, she could be thinking anything under the sun about what she had witnessed. I was embarrassed and intimidated by the fact that she intimately knew the men I was navigating relationships with, that she had had sex with them, had known them for years and seen them change and grow and had gone through good times and bad with both of them. And she was my boss. I did not know her opinion about what I should and should not be doing with either of them. She kept looking at me with this wild, disbelieving smirk that made it clear she definitely did have an opinion but I could not tell what it was.

More people were milling around now. Vendors bustled around, tidying and fidgeting with the details of an attractive market booth. Finally, Dana gave us the word to set out the goods—radishes up front, where they'd draw the eye, bagged braising and salad mixes interspersed with big bunches of greens. She had three delicate potted flowers that I had never seen before that she placed as a centerpiece on our table.

"Whoa, what are those?" I asked her, staring at the undeniably, um, *feminine* flowers. One was large and pink, another was small and yellow with red spots. They seriously looked like open vaginas.

"Orchids," she beamed. "Haven't you seen them in the greenhouse?" she asked. "I grow them because, well, because *look* at them," she breathed deeply. "Just watch. Watch them draw the customers in."

This time it was Jessi and I who looked at each other and burst out laughing.

As if on cue, a woman and her teenage daughter approached the booth. "Cool!" the girl said, reaching out to touch the big, pink orchid.

"I'd like ¾-pound of the spicy mesclun mix," the woman said, reaching into the bin.

"No, no, no!" Dana said hastily. "The bell hasn't rung yet. Besides, we need to serve you. Health Department," she said by way of explanation.

Just then, I heard a cowbell sound and noticed the woman ringing it. She walked slowly toward us, dressed in all black and wearing a mock sheriff's badge, ringing in the start of the market.

Dana handed each of us a plastic glove. "Wear this when you're bagging salad mixes," she told us, and then scooped up a giant handful of greens for the woman. She threw it on the scale and it weighed exactly ¾ of a pound.

"Done this a time or two?" the woman smiled at her.

Dana smiled back, handing her the bag and taking the woman's money in her un-gloved hand. "Thanks for supporting White Oak Farm," she said.

Within moments, buyers swamped the booth. All three of us rushed to bag greens and tally totals. We sold out of our pre-bagged half-pound bags of salad mix in the first half hour, and hand-bagged the odd quantities people wanted. The third customer wanted to buy the yellow orchid, but Dana told her they weren't for sale. "Not this week," she said. In three weeks, I'll bring my large collection of orchids to market and you can purchase them then. These are just a tease," she winked. "Come back in three weeks and take your pick of the crop!"

"One pound braising mix, six bunches of turnips, please."

"Three collard greens."

"Mild mesclun, five pounds—I'm bringing lunch to the office on Tuesday."

Transaction after transaction, we emptied coolers out into the baskets with barely a minute to stop and chat, let alone leave the booth to find a bathroom, which I was in dire need of since I had polished off my giant thermos of coffee an hour earlier. Finally, the rush slowed down and I was able to look across the busy alleyway to Joshua's booth, where a slew of women were crowded around buying cheese and milk and batting their eyelashes at him. His broad smile set off his strong jaw as he flirted with them in his polite, unassuming way, stooping to hand them blocks of cheese and glass bottles of milk. Hordes of them giggled off together, glancing back over their shoulders at him as they walked away.

"Joshua's got quite the following over there," Jessi laughed.

"Yeah, huh," I tried to sound uninterested.

Dana burst out laughing again, and I shot her a shocked glare. "I'm sorry, Kelsie!" she hooted. "I'm sorry to be laughing. It's just—it's just—," she stuttered, clutching her side. "It's just you've got yourself quite a catch there!" she finished. "And he's got quite a catch in you!" Her chuckles wound down and she turned to face the next customer at the booth, a man who stared rapturously at the pink orchid with his mouth hanging open slightly.

"What...*is*...that?" he asked slowly, never taking his eyes off the plant.

"It's an orchid," Dana said, her body beginning to convulse again. I was pretty sure she wasn't going to make it through this transaction. Seeing Dana in such an out-of-control mood was fabulous; it was a side of her we had not yet experienced.

"It's not for sale!" I blurted out, jumping in to try to help Dana.

The man glanced up from the flower just long enough to see Dana screwing up her face, struggling to keep from laughing out loud. I'm sure I looked utterly mortified at my botched attempt to save her. No matter how awkward a situation might be, I have an uncanny knack for making it more awkward by trying to right it with words. The man gave us a disgusted look and stormed away from the booth.

Dana lost it completely then, doubling over and howling so hard she drew attention from visitors several booths away. Jessi was laughing hard, too, at this point, and so I joined in with them, the White Oak Farm booth cracking up.

"It's not for *sale*?" I wailed. "It sounded like I was accusing him of wanting to buy an x-rated video!" Dana and Jessi laughed harder. "Why don't I just keep my mouth shut?" I implored them.

"He'd gone to another world with that flower, for sure!" Jessi added. "Those really are quite the draw, Dana!"

She was unable to compose herself but finally, she reined it in. At that point, though, it was too late. One of us would look at another, and we'd all be in hysterics again. Finally, Dana told Jessi and me to take a walk and check out the other booths, and she'd hold down ours by herself.

"Thank God," I said, still laughing. "I'm afraid I'm gonna pee my pants if I stay here!"

We hurried away from the booth giggling, before we could get sideswiped again.

As we walked around the little circle of booths, I saw that ours was one of the nicer-looking ones. There weren't a ton of farmers there—more craftspeople than farmers, for sure—but we all had pretty much the same things. I guess there is only so much that grows in the early spring. A couple men in cowboy hats sold elk meat and beef, and a few had free-range chickens. I counted three wineries sampling wines. Joshua was the only one selling cheese—he had a corner on that market. I thought about how intimidated I used to be, scurrying through here on my way to work at the café. Now, I recognized every single thing on the vegetable growers' tables, and the growers themselves seemed more like regular people and less like the witchy secret-keepers I used to see. We made eye contact and smiled with the farmers we passed. I couldn't believe how comfortable I felt.

Jessi took note of the prices of the items as we walked, and about how everyone set up their booths.

"You wouldn't think it, but the presentation has everything to do with how well something sells at market," she said. "I've always felt more comfortable with CSA. The market setup and mayhem has always intimidated me."

"Really?" I asked her. "I used to be petrified of this place, before I came to White Oak. I was just thinking about how much more comfortable I feel here now."

"You've got a good artistic eye," Jessi said. "I try to study how others do it, but when left in charge of my own display, it always ends up looking slightly off."

We rounded the corner back to our booth. Joshua still had a few female hangers-on milling around, but our booth looked nearly empty. Just a few bunches of radishes and two humongous bunches of collard greens left. And Dana's orchids, of course.

I tried to act casual as I sauntered up to Joshua's booth.

"Hey Kelsie! How's it going over there?" he interrupted his conversation with the two gigglers he'd been talking to.

"Good, we're almost sold out."

"I'll look forward to our lunch next week," he winked at me.

The two girls glared at me and stormed off.

"They didn't want to buy anything," he said. "I knew that would get rid of 'em."

"You sure you weren't just showing me I didn't have to worry about the competition?" I teased him.

"Well...." Was he blushing a little?

"You can really draw 'em in here!" I pushed a little more.

"Yeah, well, I sell a quality product," he answered with mock-seriousness.

"I'll say so," I replied, flitting my eyes down his broad, flannel-clad chest trying not to crack a smile. "Now what was it you were selling again?"

He threw a small paper sign at me playfully.

I caught it as it tumbled down my front. "Oh, fresh goat feta. I see." I grinned at him.

"Seriously, what are you selling?" I asked, peering over the table at the coolers behind him.

"Well, ma'am," he began, handing me a toothpick with a small cube of cheese, "This here is manchego, aged. And this is a bleu cheese. Here's the feta," he handed me another sample. "And the soft chevre, which everyone loves. This one has herbs in it, this one has some dried fruit..." All of it was delicious, but I especially liked the chevre, with its creamy texture and slightly sour flavor that goes straight into your nose.

"I'd like to buy a chunk of that!" I said, pointing enthusiastically to the chevre. "I'll use up a whole week's pay, but it's worth it!"

"You really like it?" he asked.

I nodded emphatically. "Delicious!"

"Here," he said, handing me a small bundle. "Just have it."

"No, no." I insisted. "You worked hard to make this. Let me buy it."

"How about you trade it for a kiss?" he asked.

"Ssh!" I glanced back nervously at Dana and Jessi.

Joshua looked hurt.

"I mean, not now." I said, trying to backtrack. "Not in front of Dana."

"Oh, ok." He looked confused. "Better be soon, then!" he said, handing over the cheese. "I don't generally sell on credit." He winked at me.

"I'll be sure to pay up in a timely manner. Thank you," I added, heading back across the aisle trying to look nonchalant.

I pretended to be looking for something in my purse to avoid eye contact with Dana when I heard a familiar voice say, "I'll take one of everything."

Caroline stood there grinning when I lifted my head. I rushed over to give her a hug.

Dana, this is my best friend Caroline," I introduced her.

"Great to meet you," Dana said, extending her long arm, from which a myriad of bracelets dangled.

"Dana's one of the farmers," I told Caroline, "and Jessi's an intern like me. Only she knows way more than I do about farming," I added.

"Cool," Caroline said, grabbing my arm and turning me around with a low whistle. "You're looking good!" she said to me.

I snatched my arm away from her and glanced across the aisle at Joshua to make sure he wasn't watching. He wasn't. Three women were now enraptured, sampling his cheese.

"Well, manual labor will do that to you, I guess," I told her. "Thanks, though. I feel good."

Then we heard the bell ring, signaling the end of market.

"I know you said you wanted to buy one of everything," Dana told Caroline with a smile, "but it looks like you're too late. We'll just have to give it to you now." She handed Caroline a bunch of radishes and a giant bouquet of collard greens.

"Oh, no, I couldn't," Caroline began, clutching the huge leaves.

"No, no, we insist!" Dana said with a smile.

"I could pay you for it…" Caroline trailed off weakly, halfway hidden behind the monstrous greens. I could tell she was petrified of them, which made me smile. I'd tell her how to cook them later.

"What's with that bell, Dana?" I asked her.

"Oh yes, the bell. Celia, the bell ringer, is also the market manager, and she's very strict about selling before or after the bell. Absolutely no sales are allowed even one minute before or after. A very important rule to know if you're selling at the market. And you don't want to break it, or any rule, for that matter, and get on her bad side. Trust me." Jessi and I nodded emphatically, sensing this was not an issue for debate.

"Jessi, will you go get the truck from the parking lot?" Dana asked her. "We three will start tearing down. You can back right on in here and we'll load up!"

"Wow," Caroline said, staring across the aisle. "Check out the hottie over there!" She had spotted Joshua.

Dana burst into hysterics again, nearly dropping the pile of baskets she was loading off the tables. Caroline looked at her with alarm. I didn't know what to do at that point, but Dana broke the tension by admitting that it's one of her favorite things, to bring interns to market and introduce them to the phenomenon of Joshua and the attention he gets from the women here. "You get to know him at the farm, and he's so easy to be around that you don't realize the kind of reputation he has at the Salem Farmer's market," she said, still laughing. "Women tell their friends about him, bring their friends down to see him," she continued. "Only I had no idea…" she trailed off, looking at me with this cockeyed, shit-eating grin.

"What?" Caroline pressed, her eyes darting between the two of us. "No idea what?"

"Nothing," Dana said. "I'm sure Kelsie will fill you in on your lunch outing."

"Fill you in on what?" came the deep voice again. Joshua had wandered across the aisle.

I shifted uncomfortably and pulled at the neck of my shirt while Caroline turned around and outright accosted him from toe up to his head with her eyes. Finally, when her neck tipped back far enough to see his face, he grinned at her and stuck out his hand. "Joshua Murphy," he said. "Are you a friend of these ladies?"

Caroline just about passed out, clutching my shoulder as she took his hand, mumbling," Mmm-hmm."

"Joshua, this is my best friend Caroline," I said. She looked at me incredulously. I gave her a small smirk and added, solely for her benefit, "She's the reason I can't have lunch with you today." I thought Caroline's eyes would seriously pop out of her head, her eyes looking from him to me and back again in disbelief.

"You can join us for lunch if you want...," she murmured in his direction.

"NO!" I jumped in. I watched Joshua's eyes sink a little. "I mean, no, Caroline," I flashed her a Look. "We made this plan for ourselves. I get to see Joshua all the time. I mean, not all the time—," I glanced panicked at Dana, and then at Joshua. "But more than I get to see you lately," I finished. "We could all hang out a different time."

I could see the wheels cranking away in Caroline's head as she tried to piece it all together, based on what little I'd told her already. Joshua seemed agreeable, comfortable with the ladies having girl time. He smiled warmly at me, and then at Dana. "It was a pleasure to meet you, Caroline," he said to her, tipping his chin slightly toward her. "I'd best get back to tearing down my booth." With that, he sauntered back across the aisle.

I think Dana took pity on me then, because she closed the door on the subject and focused instead on tearing down the booth, instructing us on what to pack where. Jessi pulled up with the truck, and the four of us had it loaded in no time. I thanked Dana and Jessi for putting everything away for me back at the farm, said I would see them later on, and walked down Marion Street toward our favorite hole-in-the-wall diner, The Starfish Grill.

15

We hadn't gotten seventy-five feet away from the parking lot before Caroline exploded.

"What the hell was that all about?" she demanded. "That wasn't your farmer, was it?"

"No," I began.

"Who the hell is he?"

"He's the neighbor," I giggled. "He's their neighbor."

"Are you *sleeping with* him?" she asked incredulously. *She could be so nosy!*

"Shh, Caroline, no!" We reached the door to the diner, and I held it open for her and her bouquet of collard greens. As she entered, I added with a twinkle, "not yet."

She whipped around with her mouth hanging open, about to say something else, but I just slid past her and into a booth by the window, enjoying the suspense of our exchange. Caroline makes everything seem more exciting than it really is.

Almost immediately, a skinny woman with short, curly hair and well-worn hands brought us water and menus. "Something else to drink?" she asked, eyeing Caroline's leafy bench companion.

"Coffee," we both replied in unison.

"Two coffees," she said, hurrying back to the kitchen. They don't mess around here.

"So how's your life?" I asked Caroline with a smile.

"Oh no, Kels. Uh-uh. You're not off the hook that easily."

I laughed and took a long swig of my water. I needed to remember to bring water to market next week. *Next week when I go on a date with Joshua afterward!* I would have to remember to bring deodorant too. I worked up a sweat that morning.

"Kelsie!" Caroline snapped.

"Sorry," I replied. "My mind's been racing for a solid week now, maybe longer."

"Uh, yeah. It sounds like there are some new developments since the last time we talked."

"Oh, where to start…" I said, burying my head in my hands. Now that the market was over and I was here with Caroline, I realized I was completely exhausted. All the physical work I'd been doing, getting up at 4:30 this morning, and the emotional rollercoaster I'd been on seemed to crash down on me. I wanted to curl up in a ball and pass out, right here at Starfish. Of course, Caroline would have none of that.

"If you won't tell me the story, I'll start the 20 questions," she said. "Number one, what's going on with that hot neighbor?"

"He asked me over to his house for dinner last week," I answered. "He's been kind of flirting with me since the first time I met him."

"Lucky you! He is so hot!" Caroline said.

"Yeah, huh? And nice, too. And incredibly sexy with the way he cares for his goats."

"He has goats?"

"Yeah, he milks goats. Didn't you notice the goat cheese at his booth?"

"Are you kidding?" she said laughing. "I wasn't looking at anything in his booth besides him."

"Apparently that's the case for a lot of women…"

"So he's a player?"

"Not at all, not at all. He just seems to be able to draw a crowd."

"So I noticed."

"Here's your coffee, gals," the waitress set the beige ceramic mugs down with four little plastic tubs of creamer. "Something to eat?"

"Star Burger with fries," we both responded in unison. "Siamese twins, huh?" she chuckled, scribbling on her pad. "Anything else?" We shook our heads no.

"Speaking of players," Caroline said after she'd left, "what's going on with the other farmer dude? What's his name again?"

" Craig," I told her. "He's definitely still in the player game."

"So what's been going on with him?" Caroline asked again.

"Oh lord, I don't even know where to start," I said, burying my head in my hands again.

"Is he still ordering you to take your clothes off?" she asked.

"Shh, Caroline! Not so loud!" I ducked down in the booth as several heads swiveled curiously in our direction. I took a swig of my coffee as Caroline dumped three of the creamers into hers.

"What's even *in* those things?" I asked her. "It's not really milk, is it?"

"Oh no, you're not turning into one of *those* people, are you?"

Was I? "Shit, I don't know. Maybe I am..." I trailed off. "I just don't know that I'd want to drink a dairy product that doesn't have to be refrigerated."

"Well, Miss Priss, you can judge me for my coffee condiments if I can judge you for your behavior as of late."

I laughed and clanked cups with her. "I'm sorry, Caroline. I don't care what you dump in your coffee, as long as you'll help me straighten this mess out!"

"So, spill it!" she ordered. "What's going on with Craig?"

"Well," I began, "it got really kinky for awhile. He pulled down my pants and spanked me in front of another intern in the field one day."

"Whoa."

"I know."

"I think he was upset that I said I'd like to see Joshua's farm when he asked."

"You think he's jealous of Joshua?"

"Cleo, another intern—Dana's niece—said as much. She said Dana slept with Joshua when she and Craig had first moved to the farm property, and Craig was really upset about it."

"Really! I'd be upset, too."

"Yeah, except they were supposed to be in an open relationship. And that's the thing. Craig wants to be able to do whatever he wants with whomever he wants, but he doesn't want any of the women he's pursuing to pursue anyone but him. We're supposed to be competing with each other for his attention, not making him compete with someone else for ours. That dick," I added emphatically.

"Do you really think he's a dick?" Caroline asked.

I thought about it. "I guess not," I conceded. "I don't like his double standard. It makes him less attractive."

"Does Joshua also make him less attractive?" Caroline eyed me carefully, determined to get to the bottom of this.

"Not exactly," I told her. "Wait until you meet him. He's very sexy, too, in a different way. Frankly, Caroline, Joshua scares the crap out of me. At least with Craig, I know he's not looking for anything long-term. I'd never be able to handle being in a relationship with him anyway. But Joshua...he's definitely looking for something serious."

"And you're not?"

"I don't know if I am or not!" I slurped my coffee, which frankly was horrible. I'd really gotten spoiled with the coffee at the farm.

"I guess it's not that I don't want to get serious. I'm just not sure I want to get serious right now. I feel like if I start to date Joshua, I might never have a chance to date anyone else again," I confessed.

"Really?" Caroline squeaked. "Whoa!"

The reality of what I'd just admitted started to sink in. How could I know that about someone I'd only gone out with once?

"So let me get this straight," Caroline began, her eyes twinkling. "You've been getting undressed and spanked in public by your hot but twisted boss, whom you are attracted to, but you're pretty sure you're going to end up marrying his neighbor, and you're trying to hide the fact that you're seeing him from your boss."

"No! I'm not sure I'm marrying Joshua!" I cried.

"But everything else I said is accurate?" she asked.

"Well..."

"Mmm-hmm." Caroline took a triumphant swig of her creamer-coffee. "God I'd give anything to be in your shoes right now."

We laughed as the waitress plopped our burgers down in front of us. "Need anything else?" she asked.

"Nope," Caroline said. "We've got plenty to digest here." She squirted a massive amount of ketchup on her burger and took a humongous bite, grinning at me with a mouthful of food.

I did the same, but after months of farm food, my old favorite burger and fries tasted heavy, like they were trying to cover up their lack of quality with an overabundance of oil and salt. Maybe Caroline was right. Maybe I was turning into one of *those* people.

"What about the other intern?" Caroline asked between bites of burger. "The other one you said he was flirting with."

"He's still flirting with her, all right," I said. "I'm pretty sure they're now sleeping together." I continued, "I feel kind of sorry for her, honestly. At least when he's jerking me around, I can think about Joshua and his sincerity. Shantel doesn't have anything like that, from what I can tell. She hangs all over Craig."

"Sounds like you're in a pretty good place then," Caroline said. "He holds no power over you."

"Except that he's my boss and he could tell me to leave the farm if he wanted to."

"Do you think he would do that?"

"I don't know what he'd do if he found out I was dating Joshua..." My backside hurt just thinking about it. "He tried to kiss me yesterday, and he asked me to hang out with him after work, but I told him I couldn't. I didn't feel right kissing him."

"Because you're really in love with Joshua?"

"Maybe." I shook my head. "Why did I have to fall for him so fast? I barely even know him!"

"Too bad you can't hook up with both of them," Caroline mused. "Would they go for that?"

"Caroline!" I threw a napkin at her. "No!"

She raised her eyebrows at me.

"There's no way. Craig's jealous of Joshua, and I can't imagine Joshua ever doing something like that." I thought about it. "Craig would have no problem having a threesome with me and Shantel, though."

"Would you want to do that?"

I blushed a little. "I don't think so. I've never had a chance to do that, and I'm not saying I'm not curious about it, but I'm not that crazy about Shantel, to be honest. She kinda bugs me. Besides, that's not the point. The point is I've got to figure out what to do about Craig and Joshua, not what to do about Craig and Shantel."

Caroline polished off her burger. "Seems like there's not much you can do," she said. "Keep doing what you're doing until it all blows up in your face. Sounds like it will, eventually."

Why did she have to be so honest? "Caroline, that doesn't help."

"Well, Kels, what do you want me to say?"

"I don't know...I thought you'd have some sage words of advice for me."

"Juggling two men, one who's your sadomasochistic boss and the other who's his wholesome next door neighbor? Kelsie, this is an area I haven't the slightest experience with!"

I finished off my coffee and pecked at my fries.

"You aren't going to eat those?" she asked.

I shook my head.

"Wow, you *are* in a bad way...." She looked nervously at her collard green sidekick. "What the hell am I supposed to do with these?"

I burst out laughing. "I know, Caroline, I was scared of them at first, too, but I swear Cleo, who's kinda the unofficial farm cook, puts them in everything. I eat them, or something like them, pretty much every day. They're actually really good, once you get used to them. High in vitamins."

"Right," Caroline said wearily.

"I guess what I'd tell you to do is to chop them up really finely and add them to soup when you make it. You could even put them into a can of soup when you heat it up on the stove. That's the easiest way to get them down at first. You can't taste them at all. I also like scrambling them with my eggs in the morning."

"In my soup, huh?...I guess I can handle that." She eyed them suspiciously.

"I think you'll really like them, once you give them a chance. The radishes you just eat!" I grabbed one and bit off the end, tasting its familiar, sweet-spicy juice in my mouth. It was so alive compared to the burger and fries I'd picked at for the last hour. A surge of gratitude for the farm and my life there washed over me.

Caroline tried it, tentatively taking a nibble. "It's not that bad!" she exclaimed.

"Not that bad, indeed. I'll be coming into town every Saturday for awhile now, I think," I told her. "So if you feel like coming downtown to visit, I'd love it."

"Does Craig ever come with you?" she asked.

"No, I think he'll always go to the market in Portland. Maybe you'll have to come out and spend the night at the farm to get a glimpse of him."

"Really? I could do that?" she asked.

"Yeah, Dana said we could have visitors. I've got an extra bed in my trailer."

"She seems really cool," Caroline said.

I nodded heartily in agreement. "I've learned so much from her. She's amazing."

"Well, maybe I will come out to visit. You say this Craig is interested in lots of women, huh?" she gave me a small smile.

I laughed. "Yup, likes lots of women. Maybe you'd better choose your undergarments accordingly when you come out," I teased her. "You might have to do some actual *work*, too."

"Say the word and I'm there. I wouldn't mind getting some of what you've got going on. You really are looking good, Kelsie!"

"Thanks, Caroline. I'm feeling good, too, even if emotionally I'm a wreck."

We paid the tab and hugged goodbye, and she agreed to stop by the market booth the following weekend. As I drove out to the farm, I realized there wasn't anywhere else I'd rather be going to.

16

The week leading up to my next market date with Joshua kept me pretty busy, between long days on the farm and cozy evenings snuggled up with Dana's lovely bee book. On Thursday evening, the warmest and driest day we'd had all week, we traded afternoon work in the fields for bee coveralls and veils, and we opened up the hives to check their springtime progress. Dana said enough flowers were blooming now that the bees could collect from, so the danger of them starving had passed. Still, we added sugar syrup again to any hives that had small numbers of bees, to get them off on a healthy start.

Dana had me pull the first frame out of our next hive. Using my hive tool to pry a center frame, sticky with propolis, apart from the others, I raised it steadily up, rubbing against the mass of bees scurrying about, attending to their chores. I was careful not to squish any of them. Dana had warned me that when you kill a bee, she emits a danger pheromone that warns her sisters of intruders, alerting their guard bees to attack. Dangling from the bottom of the frame was what looked like a peanut shell.

"A queen cell," Dana gasped. "The workers are raising a new queen."

I studied the peanut dangling from the bottom of the frame like a booger. “In there?” I asked, chuckling to myself.

“Yup.” She expertly pulled out another frame, studying its contents. “Lots of drone brood,” she concluded, nodding her head decisively. “Their queen must be getting old.”

She glanced quickly over the frame to make sure the queen wasn’t on it, and propped it gently against the hive on the ground. Immediately she pulled out another frame, adorned with its own peanut jewel at the bottom.

“See how this brood’s cap bulges out instead of lying flush with the frame?” she asked, brushing the bees gingerly to the sides with her finger so I could have a look. “That means there’s a drone in there. These are mostly drone brood, which could mean the queen is getting old, or it could mean something happened to her and a worker bee started laying eggs. That’s rarer but it can happen.” I nodded, trying to remember what I had read about laying workers in my bee book. “Of course, if it is a laying worker, she’s not fertile, so all her eggs will be haploid and develop into drones.”

“So she needs sperm to produce females?” I asked.

“Exactly.”

I studied the bees wandering about, lively with their sense of purpose, seeming totally content with their lot in this highly socialist life.

“How do they raise a queen?”

“It’s all about the food.” Dana replied. “Have you heard of royal jelly?”

I nodded.

“That’s the special food that makes a queen a queen instead of developing into just another worker. “

“So when she hatches, will the other bees immediately recognize her as their queen?”

“Oh no no no.” Dana laughed. “It’s a lot more brutal than that. When a queen hatches, she’ll immediately seek out any other queen cells and kill the developing queens inside them. If there isn’t another queen to pose a threat, the workers will take to her in a matter of hours, sensing her unique queen pheromones. If there is another, older queen, the old queen will most likely gather a group of followers and take off from the hive in a swarm to search for a new home to start their own colony."

"Do your bees ever swarm?" I asked her.

"Certainly. It's not really what you want as a beekeeper, but I lean toward the wild side of things, figuring the bees know their needs better than I do. Other than some simple things, like giving them enough room in their hive, I pretty much leave it up to them when they want to raise their own queens and swarm and such. I do generally put a few empty hive bodies a short distance away with the hope of catching my own swarms back again."

"That sounds like a good idea!" I said. "Do they go into your boxes?"

"I've caught a few that way," she told me. "I drop lemongrass oil at the hive entrance—something about the smell attracts swarms. I think I've caught a couple swarms from neighbors' hives," she winked.

We delicately slid the frames, still covered with bees, back into neat rows in the hive body. The bees seemed unperturbed by the disruption.

Moving onto our last hive, Dana turned to me with an inquisitive twinkle in her eye. I froze, sure she was going to ask me something about Joshua.

"Can I ask you a question, Kelsie?" she said smiling.

I nodded feebly, knees weakening, heart picking up speed.

"Sheesh!" she exclaimed. "You look like I asked to borrow your kidney!"

"Huh?—" I started.

"I wanted to know if you'd gotten to the part in the bee book about the virgin queen's nuptial flight!"

It took me a second to register and I gasped a quick breath of air. We both looked at each other and cracked up laughing. Dana grabbed my elbow, leading me back from the hive a few steps so as not to rouse the bees.

"The virgin queen's nuptial flight?" I hooted. "Dana, you are too much! You're the first person I've ever met who gets as excited about insect drama as human drama!"

She cackled along with me. "So that means you've read that part?"

I shook my head. "No, but I think I can see where it's headed."

"Good. Well then, you won't mind me spoiling the surprise."

We stepped forward to the hive again, lifting the lid and prying off the inner cover, bees spilling out of its oval opening, busily constructing the perfectly symmetrical comb against the ceiling of their abode.

"The virgin queen's nuptial flight..." Dana began overdramatically, waving her wrist in the air with a hint of pomp. A small cloud of bees danced around her palm as she gestured. A bee landed on the front of my veil, right between my eyes, and I watched it cross-eyed as it walked across the yellow netting, inspecting any potential it might hold.

"In order to mate, a virgin queen flies high into the air, sending a pheromone to attract males to her."

The bee on my veil flew away, and I returned my attention to the hive in front of us.

"As many as ten or fifteen males might visit her on her nuptial flight. In midair they copulate—each male's penis breaks off inside the queen, and she's filled with the sperm of all those males."

Dana swept the air with her hand again, more grandly this time for the finale. "The male, after losing his organ, falls to his death," she finished.

"Whoa," I answered, blushing a little at her candid description. I looked up from my frame to lock eyes with her. "I can see why you were excited to share. So she's full of sperm. Now what?" I prodded.

Dana laughed. "She returns to the hive. It's the last time she'll ever be able to fly, because now she's too big and heavy with all that sperm in her! She'll draw from her own sperm bank through her whole life, laying as many as 10,000 eggs over her time as queen."

Whew! That sounded like a lot of work. "A night of passion followed by a lifetime of duty," I mused. We closed up the last hive and hauled our gear back to the barn.

"Thanks for sharing all of this with me, Dana." I trotted along after her, always struggling to keep pace with her long gait.

"Of course!" she beamed. "It's what I love to do! And you're picking it up really fast," she said. "A real natural."

It was my turn to beam.

I returned to my trailer and a quick evening meal of salad and bread. Lying in bed, I reran Dana's version of the nuptial flight in my head again and again. "Mmm," I said softly to myself. "Way to go, Queen Bees."

Saturday morning my stomach did flip-flops beginning at 4:45 when my alarm went off, through our loading for market and the drive to Salem. I had taken extra care to look nice, donning a lacy white button down short sleeve and a soft gray knee-length skirt. The weather was supposed to be beautiful, and I decided I might as well dress up, since I didn't often get the chance at the farm. Both Dana and Jessi commented on my attire, but neither of them teased me about my date after market.

Joshua set up across from us, as usual. My second market day of salad mix sales, orchid ogling, and flirting at Joshua passed quickly, and I grew more nervous with each shrinking hour. Afterward, we tore down our booth and helped Joshua with his. Finally, Jessi and Dana headed back in the truck, leaving me alone with Joshua.

Amid the bustle of people hurrying to pack up and get home, Joshua smiled toward me and drawled out, "You look beautiful today!" Then, he wrapped me in a warm hug, stooping down and breathing into my ear. "I've been waiting all week for this!" he said. I grinned into the side of his head, feeling his hair sweep across my teeth as my lips parted to expose them.

"Really?" I asked, pulling back ever so slightly.

He pulled away and smiled into my eyes. "Really, Kelsie."

We stared at each other for a moment, an intense stare that risked exposing my admission to Caroline the week earlier about my burgeoning feelings about Joshua. I broke the intensity by blurting out,

"I'm starving! Where do you want to eat?"

Joshua smiled at me. "You're the one from Salem. Where's your favorite place to eat around here?"

I thought about the Starfish, the crappy vinyl benches and the tasteless burger we'd had there last week. I didn't want to take Joshua there. "I don't know..." I trailed off.

"There's this new place that's supposedly interested in buying from local producers on High Street near the art museum," he said. "Maybe we could try that?"

I nodded, relieved he had an alternative.

"I want to try to sell my cheese there."

He grabbed my hand decisively, Clark Kent pretending to lead Lois Lane, in exactly the wrong direction. "Which way do we go?" he asked valiantly.

I swung his arm around in a complete one-eighty. "This way, fearless leader, this way," I teased, and we walked hand in hand toward High Street and the Silver Creek Alehouse.

We made small talk on the way, the air between us electric and slightly heavy with the knowledge that we were trying each other out on the town. Joshua held the door for me when we reached the restaurant, next door to the site of my first customer service job, Robby's Deli. I could see the greasy old timers flirting with the young girls behind the counter. *Ick.*

The pleasant hostess seated us at an empty booth near a window and I waited for Joshua to seat himself first, sliding into the bench opposite him. After years of waiting tables as a relationship-challenged woman, I'm sensitive about being *that* couple who snuggles in next to each other in a booth, mocking the lonely seat across from them.

The menu overwhelmed me, and the server did the same, but we both managed to have a lovely time in spite of the pretentiousness of the place. I tried the grilled kale Caesar salad with toasted hazelnuts, chuckling to myself about how I would have gagged at the thought of such a thing two months ago. It turned out to be smoky, tangy, and delicious. Joshua sampled the Reuben, commenting on how tender the meat was and on the quality of the fermented sauerkraut. After we had eaten, he asked to speak to the kitchen manager to give him a sample of his cheeses. Troy, a lanky guy in his late 20s with dark hair and tattoos all down both his arms, came right out to greet us when he got word that a guy was here to show him his goat cheese. When Joshua introduced himself, Troy's eyes lit up.

"Joshua Murphy, I've heard you have a quality product!" he said. "I've been meaning to come seek you out at market, but I've been too busy in here to get away."

"So business is good?" I asked.

He nodded. "As good as can be expected, for a new restaurant with the absolutely *insane* model of serving high-quality local food."

We laughed.

Joshua spread out a sample of his cheeses, neatly wrapped in small packages, and proceeded to give a sample of each one to Troy, who seemed delighted by everything he tasted.

"This is incredible stuff, Joshua. Nice work!" he said. "I'd definitely like to buy from you. Let's talk via phone next week about quantities and prices."

"Fair enough," Joshua said, sliding the rewrapped pieces toward him. "Keep these then, so you don't forget about me out there in the boonies."

"You don't have to worry about that," Troy assured him. "I'll be in touch next week."

Walking back to the truck, Joshua again took my small hand in his large one, but more gently this time. He seemed elated at that interaction, that an actual chef was so impressed by his cheese. Instead of bee-lining it back to the truck, we meandered through the city streets, nonchalantly glancing through store windows and into dusty back alleys, musing about the lives of the people inside. He had worked up a sweat at market, as I am sure I had, and every once in awhile, as the wind blew just right, I caught a whiff of him, which sent a shiver of lust through my body. Mostly, we just kept walking to walk, I guess, to enjoy the feeling of having nothing to do, nothing to accomplish except spending time together. No vegetables to weed, no goats to milk, no one else to attend to, except each other. I enjoyed the time, and found myself also enjoying the feeling of being needed elsewhere in awhile. I liked feeling important on the farm. It eased my desire to feel important to Joshua. He did let me know I was important to him. He asked me about places we passed, about my connections to them and my opinions about them, and seemed genuinely interested in my insights and stories about my life in Salem. Finally, we found ourselves back in front of his pale yellow Ford.

"Will you show me your family's house?" he asked as I climbed inside the ample cab.

My easiness with him wavered a little. My family's home? So soon? I must have looked panicked because he quickly added, "I mean, if you want to. I don't mean to pry, ma'am." He beamed and tipped his head forward in his characteristic respectful nod, which was so damned cute he could probably get me to saw off my own arm for him if he dipped just right.

"Oh all right," I conceded in mock exasperation. "But don't get your hopes up."

I directed him across the train tracks, over the freeway overpass, and into our 1960s suburb, the gleeful child's bicycle track etched in the cement sidewalk along the row of ranch-style, chain-link-fenced palaces. My heart pounded as we neared my family's house. I realized I had not talked to my mom since I'd been at the farm. Frankly, I wasn't sure if she would have tried to contact me even if I'd had a reliable phone, unless it was an emergency.

"It's up here, on the left," I told Joshua, pointing to the pale, mint green home that closely resembled its neighbors. Both my mom's and my dad's cars were out front, and before I had a chance to reconcile my guilt about not stopping to say hi, Joshua was pulling his big yellow truck over next to the driveway.

"I thought we were just driving by!" I exclaimed anxiously.

Joshua looked confused. "You don't want to say hello to your family?" he asked.

Seeing the panic in my eyes, he quickly rescinded, reaching for the key to turn the engine over again.

"Should we go?" he asked me.

I nodded, glancing at the house, and he turned the key just as my mom was opening the door to check out the situation outside.

"Damn it!" I swore. Joshua looked slightly taken aback. My mom finally recognized it was me seated in the passenger seat of the truck, and walked smartly out to greet me.

"Kelsie, what are you doing here?" she exclaimed accusatorily, eyeing Joshua as he rose from his seat, his broad frame towering over the cab as he smiled a broad smile at her.

"Um, I was just showing my friend Joshua where I grew up," I stammered, extracting myself awkwardly from the cab and giving her an awkward, sideways hug.

"Your friend Joshua, eh?" she asked, rounding the truck to get a no-nonsense look at him. She stuck out her hand, more a jab toward his stomach than a gesture of goodwill. "I'm Peg. Kelsie's mom," she announced.

"Joshua Murphy," he replied slowly, tipping his head toward her. "Pleased to make your acquaintance, ma'am."

She looked downright flabbergasted, but kept her composure, turning her attention back to me.

"Is this one of your little farm friends?" she asked.

"I guess so," I mumbled, picking at something on the hood of the truck. Why did he have to pull over?

"Well, come on in," she said. "It's not getting any cooler out here."

I thought the weather felt wonderful—the first warm day since I'd been at the farm. I decided not to argue the point, and glanced over at Joshua as my mom marched back into the house. He looked sheepish, like a dog that'd eaten all your Christmas cookies, pleading at me with his eyes, like he couldn't help himself.

I rolled mine at him and tugged quickly at his elbow to follow her inside. "Let's make it quick," I whispered to him.

Mom's modest collection of wind chimes clanged their welcome as we trudged along the manicured lawn, concrete-edged with tidy shrubs, and crossed the threshold, where she quickly shut the door behind us, so as not to let anything that belonged outside—bugs, sun, air—in. We stepped into the beige-carpeted, middle-class paradise of my youth, adorned with family photos, mismatched furniture, and dad's embarrassing mini football helmet collection, housed on tiny homemade shelves with Plexiglas fronts. It was his coping mechanism for being the only male in a house full of women.

"Something to eat?" Mom half-barked at Joshua.

"No thank you, Ma'am, we just had a big lunch down at the Silver Creek Alehouse,." Joshua was polite, used to conversing with folks older than him.

"Never heard of it," she dismissed him with a wave, turning to me as abruptly. "Your father's out."

"I didn't mean to barge in unexpectedly..." I trailed off.

"Nonsense!" she raised her voice. "You're our *daughter*! Barge in whenever!" She glanced pointedly at Joshua, who smiled back, but I could see his confidence starting to falter.

"Um, well, thanks, Mom," I answered back, shifting uncomfortably.

Joshua broke the silence by pointing at a watercolor of the river's edge near town that I had painted in the 9th grade. "Nice painting," he commented. "I know that spot."

I blushed a little at the outright acknowledgement of my fourteen-year-old self. Since then, I painted lots of others, all of which I liked more than that, but they got a little less conventional as I'd gotten older. My mom always asserted she liked my younger work best. In retrospect it was probably her comments suggesting I'd gotten worse, not better, the older I got that made me give it up.

I smiled weakly at Joshua, about to tell him it was yours truly that was the artist when Mom butted in—"Our Kelsie painted that! Isn't it *beautiful?"*

He grinned at me. "You did that, eh? Not bad, not bad." He studied it in mock seriousness. "Nice attention to color and detail, to line and form."

He winked at me.

I would have smacked him on the arm, except my mom was

standing there with her jaw on the floor watching our interaction. I could tell she was stunned Joshua was interested in me. But it didn't faze her for long.

"Speaking of your art, Kelsie, I'd appreciate it if you could take your art supplies out of the garage." She smiled sweetly at me. "Kirsten's house sold before her new one is ready, and she needs to store some of her things here for the next couple of months while she's renting an apartment."

I rolled my eyes at no one but both of them saw it.

"Kelsie, don't be dramatic. Your sister needs the space, and we all need to work to accommodate her."

"Of course we do," I replied sarcastically. "We all need to accommodate Kirsten in her rise to the top."

Joshua looked taken aback. Mom shot an exasperated look at him, like, *do you see* what I have to put up with in her?

Joshua was still trying to ease the situation between my mom and me. "We can certainly load some things up in my truck, if that would help," he offered.

I shot him a look. Mom acted as though he was the sanest person ever to set foot in the house. "Thank you, Joshua, for lending a hand. At least *someone* is willing to help out here."

Anger swelled in me, so much that I started shaking. I didn't care what it looked like to Joshua. I tromped out into the garage and grabbed one of the three boxes of art supplies I had piled in a corner, the last three boxes of my stuff anywhere in the house, as far as I knew. Already, one wall donned a stack of Kirsten's boxes, neatly labeled in her tidy penmanship.

I hauled the box out to Joshua's truck and practically threw it into the bed. Hot on my heels, he followed me back into the garage, trying to grab at my hand from behind me, pleading me to look at him and ground myself, but I was having none of it. I grabbed another box and threw it at him, and took the last one into my own arms.

I stomped out to the truck, snagging my gray skirt on a sawhorse on the way, chucked it into the back, and whipped around to face my mom. "Well, nice to see you, mom," I said, my own sarcasm snarling through. "Glad I could *'lend a hand'* to help you and Kirsten out."

With that, I climbed into the cab and slammed the door, and left Joshua to fend out his own goodbye to my mom.

"It was a pleasure," he stumbled, reaching awkwardly to shake her hand again.

She mumbled something I couldn't make out from inside the cab of the truck, and walked smartly back inside the safe comfort of her absolute domain.

Joshua sheepishly entered the cab, where I sat fuming with my head down, examining the hole the sawhorse had ripped in my skirt.

He fumbled with his keys and started the engine before making an offering. "After that pleasant exchange," he said, reaching out to put a large hand on my leg, "I hardly know where to go next!"

I sat there, still shaking a little, and looked at his hand cupping my thigh like it was a rolling pin kneading out lumpy dough into something smooth and pleasant, and couldn't help smiling a little.

I gave him my own sheepish grin. "Thank you," I said, my smile spreading. "I'm sorry I kind of lost it back there." I pulled off a loose thread from the hole, making it bigger. "As you can tell, my family and I have a tenuous relationship."

"Really?" he teased. "I didn't notice a thing." I reached across the truck and gave him a playful smack on his own thigh.

"I can fix that hole for you if you want," he offered. "I'm always ripping my clothes on the goat fences, so I've gotten pretty good at mending things."

I took a hold of his hand on my thigh, scooting over a bit in the wide cab to make it easier for him to reach me, and simply held it there by way of a response.

"I've had enough of the city for one day," he said, squeezing my hand gently in his own. "What do you say we get back out to the sticks?"

I nodded, and we headed down the road toward the highway.

Gradually, the sidewalks ended, the buildings gave way to vast fields, woodland jungles, grain silos and farmhouses, all lit by the slanting late-spring sun. We didn't talk much as we followed the road, winding through neatly kept farmsteads, happy with the good care of loving tenders. Although the scenery was soothing, I worried about my family, about my relationship with them, about Kirsten and how I would probably never achieve half of what she had achieved thus far in her life. I fretted at the fact that Joshua had seen me act so childishly, so irrationally, at my mom's seemingly simple request. He'd commented on my painting, something no one outside of my family did. Moreover, he knew my special spot, the spot I'd retreat to as a respite from the daily tortures of high school and family tension. Even after my crazy display, he'd still reached out to rest his hand on my leg. Nearly an hour went by in contemplative silence, until Joshua pointed out a pretty piece of land, a 60-acre farmstead owned by a family friend.

"They're thinkin' about sellin' it," he began. "And I've been thinkin' about buyin' it." It was a huge admission for him, I could tell.

"That's exciting!" I told him, giving his hand a squeeze. "It's a beautiful property."

I could tell he was holding something back, but I decided it was best not to pry. I wasn't sure I really wanted to know what it was, after the scene that had just played out. *In due course*, I told myself. *I'll learn about his sticky parts in due course.*

Instead, we kept driving toward our neighboring farms. Worry crept up as we neared them. Would Joshua drive right down the White Oak Farm driveway to drop me off? To unload my art boxes? What if Craig saw? But wouldn't it be suspicious if I told Joshua I didn't want him to do that?

His nervousness was increasing slightly, too. I could tell by the way his hand gripped my thigh just a little bit tighter with each passing mile. What did he have to be worried about?

As we turned onto Sweet Well Road, Joshua cleared his throat and his grip tightened a little more. "I, uh, have to get home to milk," he began. "Would you, uh, like to come with me?"

My mouth broke into a huge grin. "Of course I would!" I reassured him. His nervousness was so endearing I just wanted to throw my arms around him. Plus, I could avoid the discomfort of navigating a drop off at the farm, at least for a while.

I slouched down in the seat as we went past the farm and pulled into Joshua's gravel driveway. I hoped no one was watching the road at that moment. A surge of gratitude swelled in me for the exact blackberry bramble that I had caught myself on two weeks ago. From Joshua's driveway, I couldn't see the farmhouse, except for a bit of the roofline. Joshua pulled around back to his barn and we began unloading his market booth setup. He was grateful for the help, and I was happy to be of use.

Back in his own domain, he got a bit flirtier, brushing his hands over my waist, my back, my hands as we unloaded, sending a cascade of shivers down my spine with each touch.

When we finished, he led me into his house to gather some of his milking supplies. His strong back faced me as he tended the water heating on the stove, and I could make out the sharp lines of his broad shoulder blades slicing downward in a v toward his waist through his t-shirt.

I walked up behind him and rested a hand on his back. He jumped a bit, and then moved into me, reaching behind him with his free hand to stroke my leg through my skirt. I reached my hands up under his shirt, feeling the strong smoothness of the muscles there, skin stretched taught over them. Then higher to his shoulders and rubbed them a bit, pressing myself against him, nestling the outward curve of my breasts into the inward curve of his low back, resting my head on his shoulder blades. His strong hand kneaded my body from behind, traveling over the curve of my butt and up onto my own, much smaller back. "Mmm," I moaned into him as we rocked together, kneading and rubbing against each other. Finally, he turned around to face me and pulled me to him as he leaned hard into the counter. We clasped our arms around each other and kissed deeply, our tongues entering the other's world.

Finally, Joshua had to pull away. His water was boiling, and he had to begin his milking process. I groaned as we separated, and he began filling his arms with the necessary tools for milking.

I could see the goats out on the pasture behind the barn as we approached it. About thirty big goats grazed contentedly. Smaller goats of all different sizes, from tiny babies to bigger kids, ran and jumped and head butted each other. We took our equipment into a small, tidy, cement-floored room with a row of four welded wire platforms headed with buckets. Stanchions, Joshua called them.

"The goats will climb up on these platforms," he explained, "and eat grain from these buckets while they get milked." He fetched milking pails from the stainless steel sink in the small adjacent room and filled each bucket with grain, preparing for the first set of goats to come in for their evening milking.

It was the most amazing thing! When Joshua opened the barn door, the Mama goats began to come in from the pasture and line up!

"Wow!" I exclaimed, watching them file into the barn. "What are they doing?"

"Waiting in line to be milked," he smiled, opening the door that led from the barn into the milking parlor. The first four goats filed through, knowing where they were going, and each lined up next to her own stanchion. Then Joshua closed the barn door and patted each goat individually, coaxing her up onto the stanchion platform, her heavy udder bulging and swinging as she hopped up. "This is Mulberry," he told me, pushing down a metal bar that held her head gently over the bucket of grain, which she happily started munching on. Going down the row, he did the same with the others, "Chestnut, Linden, and Ash." Each girl hopped up on her stanchion, her two nipples sticking out at awkward angles like fat antennae protruding down from her udder, and began eating her grain.

"It's incredible!" I said. "They know just what to do!"

"Yeah, huh? It's our routine. We do it two times every day. It's the same steps, every time, done in the same way, in the same order...our little dance."

Joshua seated himself on a small stool next to Ash, the first goat through the door, patting her on her back. He squirted a little disinfectant on her udder, and began squeezing her two nipples with his hands, shooting milk forcefully into the bucket below her.

"Ash here is the dominant female. She gets to be milked first, and all the other goats know it. They all have their place in line, and if someone tries to go out of turn, the others get testy with her, pushing her back into her place." After two squirts, he removed that bucket and started, quicker this time, filling a second bucket.

"It's called a stripping cup," he told me as he milked her in a rhythm. "You discard the first couple squirts from the teat to clear out any milk that might have been exposed to the outside."

Ash was wolfing down her grain, totally unfazed by what was happening on her back end. "They don't seem to mind being milked," I commented.

"No, they love it," Joshua said, squirting the last few squirts of milk out of Ash and into the bucket. Her udder was noticeably smaller. "Wouldn't you want someone to get that out of you if you were swelled up and carrying it around?"

I laughed as he moved over to Linden, toting his stool, buckets, and disinfectant spray with him. He began the process again with her.

"I like to take off my hat and lean into her while I milk," he told me. "I can listen to her rumen while she eats, and make sure nothing sounds unhealthy." I saw Linden lean back into Joshua, seeming enamored of this large man pressing his head into the side of her and squeezing her small teats in his large hands while she munched happily away on her grain.

Joshua moved quickly down the line of four. By the time he reached Mulberry, Ash and Linden had finished their grain, but Mulberry was still eating.

"Come look at this," he motioned to me with a smile. "Look into Mulberry's grain bucket. She has this slow, funny way of eating her grain. She eats a circle all the way around the outside of it, and then finishes off the cone in the middle."

I leaned over her and peeked in the bucket, where, sure enough, she had eaten a moat around the outside of her grain, and was just about to start in on the center mountain she had created.

"That's hilarious!"

Chomp. The mountain became a crater.

"Yeah, I pay attention to how fast they eat their grain, and line them up accordingly. Since Mulberry's a slow eater, I put her last in their group so she's still occupied while I milk her."

After he finished, he gave all their teats another squirt of disinfectant, and unlatched the gates on the stanchions. Each girl calmly hopped down and followed Joshua to the door opposite the one they came in. He let them into the barn area where I had first visited them and where they slept at night, and threw out a pile of hay for them on the far corner.

"They all get hay after they're milked and they get to eat it in peace, instead of having the boys and the babies all bothering them."

He led me back through the milking parlor and opened the door, where the next four ladies filed in and stood next to their stanchions. He nodded at each one as she passed.

"Cherry, Maple, Walnut, Locust," he introduced them to me. The whole process started over.

"Would you like to try milking?" he asked, patting the stool next to Cherry.

"Sure," I replied, feeling just slightly nervous at grabbing a goat's swollen teat. "You make it look pretty easy."

"Cherry's an easy milker, with a really sweet temperament. She'll be patient with you," he assured me, scratching her neck lovingly.

"You are really in love with them, aren't you?" I asked him.

He blushed a little bit. "I guess so," he said. "It's just been us for so long here, we're kind of all each other has for company."

I didn't like the intensity of where this conversation could go, so I quickly took a seat next to Cherry's swollen udder and awaited instructions from Joshua, in effect changing the subject.

"Ok, first you spray just a little disinfectant on her teats," he said, squirting the bottle gently on them. "It helps prevent diseases like mastitis."

He set the bottle down. "Then you take her teat firmly between the pads of your fingers, like this"—he cupped my hand in his and led it around Cherry's teat. "You pinch it at the top and massage downward with your fingers"—he pushed on each of my four fingers, one after another—"in a steady rhythm." I couldn't help but feel Joshua's skill, the way his fingers expertly moved over mine, coaxing milk out of her. It left little doubt about his adeptness in other such areas. However inappropriate, I longed for the time when I would feel them coaxing juices from me as well.

"Put your other hand on her other teat," he urged me. I grabbed on like he showed me. It felt warm and sort of rough, with a hint of course fuzz.

"Now massage her downward like I'm showing you," he instructed gently. I moved my fingers clumsily down, squeezing her with each one as I went.

A tiny squirt of milk shot into the bucket. "I did it!" I exclaimed, beaming.

"You did!" he laughed at me, kissing me on the top of the head. "Now do it again."

He removed his hand and watched me fumble through my first milking, reassuring Cherry with kind pats and scratches. She seemed only slightly frustrated, shifting her back end every so often.

"Thank you for being patient with me, Cherry," I said softly to her, and she twitched her ear, perhaps by way of a response.

After a few minutes, Joshua took over, squeezing any last little bits out of her before moving on to Maple, who seemed feistier from the get-go.

"It's funny how they all have their own personalities, huh?" I mused.

"Just like people," Joshua agreed, smiling at me over the back of Maple.

Those four done and led into the other barn, and the next set in. Through five sets of goats, all named after trees, as far as I could tell, which I thought was really cute. The whole process took about an hour and a half, until all the mamas were snuggled in the barn, munching away on hay. Later, he opened the door to that barn and let the boys, the babies, and the nurse goats inside.

We carried the full buckets of milk one by one to the small cheese-making room off the side of the milking parlor. We emptied them into large glass bottles and put them in the refrigerator. Then we washed the buckets in the stainless steel sink, getting them all ready to go for the next morning's milking. I appreciated how orderly everything was, kind of like working with the bees, but with lots more personality. Everything in its place, everything tidy even when it's a bit messy, a reliable routine.

Finally, I was glad it was time to go back in the house. My skirt and short-sleeved shirt were not enough to keep me warm as the evening chilled. Though the lace covered some of it, I could clearly make out my nipples through my shirt, standing on end to drink in the cold weather. I crossed my arms over my chest and followed Joshua inside.

"Hungry?" he asked as we got into the house and removed our shoes.

"Mmm-hmm," I answered.

"What should we eat?" he asked, turning to face me. I studied his hands, remembering the feeling of his fingers expertly working over mine in the barn and, in spite of myself, my nipples tightened even more.

I flicked my eyes up to meet his, and I could tell I'd given my thoughts away. "I know what I want for dinner," he smiled hungrily, crossing the kitchen in two giant steps and pushing me up against the counter, pressing into me. He smelled like milk and hard work and I groaned under the weight of him. He slid his hands quickly up under my shirt, the bottom button popping off from the girth of his forearms.

"Something else I'll have to mend," he said absently, bringing his mouth down hungrily on mine, swallowing me whole and shoving his hands harder up under my blouse. Another button popped off, exposing my stomach to the air. He tasted like salt and unmistakable masculinity and I struggled to push him away lest all the buttons on my shirt get popped off.

"Let me," I rocked him away, reaching up to unbutton my blouse the rest of the way.

"Don't worry," he said, unwilling to stop. "I promise I'll mend them."

I began unbuttoning them from the top, struggling to make space for my hands between his chest and mine, and finally he extracted his as well and helped me with the last two on the bottom. He pushed the shirt away gently, exposing me to him, and looked happily into my eyes before leaning down to take in my neck, sliding the shirt gently from my shoulders and pinching the back of my bra, unhooking it on the first try.

I pushed his t-shirt up toward his head and he pulled it the rest of the way off, exposing his own broad chest, its mat of blonde curls, and his solid stomach. I ran my mouth along the length of it, as high as I could reach, and he dipped down to kiss me when I couldn't reach any further, his abs tightening as he bent. I ran my hands along the washboard of him, sucking hard on his mouth while he brought his huge hands to my breasts, taking one easily in each hand, kneading them and pinching slightly at the nipples. He definitely knew what to do with those hands. Then he grabbed onto them and held each nipple firmly, holding me in place while he sucked and drank me in. My lower half began writhing, as my upper half was held motionless. Again and again he kissed me, squeezing my nipples tightly, firmly, not letting me shift from him. He rubbed himself against me and I thrashed against him too, my cunt convulsing at the lack of attention it was getting while the entire upper part of me was stimulated and throbbing. I moaned into his open mouth, and he kept going, pushing me to my edge.

Finally, he let go of my nipples and swiftly slid his hands down my front. He pulled my skirt up from the bottom, and moved his hand over the mound of my underwear, which was already soaking wet. He moaned there, sliding his fingers gently over the elastic lip of my panties and down into my warm wetness. He brought his other hand around my waist, and with one arm lifted me up onto his kitchen counter, spreading my legs wide and positioning himself between them. Oh, he had me now.

I reached up and clasped my arms around his neck, bringing him down to me, kissing him again. I tried to stay focused and active, but his fingers were working their magic below and my knees had gone weak. I couldn't concentrate on his mouth, on his chest or stomach, on anything except his expert hand, so large there could have been two of them down there, playing with my clit, teasing the hole of my vagina, sliding toward the hole of my ass. He pinched my clit gently, tapped on it with another finger, and kept the motion moving until I couldn't hold it anymore. I tensed up. My widespread legs were clenching hard against his, my back arching, my breasts heaving. He held me in place with his other humongous hand on the small of my back, and tickled and fondled me until I came, gasping out as warm waves of wetness welled out of me.

"Mmm," he moaned pleasurably, feeling me convulse against him, his rock hard penis practically busting the button off his jeans.

I reached over and unlatched the buckle on his jeans, undoing the button and sliding down the zipper while he held me there, his hands still on my back and on my cunt. I pushed them over his muscular bottom; the bulge of his black briefs left nothing to the imagination. Joshua shook slightly as I gently pulled them over the top of it and down, exposing the broad, ample shaft, admiring it for a minute. I tipped my head down to take it in, slowly at first, licking it little by little, teasing the tip with my mouth. He moaned and I brought my mouth over the tip and halfway down, sucking and licking the shaft with my tongue. I began moving up and down slowly.

To my surprise, he groaned loudly and pulled away, bringing his briefs back over the bulge, lifting me up to look in his eyes. "Not yet," he said, obviously pained at this decision. "I don't want to move too fast with you."

My mouth felt empty without him, and I felt vulnerable, too. I had an orgasm and he had not. I had lost control, given in to pleasure, and he had not. It gave him a power over me I didn't like. I must have been pouting, because he brought his gaze down level to mine and kissed me so intensely I felt like I saw different eras, different couples and different experiences that spanned centuries between us. An ancient knowing and a new beginning, all wrapped into one. He was waiting for me—I could sense that. And I had not shown up yet.

17

Joshua made me a cup of hot cocoa from the fresh milk we collected earlier, and poured a little splash of whiskey into it—"for extra warmth", he assured me. We snuggled together on his couch. He sewed the two buttons back on my blouse, and then he started mending the hole on my skirt, all while I was wearing them. His tongue stuck slightly out of the corner of his mouth as he concentrated on the work. His large hands moved the tiny needle and thread so intricately. I watched him as nonchalantly as I could, my heart doing little dances as I mentally replayed our scene in the kitchen. My vagina tightened with every recollection, and with Joshua poking the tiny needle under the fabric near my leg. Still, the morning was a long time ago and my eyes threatened to slide shut before he finished.

He yawned, knotted the thread on the backside of the fabric, and pulled me into him after snipping it clean.

"Thank you," I said, kissing him gently. "You're handy to have around." I rested my head on his chest and drifted off to sleep.

***

Joshua's large frame shifted underneath me, and I opened my eyes groggily to take in the unfamiliar surroundings. It was dark—nighttime—and I had fallen asleep on Joshua! He stirred, too, opening his eyes to meet mine, and smiled sleepily. "I guess we fell asleep, huh?" he asked. "You need to go back across the fence?"

I snuggled into him again, shaking my head. He felt so good. I had no reason to go back, except risking giving myself away to Shantel, or whoever else might be watching, who didn't already know about my date with Joshua.

He shifted on the couch, laid his whole body down and pulled me on top of him, my head on his chest. "The softest blanket I've ever had," he said, snuggling me into him.

I pulled an actual blanket over myself, and drifted off to sleep again, only to wake as the early sun slanted brightly through his living room window. Joshua was moving me gently off him so he could get up. Before my eyes even fully opened, my mind shot awake. The EGGS! I forgot to collect the eggs yesterday! I was having such a lovely evening, I didn't even think about my daily chore.

"The EGGS!" I nearly shouted at him, jumping up.

"Good morning to you, too!" he replied.

"I forgot to collect the eggs yesterday!" I fumbled for my shoes. I didn't want Dana to think I would slack on my farm chores if I went out with Joshua.

"You comin' back?" Joshua asked as I reached for the door.

"Huh?" I started, whirling around to face him. He looked dejected.

"Do you want me to come back?" I asked.

"I maybe had a little breakfast plan in mind, but if you need to get back..."

"Joshua Murphy, are you offering to make me breakfast?" I asked.

He gave a sly shrug. "They say it's the way to a woman's heart."

"*They* might know *me* a little too well," I winked at him. "Should I bring back some eggs, if the *chicas* haven't destroyed them all?"

"I've still got some from Miss Dana. Just bring yourself back. I need to go and milk first."

"Ok," I agreed, trotting out the back door and toward the gate. I slipped through it and ran toward the barn, hoping to beat Dana there, but she was already inside, clucking her hellos to her *chicas.*

"Dana, I'm sorry!" I said as I burst into the barn.

"Sorry for what?" she asked, startled at my entrance.

"The eggs!" I said, looking around. Someone had already collected them.

A confused moment passed between us as I realized she had no idea what I was talking about. She gave me a swift once-over, seeming to take in the whole reality of my last 24 hours in one glance, and turned the corners of her mouth up. "You must have a good friend here," she said. "The eggs were collected yesterday, as usual."

Sure enough, when I got back to my trailer there was a note on my table, on a torn piece of paper scrawled in scrappy penmanship.

"Wanted to make sure you had nothing holding you back. I got the eggs. Love, Cleo."

I'd have to do something nice for her. For now, I ran the water in my trailer to give myself a quick hand bath and changed clothes, choosing a knee-length emerald green skirt with a purple cotton top. The weather was supposed to be nice again today, a real rarity in May. I scrubbed the sweaters off my teeth—goat milk hot chocolate isn't exactly the thing you want sitting in your mouth all night—and brushed my hair, which was tangled from snuggling on Joshua all night. His smell mingled with mine on my dirty clothes, and I set them on my bed instead of in the hamper. I grabbed a bunch of collard greens from my plot in the demo beds on my way back through the fence.

As I neared the beehives behind the greenhouses, I saw a shadow coming around the other side of them—Craig.

I turned around to try to avoid him, but it was too late.

"Kelsie!" he said to my back.

I turned to face him, my heart pounding. "Oh hi Craig," I stammered.

He studied my outfit and the bunch of collard greens in my hand.

"What are you up to this morning?" he quizzed.

"Oh, uh, I was just, um, checking on the bees," I lied. God I'm a terrible liar!

"Checking on the bees, huh?" he asked again with a small smile.

"Well, not really *checking* on them," I continued. "More like looking at them."

"They're so fascinating!" I finished, trying not to show my nervousness.

"That they are…" he said, taking a couple of steps closer to me. "You look nice this morning."

"Thanks," I said, glancing over toward Joshua's place. He was probably still in the barn doing the milking.

"It's not often I get to see you dressed up," he said, stepping closer again. "Any special occasion?" he asked, running his hand through his dark hair.

My heart thumped harder. "No, no special occasion…" I trailed off. I couldn't think of even a lame excuse.

He was standing right next to me now. I could smell his ocean smell. Did he know? *He's trying to get me to slip up,* I thought. *Just say something and go back toward your trailer. You can sneak over again once he's gone.*

I remembered the bunch of collard greens in my hand. "Well, I'd better go make my breakfast," I said to him, turning back toward my trailer.

"Yeah, you'd better do that," he replied, winking at me. "Now that you've seen what you were looking for."

Suddenly I got it. *He thinks I was* trying *to run into him! Better than the alternative,* I thought. I smiled back, more confidently now. "Nice seein' ya," I said, bounding off toward my trailer.

I hid behind a tree in the small grove separating the demo beds from the greenhouses until I saw Craig heading back toward the farmhouse, and then I snuck back the way I came and slipped through the fence onto Joshua's farm. I didn't know it, but someone else was watching me while I was watching Craig.

18

As soon as the blackberry bramble on Joshua's side safely hid me, I relaxed a bit, popping my head into the barn as Joshua was finishing. Together we cooked up a delicious meal of potatoes, eggs, and collard greens topped with his chevre. Once again, it struck me that we were eating a meal entirely of our own making. Everything from the veggies to the eggs to the butter we cooked them in was grown on these two neighboring plots of land. I couldn't help but feel proud of us.

After breakfast, we parted ways. I had some catching up to do in my plot in the demo beds, and Joshua needed to do some fence mending so he could move his goats into a new pasture. He offered to help me haul the art supply boxes we had picked up from my Mom's house over to my trailer, but I assured him it wasn't necessary. "I don't want to get in trouble with Dana and Craig for hanging out with you when I should be doing farm work," I said, which wasn't totally a lie. "I'll just take this box and get the next one the next time I'm here."

"That works for me, I guess," he said. "Means you'll have to come over here again soon."

After a passionate good-bye kiss, I snuck back through the fence, back into the world of White Oak Farm.

***

Monday we entered what Craig referred to as the "last leg of the rat race." Now that the danger of frost had passed, there is a rush to get all the hot crops in the ground, while harvesting for market and, now, for the CSA, which started last week. During all this, we needed to keep everything weeded and watered. We would transplant literally thousands of tomatoes, peppers, eggplant, tomatillos, ground cherries, squashes, cucumbers, melons, and basil, along with our regular successions of lettuce for salad mix, and in addition, seed pole beans, bush beans, soybeans, corn, and more squashes. All of this had to be done within a matter of weeks. The days were longer now, so we would start earlier and end later.

After an intense morning riding on the back of the tractor with Jessi, plopping butternut squash starts into the ground in the holes that the tractor's attachment punched into the earth by the hundreds, we broke for a lunch of what Dana called "Whatcha-got Salad"—mixed greens topped with hard boiled eggs, fresh herbs, toasted nuts, topped with the roasted remnants of last year's harvest—potatoes, a couple carrots and parsnips, rutabaga—like an extravagant vegetarian version of a chef salad. The crown jewel was our first harvest of baby beets, perched atop the whole thing like earthy sweet rubies. Happy to have a break from the unrelenting focus required by the squash planting, I savored my food and the company of my fellow farmers. Unlike a human working, a tractor never stops to stretch its back or reach a foot back to correct a mistake. It keeps going, on and on, in a relentless, mechanical monotony. I found it tedious and tiresome in a way I hadn't experienced. In contrast, the quiet and fluid movements of our crew without machinery welcomed and soothed me.

That is, until Shantel opened her mouth.

"So Kelsie, why were you going over to Joshua's yesterday?" she asked sweetly.

I froze, my fork suspended in mid-air, interrupted en route to my mouth, which hung open at her audacity.

Cleo shot her a death glare. Dana cleared her throat loudly. Craig's neck whipped fast in my direction, his eyes ablaze. I might as well have been a beet, my face burned so hot.

Cleo again came to my rescue, putting a hand on her skinny hip and aiming her fiery glare at Shantel. "As if it should matter to *you*," she began, "I asked Kelsie to run over to Joshua's to grab some milk when I ran out in the middle of attempting a crème brulée." She oozed disgust and condescension, finishing her explanation with a whip of her hair over her shoulder and stormed off toward the sink with her empty bowl, mumbling and growling under her breath.

I nodded feebly at the table of inquisitors boring holes in me. When I met Dana's eyes, she smiled sympathetically at me. Craig seemed suspicious, Shantel unconvinced, but the tension lightened when Dana announced the topic of the June Luscious Earth workshop—honeybees. "After our last experience working with them, Kelsie," she smiled at me, "I realized—or rather, remembered—that they are truly one of the most erotic and fascinating creatures on the planet."

"Aunt Dana," Cleo butted in, obviously delighted with the change in conversation, "you could uncover the inner erotic and fascinating nature of this table."

A hearty laugh went around it as Dana explored the grain of the wood with her strong fingers. "It is certain," she began, her eyes gleaming as she went around the table looking at each of us. "The solid wood, given by an old oak tree, serves as the centerpiece for all our favorite farm meals..." We giggled uncontrollably. No one was more relieved than I. She could fondle that table all day if it kept the attention off me and Joshua.

That evening in my trailer, I fumed over Shantel's indecency. Would she really stoop that low? Little did she realize I was fast losing my desire to attract Craig anyway. She could have him, for all I cared. But that she would backstab me really got to me. I felt trapped in my trailer, knowing she was inside hers, possibly spying on me, waiting to reveal the next move I made to visit Joshua.

As a distraction from my entrapment, I opened the box of art supplies from my parents' house, and walked down memory lane as I unpacked the contents one by one. From the time I still colored outside the lines, all I ever wanted to be was a painter. But my mom was good at pseudo-well-meaning guidance away from things we were passionate about and toward things that made money and offered security. "I'll not have my daughters dependent on *men* for their financial security," she would tell us. I remember her commenting at a high school art show that there were a lot more talented painters in the show than I, and even they weren't going to be able to make a living at it. I would be wise to enroll in a foreign language elective instead of wasting my time on art classes.

The entire month of May passed in a blur of work and, occasionally, sneaking over to Joshua's for dinner and a sleepover. Although he'd let me go further, he still stopped short of intercourse, making this officially the longest I had ever dated anyone without sleeping with him. On a brighter note, Craig was totally stressed about work. He barely had time to sleep, let alone hit on me or Shantel, who was obviously upset with the situation.

And best of all, I started painting. Several nights a week, after shoving down some sort of quick and unexciting dinner after another strenuous day, I cozied up to my tiny table and escaped into the happiest activity of my childhood, chewing thoughtfully on the end of a paintbrush as I brought a world to life on what started out as a plain white canvas. Inspired by Dana and White Oak Farm, I was painting bees. Close-ups, so close you could see the hair on their fuzzy bodies. Drinking nectar with their long tongues, cleaning big globs of pollen off their bodies and packing it into the pollen baskets on their back legs, dancing their waggle dance. Dana told me how a bee that scouts out a good source of flowers will come back to the hive and perform a dance to give the other bees directions to the flower patch. *And the bees know exactly where to go!* They can tell how good the patch is by the intensity of her dance, and they will send the correct number of foragers to the patch. I was inexplicably happy knowing that happens, and was trying to capture the movement of the dance on the canvas.

At her Luscious Earth workshop, I presented Dana with my first painting—a golden-colored bee unfurling her long tongue—her *proboscis*—to drink from a blue-purple *Phacelia* flower. I tried to give the flower a phosphorescent glow, because Dana had told me how bees can see the ultraviolet spectrum invisible to humans. She said that flowers don eye-catching patterns that lead a bee to the center, where the nectar is, most of which are invisible to humans. I adorned the *Phacelia* with bright blue nectar guides shimmering with patterns, so we could see some of the beauty that bees see. An unexpected benefit of studying bees is that we also learn about the native wildflowers that feed them.

Dana invited participants to dab honey on bare parts of their bodies and invite honeybees to come drink from them so they could feel their small legs, their furry bodies, their imploring tongues, the buzz of their wings, and the rush at the potential of their intense sting. Dana, enamored of baring flesh to the universe, removed her shirt and invited bees to form a belt around her belly by painting it with a wide band of honey. Several older women and two hippie-type men also removed shirts and enjoyed the sensation of the bees on their soft, wrinkled bellies. I opted to welcome them onto my arm while keeping my boobs hidden safely beneath the double barrier of shirt and bra. I found myself much more comfortable with the whole ordeal than I had during that first pumpkin workshop, and reckoned I was growing, even if I wasn't ready to go frolic naked through the woods just yet. I enjoyed myself immensely, as always, though I did feel like I already had my own private Luscious Earth workshop with Dana, working with the bees for the prior couple of months.

During the workshop Dana worked herself into a frenzy, imparting every sexy tidbit she could think of about *Apis mellifera*, including a more detailed version of the virgin queen's nuptial flight, the waggle dance, the long, unfurling proboscis, the bees' communication by pheromones, the roles of the drones, and the cultural significance of honey and bees in ancient cultures.

As most of the participants headed off toward their own abodes, I gave Dana the painting. She burst into tears.

"Kelsie, this is absolutely breathtaking!" she exclaimed, wrapping me in an exuberant embrace.

Then she began whirling me around in the evening sunlight. We laughed, flailed our arms and legs, shook our butts and our breasts, danced each other around until we collapsed breathless against the wall of the greenhouse.

"Thank you so much, Kelsie!" she beamed at me, panting, the sunlight twinkling off her silver earrings. "This is an exquisite gift, a reminder of the luscious intricacies of the earth and its gorgeous and complex web of inhabitants. I will hang it with honor, and honor it always." And I knew she would.

Cleo came knocking on my door when I returned to the trailer, and helped herself to a beer and a seat on my crowded little couch amid paint tubes and half-finished canvases.

"Good workshop tonight, huh?" I asked her, opening one myself.

"As always. It's so cool you're learning about the bees!" she told me. "Aunt Dana told me she's hoping you will take some hives on yourself after you're done with the internship."

"I gave her my first painting tonight," I said. "Of a forager bee drinking from a *Phacelia* flower."

"Oh," Cleo said laughing, "I bet she was beside herself."

I chuckled, too. "Yeah, she grabbed me and made me dance with her after she saw it."

"Not that I minded," I added quickly. "I'm so grateful for her."

Cleo took a giant swig off her beer. "You know who I'm *not* grateful for is Shantel," she blurted out. "I swear I almost punched her last week at market. I wish I was hanging out with you and Jessi there."

In spite of myself, I was dying to hear more gossip. "Why did you want to punch her?"

"Oh God, when *don't* I want to hit her?" she asked, her hair leaping up off her bright yellow t-shirt. I couldn't help smiling.

"I don't know what her problem is," Cleo continued. "She left the booth at least once an hour last week, in between begging Craig for attention and *sort of* helping customers. Meanwhile, I'm running my ass off trying to keep everything stocked and help everybody, and Craig seems super distracted, which isn't even like him—usually he's totally on it at market. Now the only time he seems to snap out of whatever weird mood he's in is when some young hot chick comes up, which just pisses Shantel off more and more...it totally sucks!" She slammed her head into the couch cushion for emphasis, mumbling, "Aaarggh!"

"Aw, Cleo, I'm sorry," I said, unsure of what to say. I'd been enjoying my relative break from both Shantel and Craig—the relentlessness of our work didn't allow for much chitchat or flirtation—but hearing that made the old feelings well up inside me again. Craig and Shantel together, Craig flirting with other girls. I didn't really want to think about that.

"Whatever," she said with a sigh. "I don't really want to talk about it anyway. Fuck 'em. Let's talk about something more interesting..." She shot me a sly smile. "What's going on with Jo-shu-a?" she asked, raising her dark eyebrows on each syllable.

I threw a paintbrush at her. "That reminds me of something my friend Caroline would say," I laughed. "I'd love the two of you to meet each other."

"Any friend of yours..." Cleo replied.

"My birthday's in a week," I mused. "I was thinking of inviting her out to spend the night. She said she wanted to, and I've wanted her to see what my life's like."

"Rad," Cleo agreed, swigging her beer. "We could use some fresh blood out here...it's gettin' a little claustrophobic."

It was dark, my signal to pass out in order to be relatively rested for another day of tough work. Cleo's eyes were drooping a little, too.

She ran her fingers over a half-finished bee painting. "You're really good, you know," she offered. "They look alive, almost better than alive."

"Thanks, Cleo. I'm really enjoying myself. Fuck my mom. She tried hard to get me to give up painting in lieu of a more lucrative career." I contemplated my $50/week farm stipend. "If only she could see me now..." I laughed.

***

The next night I called Caroline and invited her out to spend my birthday on the farm. She happily agreed, informing me she'd picked out some new underwear for when she got an invitation. "You never know—that Craig might need some extra company while I'm there, huh?" she'd joked.

"Be careful what you wish for," I warned her.

***

On my birthday, the weather was awful, pouring rain all day and nearly drowning some of the small transplants struggling to get their roots anchored. Several young lettuce starts washed out of their holes, laying helplessly on the mucky surface of their bed, their bright white roots exposed to the air. Luckily, the peppers and eggplant had taken root before the latest days-long downpour. By contrast, the squash and bean seeds, both having germinated several weeks earlier, seemed ecstatic about the weather. I swear I could see the zucchini leaves getting bigger before my eyes, glowing bright green and vibrant. The beds and paths were mucky so we spent the day cleaning the barn and the packing shed that had been annihilated in the rush to get everything in the ground.

"Hey, birthday girl!" Cleo called to me over the rain pounding on the roof of the barn while we stacked pots and cell trays. "Aunt Dana and I were thinking how it'd be cool to have an exhibition of your art at this year's harvest festival!"

"That would be awesome!" Jessi agreed. Even Shantel seemed supportive, between the frequent trips out of the barn that had become her signature move these last few weeks.

"I don't know ..." I began.

"Of course, you don't," Cleo asserted. Dana walked in, her raincoat dripping. "I swear you'd sell yourself short to a midget."

She cracked us all up. "What on earth are you talking about?" Dana asked.

"Kelsie," Cleo said flatly. "She, of *course,* isn't sure anyone would want to see her paintings at the harvest festival."

"I didn't say it like that..." I defended myself.

Dana patted me on the shoulder, her long hair curling slightly in the humidity. "There's no pressure, Kelsie. I'm just thinking it would be a supportive place to showcase your talents! You don't have to if you don't want to," she assured me.

Caroline arrived in the late afternoon. I heard her car pull up in the gravel driveway and I ran out of the barn to greet her. She waved excitedly through the windshield as I approached.

"I'm glad you found us!" I said, practically yanking her out of the car for a hug. She pulled her raincoat up over her brown curls and looked around. "It's pretty!" she offered. "Which one's Joshua's house?"

"Ssshhhhh!" I shook her, glancing quickly around. "Don't talk about that!"

"Sorry," she giggled. "So not much has changed since our last meeting, eh?" she teased, swatting me on the butt.

The other women emerged from the barn to greet Caroline. Dana, with her long stride, reached her first, and wrapped her into a warm hug. "Welcome to White Oak Farm, Caroline," she beamed. "We're so glad you could join Kelsie out here for her special day!"

I surveyed them. "You already know Jessi," I offered. Jessi nodded hello at her. "This is Cleo and Shantel."

Caroline said her hellos to all of them, looking around for someone else, after giving Shantel a very serious once-over.

"I think Craig's in the greenhouse," I mumbled at her. "I'll introduce you later."

"We might as well call it a day," Dana suggested. "The weather isn't getting any better, and the barn doesn't need to get any cleaner. I'll leave you ladies to your birthday celebration and try to catch up on some CSA paperwork." She smiled at Caroline. "So glad you're here. Make yourself at home," she said.

"Yes, Caroline, so nice to meet you," Shantel said sweetly. "I'll see you at dinner. I'm going to see if Craig needs any help in the greenhouse!" And with that, she ran out the door. Cleo rolled her eyes so hard her whole head rolled with them. The rain had really done a number on her hair, giving her a heavy metal kind of look. "Why did you have to invite her?" she snarled at me.

"What, was I going to invite everyone *but* her?" I retorted.

Jessi grabbed her hand. "You'll survive it somehow," she joked, pushing her slightly.

Cleo tousled Jessi's hair. "We'll see...you might have to pull me off of her after a couple drinks, ...I'm just sayin'..." They took off hand in hand toward the trailers.

I was a little preoccupied with the thought of Shantel and Craig in the greenhouse together, but I pushed it out of my head and helped Caroline with her bag while she grabbed a sheet cake from the back of her car. It was from a grocery store, a huge white cake dabbed with pounds of frosting and even more food coloring. Under the phrase," Happy Birthday, Farmer Kelsie!" was a plastic figurine of a woman in overalls, with a frosting pitchfork and a host of bright frosting farm animals—pigs and chickens and goats. It looked disgusting, almost inedible, but hilarious.

"Thanks, Caroline!" I laughed as she emerged with it.

"I had them decorate it especially for you!" she beamed.

"Let's take it to my trailer, then I can show you around," I said, showing her the way.

She came up next to me, whispering too loudly, "Yeah, I want to see what's in the greenhouse!"

"Sssh!"

She burst out laughing.

"Hey, wait up, Kels!" she said. "Lord you've picked up speed!"

I chuckled, slowing down. I guess I wouldn't notice it, always struggling to keep up with Dana, but it makes sense. There's always so much to be done around here, and so far to go between tasks that we all probably walk a little faster than we did when we arrived.

I led Caroline through the demo beds, and pointed out my personal garden bed, which boasted a small patch of ripening June-bearing strawberries getting soggy in the rain. I stooped down, picked a bright red one, and popped it into Caroline's mouth.

"Yum!" she exclaimed. "This stuff's all yours, eh?"

"Mmm-hmm." I chomped down on one. "And look! I've got my first little zucchini coming on!" I pointed at the peanut-sized green fruit with a huge, soggy, yellow flower attached to its butt.

"Cool!"

"And my trailer's around this hedge," I led her, propping open the door so she could get inside with her massive cake.

"It's cozy, all right," she said, looking around. Right away, she noticed the bee paintings, leaning up against a window. I had cleaned up all the painting stuff so there would be room for both of us.

"Wow, these are amazing. Who's the artist?" she asked.

"Uh, I'm painting them," I said shyly.

"What?" she whipped around. "Since when? I didn't know you could paint!"

"I used to in high school, but then I sort of gave it up."

"Good thing you picked it back up. You're really good!"

"Thanks, Caroline. I'm really enjoying it. Actually," I paused, "Dana and Cleo think I should have an art show at our harvest festival this year. They asked me today."

"Totally," she said matter-of-factly. "You'll be a wild success!"

"I appreciate your optimism, Caroline," I said. "I'm thinking about it. Wanna go check out the rest of the farm?"

I felt like a kid showing her mom around her school, pointing out every feature—the chickens, the bees, the fields, the new starts, the salad mix, on and on, sharing way more than Caroline ever wanted to know about each of them.

"Cool. Interesting. Pretty. Wow," she'd say politely after each diatribe.

Finally, I gave in. "I know what you really want to see."

Her eyes lit up. "Let's go," I said in mock exasperation, dragging her toward the greenhouse. I quietly pointed out Joshua's place and the gate in the fence as we passed it, circling around to the front of the greenhouse. I couldn't tell if Shantel was still in there, and I definitely didn't want to go barging in on them if she was.

I knocked timidly on the door.

"Come in," Craig's voice came. I poked my head in. He was, as usual when in the greenhouse, shirtless. He broke into a huge smile when he saw me, I guess figuring I'd come to my senses at last.

"My friend Caroline is with me," I started, opening the door. His eyebrows rose a bit. "She wanted to—I mean, I wanted to introduce you to her."

We stepped into the warmth of the greenhouse and Caroline almost fell on her own jaw as the smooth, shirtless Craig stepped forward to shake her hand. He flashed her a bright smile, setting off his dark skin. Even I had to admit it was hard not to get a little turned on by him.

He took her hand in his. "Pleasure," he said, eyeing her up and down.

She had no problem doing the same, staring at his smooth, muscular chest before bringing her eyes up to meet his. She held his intense gaze. "Likewise," she said, subtly licking her lips.

Whoa, I thought. It had been awhile since I'd seen Caroline in action.

"So you want to get a taste of White Oak Farm?" he asked her.

She nodded eagerly. He took the opportunity.

"Kelsie's gotten a good feel for it, haven't you?" he asked, sliding his hand onto my ass. My knees went weak. Caroline gaped at me. My cunt throbbed, thinking about the last time I was alone in here with him. Part of me wanted to push his hand away, and part of me wanted to shove it inside me. *How does he do it?* I wondered. Joshua's sincere smile flashed in my mind and I stepped out of Craig's reach, swallowing hard.

"Caroline's never done any farm work," I changed the subject. "She said she was up for anything." I winked at her. She winked at Craig. That seemed to satisfy him.

"I love to enlighten the newcomers," he said, almost imperceptibly flexing his biceps. That was enough to turn me off, but it made Caroline more excited.

"Well, I'd love to learn," she replied, quickly flitting her eyes to his penis.

Jesus, I thought. She doesn't mess around. Craig seemed impressed as well.

"Be in here tomorrow morning, 8 am sharp," he told her. "Don't be late."

"I'll see what I can do," she said nonchalantly, turning to me. "Wanna continue the tour, Kels?"

And with that, she turned and walked out the door. This time it was me scurrying after her, nodding at Craig on my way out. "See ya," I mumbled.

Caroline was practically running toward my trailer and by the time we reached it I was laughing so hard I could barely keep moving. She flopped herself down on the sofa and let out a scream.

"Holy shit that was intense!" she squealed.

"You're tellin' me!" I hooted. "I've never seen that side of you!"

"Neither have I!" she laughed back, panting. "But I thought, hell, if Kelsie can do it, I can too!"

I laughed harder. "I certainly have never done it like that," I assured her. "I'm way too chicken for that. You were incredible!"

"So now what?" she asked, her eyes bright.

"Now you're going to go get a 'lesson' from him in the greenhouse tomorrow," I replied.

"Holy shit!" she exclaimed again. "I am *so* glad I bought new underwear!"

Cleo had offered to make me whatever I wanted for a birthday dinner, and I had chosen the sweet and sour chicken we'd had at her summer-in-winter party, since I knew Caroline would like it. I didn't want to feed her anything that totally freaked her out. Still, I wanted to show her how good farm food was. My contribution was an Asian snow pea salad with sesame seeds and my new farm favorite, garlic scapes.

"It's the flower stalk of the garlic plant," I told Caroline, pulling a handful of the whimsical, curling, snakelike green stems out of my fridge. "Smell 'em," I said, handing her a few.

"Mmm, they smell like garlic!" she said. She slid one on her wrist like a bracelet. "Maybe I should wear this on my date with Craig tomorrow," she joked.

"Good idea," I kidded back. "Offer you some protection from that vampire."

She giggled.

"Seriously, though, he'll expect you to work," I warned her.

"I fully intend to *work*, Kelsie."

I burst out laughing again. "I'm so glad you came here!" I told her. "I've been dying to introduce you to this place!"

"It really is beautiful, and sexy! I can see why you love it so much," she mused, fingering her vegetable bracelet.

"Wanna help me pick some peas?" I asked her. She nodded, slipping her raincoat back on.

Happily, when we walked outside, we found the rain had stopped. There was a mist settling over the fields in the distance that made them look gorgeous and eerie at the same time. I led her to the pea patch, where we picked a few and snacked on some straight from the vine.

"These are good!" she said, her mouth full of peas.

"Indeed," I agreed. "Isn't it cool to be able to eat your food right off the plant?"

As we returned to our trailer, we got a clear glimpse of Cleo and Jessi having some fun in Cleo's through her window, legs and arms flailing in the air.

"Whoa," Caroline said. "Everyone around here's gettin' it on."

"Except me," I said with a sigh.

She whipped around to face me. "What are you talking about?" she demanded.

"Joshua hasn't wanted to yet."

"Why the hell not?" she insisted.

"I don't know," I sighed again. "He says he doesn't want to move too fast with me, that he's scared of messing up a good thing."

"Too fast?" Caroline exploded. "Jesus! Haven't you been dating for at least a month now?"

I nodded. "Six weeks."

"What the hell is his problem?" Caroline isn't one to wait around. Or to mince words, for that matter. "If you ask me, a surefire way to 'mess up a good thing,'" she drew quote marks in the air with her fingers, "is to withhold sex." She pulled a bottle of wine out of her suitcase. "That makes me want a drink," she said, exasperated. "I feel like I should march right over there and tell him to *get moving*!"

I laughed. "Thanks for the offer, Caroline. But to be honest, I'm kind of enjoying the suspense of waiting. It makes every time together exciting."

"Exciting? No sex is exciting? I'll have to give that one some thought," she rolled her eyes playfully, pouring herself a huge glass of wine, and then one for me.

We chatted about the parts of each other's lives we'd missed out on over the last few months, tried to get caught up on the details, until Cleo and Jessi came knocking. Caroline gave them both a knowing smile as they entered the tiny trailer and snuggled in around the table.

"Hey ladies," she said, clutching her wine glass. "We were discussing how Joshua won't put out."

Wine bubbled up into my nose and splattered out my mouth. "CAROLINE!" I yelled. Cleo and Jessi doubled over. "SHUT UP!"

"Well, it's true, isn't it?" she retorted. "I'd think you'd want a little sympathy from your friends."

"Believe it or not, Caroline, not every single person in this world believes you must have sex within a few weeks of dating someone to be all right with the world. Furthermore, you can NOT bring this up when Shantel gets here. She doesn't know about Joshua and I want to keep it that way."

"Why?" she asked.

"I don't know," I paused. "I don't trust her. I feel like she might tell Craig."

"Well, he's gonna have to find out sooner or later, right?" she asked.

"Yeah, but..."

"Things can get a little too incestuous out here," Cleo summed it up.

"Exactly," I said. "Thanks, Cleo. And whatever. Joshua wants to take me out after this week's market for my birthday. Maybe...."

"Let's hope so!" Caroline wailed. "Let's toast!" She held up her wine glass. "To Kelsie getting laid!" she bellowed.

Just then, a timid knock came at the door.

19

Everyone fell silent as I shot Caroline a "damn you!" look. Cleo started snickering, but my heart was beating like a drum. Caroline seemed pretty unfazed. I opened the door for Shantel, who appeared to be processing exactly what to say. She took a deep breath and stepped inside.

"Hi, everyone," she nodded at the table packed with women. "Happy birthday, Kelsie." She awkwardly shoved a card into my hand, and I fumbled to open it. "Thanks," I mumbled, my heart still pounding. She definitely heard Caroline's toast. Caroline broke the silence by recounting her experience picking peas. "It was really cool!" she told the girls. "We just ate them right off the plant! I've never done that before..." Inside Shantel's card was a coupon for a one-hour massage from her. Just what I wanted to do—have her perfect hands that have probably rubbed all over Craig's body rub on my back.

"Thanks, Shantel," I said again. "Have a seat!" I tried to sound cheerful. "Would you like some wine?"

"No thanks," she said. "Do you have any tea?"

"Oh, uh, probably," I stammered. Who doesn't drink a glass of wine at somebody's birthday party? Why did she have to be so damned prissy? I found the tea in the cupboard and set some water to boil.

"So, Caroline, you like White Oak so far?" Shantel asked her sweetly.

"Definitely," Caroline replied. "Kelsie showed me all the goods, but I've gotta say, the best ones were in the greenhouse!"

I shot her a *look.* I saw an accusatory fire flare up in Shantel's eyes, but she struggled to remain calm. I shifted on my feet. The tension was thick in the trailer, way too thick for such a small space.

"Oh really? What did you like about it?" she asked Caroline innocently.

Caroline began to grasp the delicacy of the situation. "Oh, uh, the, uh, plants in there," she stammered, an unconvincing lie because we had planted out most of what was in there. She took a swig of wine, and turned to Cleo for support.

"Cleo, Kels tells me you're from Portland?"

Cleo nodded eagerly, grateful for the change in subject. "Yeah, it's quite the alternate universe over there."

Caroline laughed. "I'll say. The land of tattoos and circus freaks."

"Actually," Shantel butted in, "*Craig* has been showing me around there after market sometimes, and it seems like a really nice city." She batted her eyes at me.

Cleo about had it. "Yeah, well, *Craig* has his own agenda in mind, and you're not exactly the kind of person who's gonna appreciate the more gritty side of the city," she informed Shantel with a smirk.

"Ok, ladies," Jessi butted in. "This is Kelsie's birthday—keep it to yourselves. We're here to celebrate her."

Shantel's tea water boiled, and I shoved a tea bag into it and practically threw it at her. "Here," I barked. I was fuming at Shantel, trying to keep my cool, but before I could stop myself, it was coming out my mouth.

"Yeah, Craig must love showing people around Portland. He's been asking me to go there with him for weeks now," I lied, pretending to inform Caroline but watching Shantel's reaction out of the corner of my eye. Why was I doing this?

Her eyes sank. I know I'd hurt her feelings, but she was trying to do the same to me, I told myself. Still, I felt bad.

"Anyway, enough about him," I changed the subject. "Has anyone noticed Dana in the B&B cabins lately?"

Cleo and Jessi both cracked up. "What does she do in there?" Caroline asked.

"She offers extra attention to certain visitors who want it!" Cleo squealed.

"Really?" Shantel and Caroline asked in unison.

"Really," Cleo stated. "Aunt Dana believes her love is too great for one person, so she wants to share as much of it as possible with as many people who want or need it."

"Whoa," Caroline mused. "I wouldn't mind getting paid extra for that job."

"Yeah, huh?" Cleo asked. "They'll pay top dollar for that. Can you imagine being alone with all Aunt Dana's passion in one of those tiny cabins? Seems like she'd blow the walls off the room!"

We laughed at that as Cleo shimmied out of the bench seat. "I bet the chicken's done—I'll go grab it from my trailer," she offered. "Be right back!"

We stared at our glasses, lost in our own thoughts, until Caroline blurted out, "This place is so hot! There's sex all over here!"

"Farmerotica," Jessi declared, cracking us up. "This place has a reputation even on the east coast!" Cleo came back with a humongous plate of chicken and we sat down to eat my birthday feast, after which Shantel excused herself abruptly, avoiding eye contact with me while mumbling another "happy birthday" on her way out the door.

***

That weekend after market, I met up with Joshua for our birthday date. The weather was incredible—hot for this part of Oregon, and we'd both worked up a sweat.

"I have a surprise for you," Joshua said, stooping down to kiss me the second we'd left the market lot. He led me to his truck and opened the door for me to climb inside the now-familiar cab. He had a twinkle in his eye as he headed back out toward the highway, turning down an old dirt road. Suddenly, I knew where we were headed. It was my special spot, the spot I'd painted that hung in my folks' house. The spot he said he knew. Sure enough, he turned and followed the river for miles, pulling over just where I always had as a teenager.

"You weren't fibbing when you said you knew my spot," I said, squeezing his hand. "I haven't been back here in probably 5 years."

"Well, you're in luck," he said, climbing down from the cab and leading me through the woodland to the river's edge, looking like I remembered it. Huge boulders lined the banks, the clear water winding between them. The soft green leaves of the trees twinkled in the breeze, the sunlight flitted off each small ripple in the water.

"The surprise is over here," he said, leaping like a mountain goat from boulder to boulder. I followed behind him at a slower, more cautious pace.

Behind a large boulder, he'd set up a picnic in one of the only patches of sand on the river bank. A blanket was held in place by rocks; a cooler and a vase of flowers nestled in the sand.

He hugged me, lifted me off the ground, and twirled me around once. "Happy Birthday!" he said.

"It's so gorgeous!" I said, tears welling up in my eyes. "So....perfect...."

"Best hold judgment on that 'til after you've tried the food," he teased, sunlight glittering off his blond hair, his strong jaw set in a huge smile. He'd obviously been planning this for awhile.

He unpacked the cooler—Cleo's homemade crackers, several kinds of goat cheese, prosciutto, figs, hazelnuts, fresh strawberries with chocolate for dipping, and a couple IPAs.

We spread out on the blanket, took off our shoes and buried our toes in the warm sand. We ate and drank, laughed, kissed, and talked under the clear, bright sun.

Joshua decided to swim, stripping off his white t-shirt and jeans, and giving me a sideways smile before shimmying out of his black briefs and diving into the small swimming hole framed by smooth, impossibly huge boulders. He surfaced, shook his head, and let out a short "whoop!"

"Come on in, Kelsie from Salem! It feels great!"

I knew *he'd* feel great in there, and wasted no time shedding my own layers and jumping in. The cold water took my breath away for a second, shocking my warm flesh with a rush of energy and refreshment. I swam over to him and he pulled me close; two naked bodies rubbing together while we treaded water. We kissed, swam, kicked and played, until I started to get cold.

"I think it's time for me to assume a lizard pose," I told him, making my way for the warm rocks on the edge. I pulled myself up onto a particularly large one, and he followed. My heart pounded as he brought his whole naked, wet body up onto the rock and over the top of me. This was it.

I looked into his eyes. He held my gaze and gently spread my legs wide with his own. Droplets of water dripped from his curls onto my chest, sliding over my breasts, diving into the insatiable rock beneath me. My bare back pressed into the warm rock, gritty with a fine layer of sand, sending thousands of tiny pricks of sensation down the backs of my legs.

I felt the warmth of the tip of his penis around my opening, and softly, slowly, he pushed himself into me, filling me completely. My back arched into him as the entire length of his penis slid inside, his broad chest heaving as he let out a low groan of pleasure. Finally, Joshua Murphy was inside me. We rocked together, rubbing me up and down against the rock. He brought his mouth to mine and entered me there, too, our tongues wrapping around each other. He reached a core inside me and held himself there steadily, surely, as the sensation got stronger. I writhed and he held me secure, pressed me harder into the rock, nearly crushed me with his bigness. I was splitting, cracking open, and he stayed. Stayed. Stayed, until finally I let go, clenched my legs tight around him and exploded, spilling my juices onto him. Again, he moaned, moved quicker until he got tight, too, then pulled himself out of me and shot his orgasm up between my breasts.

He collapsed on top of me, both of us breathing together, holding each other for dear life. I felt tears again well up in my eyes at the intensity of our connection, at his patience, his strength. He kissed me deeply, then rolled over onto the rock beside me, and we both lay there naked, offering our satisfied bodies to the sun and the river.

I nestled myself into the side of him and rested my head on his broad chest, sighing with contentment.

Joshua cleared his throat. With my ear pressed into his chest, I heard his heart begin to thump quicker. My own heart began racing, unsure I wanted to hear what was to come.

"Remember the Johnson place I pointed out to you on the way home from market that time?" he began. "The one I was thinking about buying?" I could actually smell nervous sweat seeping out of his armpit. I lifted my head off his chest, looked at him, and nodded.

"Well, I think Old Man Johnson has decided to sell it to me, at the end of the season."

My eyes lit up. "Joshua, that's great!" I exclaimed, squeezing him across his chest. "Your own land! Congratulations!"

He nodded queasily. "Yeah, it is great," he trailed off. "Something I've been working toward for a long time..."

"So why the worried brow?" I asked him gently, rubbing his broad, fuzzy chest with my palm. "You look more scared than happy about it."

"Well, that's the thing," he said, taking another deep breath and staring up at the passing clouds. "My own farm is something I've always dreamed of having, but..."

"But what?" I encouraged him.

"But I never saw myself doing it alone," he finished, releasing the rest of the huge breath he'd been holding. He turned his head toward me nervously.

I panicked, rolled off his chest and onto my back, my mind racing. Now it was my turn to disappear into the clouds overhead. Why was he doing this now, so soon? We'd only known each other for a couple months. What was he expecting me to do, jump right into his arms, onto his farm, and live happily ever after? He reached out and took my hand in his. It felt like it was swallowing me whole, that hand. I was drowning in it. I pulled away again.

"Kelsie, please—" he started, rolling over to face me. My heart just pounded louder, tears welling up in my eyes. "I didn't want to upset you," he said, reaching over to trace the outline of my arm, up to my chin. He turned my face gently toward him and looked into my eyes. "Maybe I shouldn't have brought this up so soon..." he started.

"Yeah! You shouldn't have!" I said, half-crying.

"It's just that I really like you," he continued. "I've been ready for so long to do this, to start a life and a farm with a woman I love."

I rolled onto my side, with my back to him, gathering my naked body up into a small ball on the rock, and began to weep. Love? How could he be so sure, so fast?

Joshua slid in behind me and brought his strong arm over the small of my waist, cradling me in his large embrace. He felt so nice, so safe, holding me there. Oh why did he have to start this conversation so soon? I cried gently, and to my surprise, I felt his body shaking a little, too. He sniffed, and I turned around to face him once more. He had tears in his eyes.

"Oh, Joshua," I said, throwing my arms around him. "I really like you, too," I told him. "But it seems so soon to be talking about stuff like that." A tear slid down his cheek, plunging off his strong jaw onto the rock below. "I'm sorry..." I trailed off, not knowing what else to say.

Then we heard a crackling in the forest behind us, and we simultaneously shot up and grabbed our piles of clothes, fumbling with each piece as we hurried to throw it back on as the voices got closer. I threw on my jeans and yanked my shirt over my head just as a woman with three kids came bursting through the thicket of forest behind us. The two boys were arguing, chasing each other with sticks. They skidded to a halt as they spotted us. My bra dangled from my hand. A still bare-chested Joshua struggled to zip up his pants. The woman and the little girl followed the boys, obviously as flustered as we were. "Oh!" she yelped, grabbing the girl's hand instinctively.

"Um, hi there, ma'am," Joshua nodded, regaining his composure. "We were finishin' up here if y'all were wantin' to take a swim."

"Uh, yeah," I said, shoving my bra into my back pocket. "We're leaving."

"YEAH!" the boys yelled, already in their swim trunks. "Race ya!" one said to the other, and they tore off toward the water, cannon-balling their little bodies into the deep, refreshing blue.

We quickly gathered up the picnic and hopped back along the boulders on the bank to the truck in silence. Joshua fired it up and took off toward the highway without a word. I wasn't sure what to say, if anything. He had opened his heart to me and I had shot him down. I thought he might be angry with me, but he simply looked sad as we bumped along the dirt road, listening to our own thoughts and the tires grinding on the gravel.

We rode almost all the way back to White Oak in silence, Joshua finally speaking as we turned onto Sweet Well Road.

"I'll wait for you, Kelsie," he said, looking at me intently. "But I won't wait forever." He neared the farm and slowed down as we approached the drive.

I nodded. "I understand," I said. As he stopped the truck at the end of the drive, I leaned over and kissed him on the cheek. "Thank you for a wonderful birthday," I said, squeezing his hand. I didn't know what else to say, so I slid out of the cab and walked up the drive, glancing back over my shoulder as Joshua drove off and turned into his own driveway next door.

When I turned back around, Craig was leaning on the greenhouse door, watching my every move.

20

"Well well, Kelsie," he said as I passed him. "It's all starting to make sense now."

He turned to follow me beyond the greenhouses. Anger boiled in me, and all the hurt and frustration about what just happened with Joshua came rushing to my eyes. I clenched my fists and spun around to face Craig.

"Not now," I barked at him, shaking. "Just leave me alone!" With that, I took off running, through the demo beds and into my trailer, where I slammed the door and fell face down on the bed, sobbing. I cried and cried, until, eventually, I drifted off to sleep.

***

The next morning, I awoke in fear. What had just happened with Joshua? Had I blown it? How could I be ready to commit now? And what about Craig? What's he gonna do to me now? Now that he knows. I stayed in bed all the morning, squandering my only day off, scared to leave my trailer. What was I doing here? I loved the work, but I had about all I could handle of these two intense men. I wanted to be with Joshua—but I didn't want to commit to a life with him yet. And Craig—this whole thing was bound to blow up eventually. I had no idea if he would fire me outright, or demand I stop seeing Joshua, or what.

To my complete surprise, the next day at work, Craig didn't seem upset. He was extraordinarily respectful and nice to me while we packed CSA boxes. Instead of making snide comments and sneaking smacks on my butt as he usually did, he simply told me what he needed done—pack two summer squashes per box, make sure to put the lettuce mix on top so it doesn't get smashed, pack the calendula flowers in a separate bag so they don't get wet and soggy in with the lettuce—and then he left me alone to get my work done. He mentioned the crops he anticipated we'd start harvesting next week—basil, cucumbers, our last round of Chioggia beets. He showed me little tricks to help the packing go faster. In short, I felt he was treating me more like Jessi and Cleo. Not exactly equal to him, but certainly as a serious farm employee and not just a girl he wanted to fuck. He didn't once mention Joshua. It frankly confused the hell out of me.

The next few days I tried to immerse myself in work, to get Joshua out of my head and to focus on what I came here to do in the first place. We were trellising tomatoes, pounding post after post into the beds and weaving thick string between the plants to force them to grow upright and not sprawl out along the ground. *Like us*, I thought to myself as I cinched the ropes tightly between the posts, hoisting the young plants into a stable, upright position down the row. We try to keep growing upward toward the light, occasionally needing someone to come along and prop us up when we're too weak to pull ourselves upright. Craig explained that they grew many of their tomatoes under movable hoop houses to keep the rain off the plants and to heat them up because tomatoes preferred hot and dry weather.

Working in the hoop houses in the June sun made me sweat, moistening the front of my shirt as I bent over to tie the ropes. I caught Craig looking at me once but he didn't say anything. He returned to propping the tender tomato plants up between the strings as I rolled them out between the poles.

The moon rose in a sharp crescent beyond the edge of the fields that evening, before the sun touched down on the opposite horizon, beckoning me out of my trailer. I strolled around the dimly lit fields surveying our hard work. Row after row of different vegetables glowed peacefully in the shy twilight, patiently awaiting the morning and their next sunlit meal. Beyond the fence I could see that Joshua's goats had gone into the barn for the night. I pictured him sitting at his small table, eating or reading, or maybe washing up from the evening milking. Deep down, I knew I loved him. It all felt so new. Joshua, farming, this whole new direction in my life. Satisfying hard work, feeding hundreds of people good, healthy food, and getting healthier myself had made me confident in an indescribable way. What was I so scared of with him?

I wandered back through the demo beds and over toward the beehives near the back of the greenhouses, head down, scuffling over the ground, lost in thought. I didn't notice Craig, out for an evening walk.

"Hey Kelsie," he said, practically right next to me before I realized it.

I jumped. "Craig!" I said. "I was just—out—uh—" I stammered.

"Enjoying the evening?" he said.

"Yeah, something like that," I mumbled.

"This is one of my favorite times of day to observe the farm," he said. "Everything looks so beautiful, and you don't see all the weeds that are visible in the heat of the day," he winked at me.

"Yeah, it is really pretty," I mused, wondering where this was going.

"So, you're hanging out with Joshua, huh?" he asked. I knew I couldn't avoid it forever. I took a deep breath.

"Well," I began, uncertain of how much to tell him. "I was. I'm not totally sure what's going on now."

"I knew he had a thing for you the first time he met you," Craig said.

I didn't tell him that I'd met Joshua once before the day he came out into the field with me and Shantel. I winced as I remembered what Craig did to me as he processed that observation that day.

I tried to sound casual. "Yeah, I bet this revolving intern thing works out well for him. New blood every year." I raised my eyebrows a bit at Craig.

He let out a hearty laugh. "No, Kelsie, that's more my *modus operandi*. Joshua's a straight shooter. In all the years we've been out here, you're the only one he's ever taken a serious interest in."

That seemed unlikely to me. "Really?" I asked him.

"Yeah," Craig nodded. "Not that a lot of the interns haven't tried to get him interested in them." He chuckled. "If only I had half the country boy charm of that man..."

It was my turn to laugh. "You do have a, uh, *different* approach," I teased him.

"Don't tell me you didn't enjoy it," he countered, "At least until Superman swept you off your feet."

"Well," I grinned back at him, trying to be diplomatic. "I can't deny any of what you just said. Only now..." I trailed off.

"Now you're coming to your senses and are ready to get back on the Craig Mazariegos program?" he playfully grabbed my arms and pushed me up against the greenhouse, smiling down at me.

Gratitude for our friendly interaction and Craig's lighthearted sense of humor washed over me. "What about Shantel?" I poked at him. "She seems to be keeping you pretty busy."

"I'm here now, aren't I?" he retorted.

I mock groaned and nodded, still pinned against the greenhouse by him. "That you are, Craig. That you are."

Just then footsteps crunched on the gravel on the far side of the greenhouse and before I could react, he came around the corner. Joshua. He had a bouquet of flowers in his hand, and he dropped them when he saw me and Craig.

I pushed Craig away. "Joshua!" I half-screamed. "This is not what it looks like!" *God, that sounded so cliché.*

"Sure, Kelsie," he said, shaking his head. "This explains your reluctance. I get it now."

He turned to leave. I ran after him. "No!" I yelled, catching up to him and grabbing his arm. "Joshua, I swear!"

He shook me easily free and turned to face me, tears welling up in his eyes. "I get it now. I get it." He spun and stormed through the gate, slamming it behind him. I began to shake, and took off running past Craig back toward my trailer.

"Kelsie!" he called after me.

I couldn't stop now. Tears pricked my cheeks and, for the second time that week, I flung myself face down on my bed and cried myself to sleep.

***

After work the next day, I dashed into the barn and called Caroline, but I got her answering machine.

"Caroline, this is Kelsie," I wavered after the beep. "Please, please, please pick up...." Nothing. Finally I hung up. I stared at the receiver for a few minutes, fighting back tears, and decided to try again. I really needed to talk to her. I dialed her number again and she picked up on the last ring.

"Oh Caroline," I wailed into the phone, "I've really fucked things up now." And I burst into tears.

"Ok, Kels, don't panic!" she said. "What's going on?"

"Joshua just saw me with Craig!" I said.

"Oh shit."

I could hear her mumbling something.

"Caroline, do you need to go?" I asked her.

"I do have a, uh, friend over," she began, giggling slightly, "but I can tell you really need me. Can you call me back in 15 minutes?"

"Sure," I said, and I hung up the phone.

I pretty much sobbed and stared at the phone for fifteen minutes and then called Caroline again.

"Ok," she said when she picked up the phone. "He's hanging out in the bedroom watching a movie. So Joshua saw you fucking Craig?"

"No! Not at all! We weren't even doing anything?"

Caroline paused. "So, Joshua saw you not doing anything with Craig? What's the big deal?"

"I mean, I could see how he could have thought that," I said, "but we were actually having a friendly conversation."

"With that man? Yeah right," Caroline said. "My backside still hurts from my visit out there," she hissed.

"Not that I mind," she added quickly, giggling again.

I suddenly felt so selfish dumping all my problems on Caroline, especially when she had a date over. "Caroline, we can talk about this later," I said, starting to tear up again.

"For hell sake, Kelsie, you're my best friend!"

"Oh, Caroline—" I started.

"Whatever. I'm here for you. So you weren't actually doing anything with Craig but now Joshua thinks you were. So go, explain it to him, and apologize."

"I tried to explain it to him, but he was too mad to hear it. Plus, he'd ..."

"He'd *what*, Kelsie?!"

I paused.

"You two finally had sex?" she pushed.

"Well, that too."

She half-shrieked into the phone. "I knew it! Well, what else?!"

"He basically...how should I say it? He basically asked me to move in with him. Actually, to start a life and a farm and a family with him."

Silence. Finally she came in. "Whoa," she said.

"Yeah."

Another pause.

"So what did you say?"

"I...didn't...." I began. "I didn't say anything, really. Except that it seemed really soon to have that conversation."

"Was he okay with that answer?"

"Not really. He said he would wait for me, but that he wouldn't wait forever. And now he just saw me--," I began crying again. "Me and Craig..." I stuttered. "Caroline, he was bringing me flowers when he saw us!" I sobbed harder.

"Oh, Kels," Caroline said. "Oh, I'm so sorry."

"Now I have really fucked things up."

"I don't mean to make it worse, but what about Craig? How did he take the news that you were hanging out with Joshua?"

"It's weird," I said, blowing my nose on the handkerchief that I started carrying in my back pocket. "He seems totally fine with it. He actually has been treating me better since he found out."

"Huh."

"Yeah, I don't know what that's about. I guess it's no fun for him if I'm not interested."

"I sure am interested," Caroline started giggling again.

"Yeah, well, I'm sure he and his strong hands will be here any time you want to come back and visit."

"Those hands," Caroline sighed. "Well, speaking of such things, I should get going..."

"Thanks for talking with me," I said.

"Sure. It'll all work out, Kels. Stay honest with yourself. All your actions will be right if you do."

"I'll try. I love you, Caroline."

"I love you, too. Bye."

I hung up the phone. Stay honest.

Twilight flushed the farm with low, warm glow as I left the barn. The chicas were all tucked in, and the cabins looked pretty deserted. As I meandered back toward my trailer through the demo beds, I heard a sniffling off to the side, then I saw a silhouette hunched over one of the beds crying. Shantel.

Shit! I panicked. *What do I do?* She was obviously upset and I couldn't very well pretend that I didn't notice her. I slowed down and veered toward her.

"Shantel, are you okay?" I asked cautiously as I approached.

"Oh, hi Kelsie," she sniffled. "No, I'm not so good..."

Sheesh! This farm is a fire hose! We could drown the place with our tears!

"Do you want to talk about it?" I asked her.

She looked up at me, her eyes huge and frightened. I could tell she wanted to confide in me, but was weighing that decision.

Finally, her tears got the better of her.

"I'm pregnant!" she wailed in a hushed, strained voice. "Craig got me pregnant!"

The air left my lungs. "Holy shit," I whispered.

She sobbed quietly while I took in the information.

"Does he know?" I asked. "How far along are you?"

"Six weeks," she replied. "And, yes, he knows."

I couldn't believe he knew and hadn't said anything. Then again, I absolutely could believe it.

"What does he say?" I asked her.

She looked at me closely, attempting to classify me as friend or foe. I reached out and put a hand on her shoulder. I might not be crazy about her, but nobody needs a cold shoulder in this kind of situation. She fell forward and buried her head into my chest.

"Oh, Kelsie, I'm so scared!" she sobbed. "I don't know what I'm going to do!"

I held her and stroked her hair.

"Craig doesn't want me to keep it!" she said, still sobbing. I pushed her away and looked into her eyes.

"He what?" I said softly. She nodded.

"Wow," I said, staring at her, letting the full implications sink in. "Whoa."

"Yeah," she said, shaking her head.

"What do you want?" I whispered.

She shrugged a little. "I don't know exactly." She took a breath. "I think I want to keep it!" she whispered.

"Do you?—Have you?—"

"Have I been through this before?"

I nodded.

She shook her head no.

"I've always wanted to be a mom, always knew I'd have kids," she said. "And I want to do this with Craig, but he—"

"But he doesn't," I finished for her.

She nodded.

Anger bubbled inside me again. "Why does he have to be such a selfish bastard?" I asked.

She gave a small smile. "It feels good to be talking to you about this. I am so sorry for the weirdness there's been between us."

"Yeah, well," I said, bristling a bit.

"At first it was kind of a game, to see if I could get him to choose me. Then I let him go further than I should have, and now I'm in this mess and he'd still rather choose you, or some other girl he hasn't already won over. It's like, once he gets you, he doesn't want you anymore." She trailed off, beginning to cry again.

"Shantel," I began, "I'm not interested in Craig. I've been dating Joshua next door."

She eyed me. "Really? I thought so..."

"Yeah. Only I really hurt his feelings and I'm not sure if he wants to be with me anymore."

"Looks like we're both in a mess," she said, guffawing a little. She had snot dripping out of both nostrils, and looked more like a scared little girl than the confident, flirtatious, gorgeous woman that I thought she was.

"Promise me you won't say anything to anybody?" she asked.

I agreed.

21

Joshua was not at market on Saturday, the first time since it began and, as much as I wanted to believe it wasn't on account of me, inside I knew it probably was. Dana seemed to sense it, too, though she didn't push it.

Instead, she busied herself discussing the details of the farm's annual summer solstice party the following week. I had really looked forward to having a bunch of people and a party on the farm, but now with everything gone wrong with Joshua, I was having a hard time maintaining my enthusiasm.

"...and Eric and Ryan are coming up from Ashland with a whole pig! We'll roast it in the ground, and Cleo will organize the cooking of the accompaniments..."

I stared blankly across the aisle at Joshua's empty stall, missing him terribly. Why did I have to push him away like that? What was I so scared of?

"...Right, Kelsie?" Dana playfully waved her hand in front of my face.

"Oh, huh?" I asked, blinking. "I'm sorry, what? I'm having a hard time concentrating today..." I trailed off.

Dana put her hand on my shoulder. "This too shall pass," she said, giving me a slight squeeze. Tears welled up in my eyes.

"I hope so," I choked. Thankfully, several people mobbed the market stall then, forcing me out of my head and back to the table of gorgeous vegetables between us. Peas, radishes, huge lettuce heads, salad mixes, mustard greens, garlic scapes, cilantro, chives, kale, calendula flowers all spilled abundantly from baskets, onto the colorful tablecloths below, seemingly trying to jump into the bags of passersby. It was an incredible sight—so much food, all of which had grown from a handful of tiny seeds, with a little coaxing from us and the miracle of soil and water and sunlight combining.

"Now I can handle the collard greens," Caroline's familiar voice rang boldly out behind me. She always speaks with a little bit of a swagger when she's working on cracking a joke. I could practically feel her teeth spilling out of her lips from smiling so hard. I turned around to see her holding a huge, purple kohlrabi in her open hand. "Peas off the vine, sure," she went on. "That crazy lettuce stuff that tastes like wasabi? Not my style but still impressive." She paused for effect, staring at the large, odd orb with leafy stems protruding upward like a hot air balloon. "But this...this is too weird to be real."

A few passersby laughed along with us.

"I mean, seriously!" she said, shaking her head. "It looks like a UFO!"

"The sweetest UFO you've ever tasted," Jessi mused.

"People really eat this?!" she asked incredulously. I admired her lack of self-consciousness about how ignorant she was to the world of vegetables. Before I began my internship, I never would have walked up and asked somebody what the vegetables on their market table were, let alone poke fun at them.

"As a matter of fact," Dana replied, reaching into a cooler under the table, "we happen to have some in our emergency market snack bag." She held the Tupperware of chopped kohlrabi soaking in cold water out to Caroline, who gingerly took a chunk, eyeing me suspiciously. I gave her the nod.

"You'll love it!" I said.

She crunched down on the sweet, slightly spicy chunk and I saw the relief pass over her face as she realized it wasn't bad.

"This is seriously what the last four months of my life have been like," I laughed at her. "Nervously popping one strange food after another in my mouth and being surprised that I like it."

"Just wait for the solstice party," Dana said with a twinkle. Folks come from miles around to enjoy the food. "Are you coming, Caroline?" Dana asked her.

"How could I say no?" She winked at me. "It sounds like a *spanking* good time!"

I flushed bright red, but Dana didn't seem fazed. "We'll have to harvest our inaugural batch of honey so we can make some mead at the party!" Dana declared excitedly to me.

"Mead? Cool," Caroline said. "I'd love to learn how to make it."

"Good, then it's settled," she announced. "We'll put you and Kelsie on the mead crew at the party."

***

After stewing about Joshua for several more days, I decided to make a move. I *am* in love with him, I admitted to myself, and I should not let my fear of jumping in too soon get in the way of expressing my love to him. I know I hurt his feelings when he saw me with Craig, but I hoped he would forgive me and get over it. At least, that's what I told myself while preparing my personalized invitation to the solstice party for him.

Dana and I ended up harvesting a crop of honey a couple days before, which was actually a lot less fun than I originally imagined. We had to move the heavy boxes of honey—supers, they're called—from the hives into the barn, then cut the wax cap the bees apply to seal the honey in the cells with a hot, electric knife and load them into a stainless steel centrifuge bolted to the floor. After we loaded ten frames, we ran the centrifuge, which whirled the frames around, shooting the honey from them and splattering it onto the walls of the centrifuge, where it then drained through a spigot to the bottom and into our buckets and jars. The whole process was incredibly sticky, covering ourselves, the barn floor, and numerous pieces of equipment with honey, which then had to be washed with warm water carried in from the outdoor kitchen.

"Someday I'll have a hot water sink in here," Dana said. "The health department wants me to have one, and believe me, I prefer to own one, too, but the cost of plumbing hot water out here is hard to stomach when we have hot water in the kitchen not seventy yards away."

My favorite part of our afternoon of honey-gathering happened after running each batch of frames through the centrifuge. I loaded the empty frames back into the super and set it outside the barn, where the bees would inevitably find it and lap with their tiny tongues every precious speck of honey that we could not get with our big, human processes.

Within minutes of putting another super outside, dozens of forager bees would come and begin to drink it up, their little bee butts high in the air, wafting out a 'this-is-a-great-spot-come-get-it!' pheromone to lure their sisters to the treasure. It would take them several days to recover every little drop, which satisfied me in a very profound way. Not one drop of honey would be wasted through this process, if it was up to the bees. And, given that a single honeybee might produce only a half teaspoon of honey in her entire life, a drop of already finished honey constituted a sizeable portion of her life's work. All that made it difficult to ignore the fact that we wiped up several bees' lifetime contribution off the barn floor with every batch. Dana made a point never to use soap to clean the floor or the equipment, and she left the cleaning rags out near the empty hive supers so the bees could take whatever little specks of honey they could find.

It made the honey in the jars that now lined my kitchen counter extremely precious. Dana had given me several pints to dole out to friends and family to share my newfound skill and the bees' handiwork. I decided to share the first one with Joshua, attaching a note to the jar of amber-colored treasure. "I'm still sweet on you," I wrote. "I'd love to see you at the solstice party this Friday! Love, Kelsie from Salem."

I snuck down the drive way at dusk, when I thought Joshua might be doing his evening milking, and crept up to his front step, where I left the jar and the note. I ran back to the farm, my heart pounding, and settled into alternating sinking and hopeful feelings, wondering if I would see him on Friday.

***

The day of the solstice party was hectic, since we had to harvest for market in the morning, and then get ready for the party. As promised, Eric and Ryan showed up mid-morning with a whole pig from their free-ranging pig orchard near Ashland, where the pigs foraged for acorns in the white-oak-dominated woodlands surrounding their farm, their diet supplemented by any rotting pears that fell from the inter-planted pear trees, as well as whey purchased from a nearby dairy specializing in cheeses.

Craig built a fire in the rock-lined pit early in the morning so the rocks would be hot when the brothers showed up with the pig. They stuffed the pig with clean, hot rocks, and laid it in a bed of hot rocks covered with grasses and a few sprigs of herbs. They placed wet burlap over the top of the pig, and then buried it with a few shovels full of earth to steam cook in the ground. The whole process created a festive air and, as the afternoon harvest finished up, I found myself eagerly awaiting the party. I even dressed up a little, wearing a summery, flower-printed skirt and a short sleeved blouse. I wove a few fresh calendula flowers into my hair, and gave Caroline some.

The warmth of the evening welcomed visitors, who strolled around the farm and lingered late into the evening. The food was divine, the mead flowed freely, and folks danced around the fire and sang and laughed into the wee hours of the morning. It would have been a great night, except that Joshua did not come.

My heart leapt into my throat when I saw Joshua's pale yellow pickup pull into his market stall the next morning. He set up his booth without so much as a glance in our direction. Dana was too exhausted to notice—I think she might not have gone to sleep at all the night before. Having him right there ignoring me sent a knife right through me.

We set up our tables, displaying our usual rainbow of leafy

greens and the last of the radishes, along with two new, exciting delicacies—the first basil harvest, wafting its unmistakable heavenly aroma out into the gathering crowd, and our first raspberries! Red treasures delicately placed in small baskets by a veritable marathon of difficult picking yesterday. I would have never guessed that I would enjoy picking such a delicious fruit so little. I had bounded out into the raspberry patch with Cleo, excited at the prospect, and within minutes found my bare arms and hands scratched by tiny stickers on the stems. I wanted only to hurry up and get out of there. The berries were small and it took a long time to fill a pint. The worst part was trying not to eat all of them on their way into the basket.

"Pick a pint, then eat a handful, that's my motto," Cleo shared. "It gives you something to look forward to."

"Yeah, sure," I said, trying to extract a nearly-invisible thorn from my forearm without spilling my half-full pint. "My motto from here on out will be: When picking raspberries, wear a long-sleeved shirt."

It took us over an hour to harvest a few flats, and I dreaded the next time I'd have to do that job.

Seeing them laid out lushly at the farmers market table made our hard work slightly more worthwhile, but I still harbored a small amount of animosity toward the poor things.

Joshua had set up his booth and now his large frame fidgeted around trying to keep busy to avoid just standing there, facing in our direction.

"Well, look who showed up!" Dana called over to him, walking across the aisle to say hello. "Where were you last night?" I heard her say as she approached. "We missed you!"

Joshua looked sheepish. "I'm sorry, Miss Dana," I heard him mumble. "I just couldn't—er, I just had some other stuff to do."

"Well, the party wasn't the same without you." She reached over and squeezed his shoulder. "We *all* wished you would have come," she said pointedly. "Good luck today!"

Now it was my turn to pretend to be busy. This was going to get really awkward really fast. As the bell rang to begin the market, I briefly entertained the idea of seeing if I could switch with Cleo or Shantel and work at the Portland market instead.

A woman walked up to the booth and eyed the pints of raspberries. “$5 for a pint, huh?” she said huffily. “I can get twice as many for that price at Costco.”

Anger welled up inside me. I still had little welts all over my forearms from picking them and I thought about the hours we had spent and started shaking. I wanted to jump across the table and punch her in the face.

“Well, this isn’t Costco,” Dana butted in, snapping at her. “This is small-scale local agriculture, the kind of healthy livelihood that’s hanging on by a thread because of places like Costco that demand cheap, industrially-produced food that exploits everybody from the workers in the field to nature herself. If you can’t tell the difference, head on back to Costco and buy those half-dead, chemical-laced raspberries from Argentina and move out of the way so we can sell our special food to folks who actually care about local, organic agriculture.” With that, she turned to the next customer in line, beamed a big smile, and asked, “What would you like?”

The woman stood there blinking at us in complete shock. I stifled a laugh and followed Dana’s lead, turning to the customer next to her. “What would you like?”

As the woman shuffled away, completely baffled, Jessi elbowed me in the side and flashed a big grin. I felt so proud to be sharing that booth with Dana.

The crowds began to die down around noon, as usual, and again the ache about the awkwardness with Joshua returned. I struggled to remain positive, to remember that he wasn’t the only reason I was here, and that things would work out eventually if they were meant to. Still, my eyes darted instinctively every time I’d hear his voice wafting across the aisle, and my body ached watching his broad frame moving adeptly inside his small stall. I could practically smell him from our booth, and I longed to grab him and pull him to me. By the time the market was over, I’d had enough of us avoiding each other.

I collected myself and marched across the street to Joshua’s booth before I could lose my nerve, my heart pounding.

"How did it go today?" I asked him, trying to be casual.

"Fine," he said, busying himself with wrapping up his sample cheeses, avoiding my eye.

I tried again. "Um, did you get the honey I left for you?"

"Mmm-hmm," he nodded, still not looking up. He turned around to load his samples into a cooler. My heart sank.

"Joshua," I said, talking fast, "I don't care if you believe this, but I have to say it. I am not interested in Craig." I rushed on in a hushed voice, his back still turned to me. "I'm actually in love with you. I just didn't want to admit that so soon and risk ruining the good thing we have—er, *had*—going," I stammered.

He whipped around and faced me, his eyes ablaze.

"That ain't what I saw," he countered, shaking his head. "That's not what I saw."

"Joshua," I reached out and laid my hand on his, feeling the strong sinew beneath my own calloused palms. I didn't care who was watching at this point. "You have to trust me. If you don't trust me, it would never work out anyway."

He held my gaze for a minute without saying anything. I saw tears glinting the corners of his eyes. His head shook slightly and his shoulders trembled a little.

Finally, he looked away, resumed packing up his booth. "I'd best be gettin' this torn down. Don't want the market Nazis on my case," he mumbled.

I got it. I walked back to Jessi, waiting with our stuff while Dana brought the truck around, tears streaming down my cheeks.

Jessi put her arm around me. "It'll be okay," she said. "I don't know exactly what's going on, but I know that he's a fool if he doesn't come back around."

I sniffed. "Thanks, Jess."

We loaded the truck and drove back to the farm. I looked away when we passed the Johnson place, home of Joshua's future farm and family.

***

The weeks dragged on, one after another—Joshua continued to

ignore me at market, Shantel was still a mess, and Craig remained as obtuse as ever. The actual work on the farm was one of the only pleasurable parts. I busied myself learning everything I could about the crops, with warmer weather bringing new summer treats each week—garlic, cucumbers, onions, green beans, jalapenos, Japanese eggplants, and my new favorite, ground cherries. Little yellow pineapple-flavored balls in paper husks like tomatillos that make the perfect snack.

Dana had what she called a "stroke of divine genius" and decided we should display one of my bee paintings each week in the market booths, to draw attention to the booth and create a buzz, for lack of a better word, around the harvest festival and my debut as an artist. I agreed to give her two paintings a week to display, one for each market booth.

"What if somebody wants to buy one?" she asked me.

I blinked at her. "Are you kidding?" I responded. "Sell it to them! I'm not exactly raking it in out here," I joked without thinking. I stumbled. "I mean—"

Dana threw her head back laughing. "It's ok, Kelsie! You're right, your compensation at the moment isn't in monetary riches. You set the prices, and if someone wants one, we'll send them happily on their way with one of the best purchases they've ever made."

At first I felt shy about even showing her the paintings but, after a few weeks, I'd grown accustomed to loading them into their respective trucks, the same as any veggie we were taking to market. One week someone actually bought one in Portland. For $300! I couldn't believe it! It was one of my favorites, a forager dancing for her sisters about a newly blooming patch of flowers across the field while they looked on with excitement.

Still, the heat and the tedium of harvesting some of the summer crops, like cherry tomatoes, started to wear on my resolve. When Dana invited me to attend a beekeeping conference in Portland for a long weekend, I jumped at the chance.

"I'd go," she said, "but I thought you'd get more out of it than I would." She nudged me in the side. " Make no mistake I'm trying hard to lure you into beekeeping as a part of your future career as a farmer.

It's partially for my own benefit. I need someone else to learn how to do this."

At this moment, I couldn't think of anything I'd rather do than get away from the farm for three whole days. "I'd love to go," I gratefully accepted. *Come Saturday and I'm out of here!*

In the evening after the Friday harvest, I snuck into the barn to use the phone. I thought it'd be fun to see if Caroline could join me in Portland for an evening, but I couldn't get a hold of her. As I cracked open the door to leave the phone cubby, I saw Dana and Craig approaching the barn, deep in a heated conversation. Instinctively I drew back into the room as their voices got louder, peering out through the cracked door.

"Damn it, Craig!" Dana was saying, her face hidden behind a huge stack of totes from yesterday's CSA harvest. "You have really done it now!"

He followed her sheepishly toward the back of the barn carrying his own stack.

"I don't know how much more of this I can take!" she continued, now hidden behind the barn wall. I heard her slam her stack of totes down. "I've abided your reckless flirtatiousness, allowed you the freedom to be who you are, but this is too far. You've put the farm and our livelihood at risk, not to mention her well-being!"

They walked back into view, squaring off in front of the huge, open barn door.

"I know, I know," he said, his head dipped surprisingly submissively. He looked more like a child being scolded by his mother than Dana's confident farming partner. My heart beat in my chest. *Are they talking about what I think they're talking about*?

Suddenly a lone, burly figure came into view at the far edge of the field beyond Dana and Craig, and headed this way.

My legs began to tremble slightly and I caught my breath in my throat.

"If we are to continue here together, Craig," Dana continued loudly, her strong hands gripping her slender hips, "we have got to come to an agreement about what is and is not appropriate regarding the interns."

Joshua's large frame moved closer, but Dana and Craig were so lost in their own conversation that they didn't see him approaching.

"You are their *boss*, Craig, and you know as well as I do that it's an abuse of power to come on to them, let alone fraternize with them!" She continued softly. "How scared she must be..."

"I'll do right by her, Dana, you know I will," Craig said.

Dana raised her eyebrows at him. "At this moment, Craig, I have serious doubts about that."

He lowered his eyes.

"I'm starting to worry about you, too," she said. "This shit was passable when we were in our twenties, but it is undeniably time for you to grow up. When I think about all the years of hard work we've put into this place," her voice grew louder again. "All we've built together, all we've shared. I am *shocked*—no, *horrified*—that you would risk throwing it all away like this!" She stood still as a stone, unwavering, facing him in fury. Craig seemed at a loss of what to say. Joshua had stooped down to drop what looked like milk pails near the chicken yard, but was now approaching with a large object, not twenty yards away from the barn. Dana revved up again.

"It would be one thing if you wanted children, or if you even loved her!" she bellowed. "But instead you were reckless. You strung a young girl along, a girl who came here to learn *how to farm* from you. You took advantage of her vulnerability, failed to use protection, and you GOT HER PREGNANT!"

Joshua immediately stopped in his tracks, now just a few yards away from the barn door.

"Now we've lost a good intern! She told me today before she left that she feels she's got no choice but to go back and live with her family while she figures out what on earth she'll do! What the hell are you going to do about that?!" Dana implored him.

Shantel, gone?!

Slowly now, Joshua moved forward, his boots crunching on the gravel, slicing through the silence that now shuddered through the barn as Dana glared at Craig. They both started at the sound, whipping around toward him.

"Who's pregnant?" Joshua asked quietly, calculatingly as he approached, studying first Dana, then Craig, obviously distressed.

"None of your damn business," Craig snapped at him furiously. He glared down at the metal cylinder in Joshua's hands.

Joshua came to his senses, realizing he'd walked in on a very personal conversation. He turned to Dana. "Uh, Miss Dana, I just came to return this fence post pounder I borrowed all those weeks ago," he mumbled.

"Yes, fine, Joshua. Thank you," she said curtly, reaching out to take it. "We'll put it away."

He nodded, understanding the cue. "Sorry to barge in on you," he said quickly, escaping toward the fence gate in the setting sun.

I let out the breath I'd been holding slowly, sure Dana and Craig could hear my heart knocking around in my chest. She picked up the post pounder and walked it back toward the back tool wall. "You've got some serious soul-searching to do, Craig," she called over her shoulder at him. "And so do I, I suppose."

With that, Craig walked out the barn door, head hung low.

Dana exited the barn, holding her hands wide toward the sky. She tipped her head back and let out a large, audible moan. Her long frame swayed in prayer like a tree trunk, silhouetted against the last light of the day.

22

As much as I was ready to get the hell off the farm for a few days, especially in light of the escalating drama, I honestly couldn't wait to get back after the conference. I laughed at my own eagerness as I turned onto Sweet Well Road, getting closer to home, as I now considered it. The conference was so incredibly cool. I got to meet beekeepers from all over the country, and attend some really excellent workshops. The food was delicious the entire time, and every meal had something made with honey in it. I tried honey chicken, honey-glazed carrots, honey butter with biscuits, honey-lavender lemonade, honey wheat beer, pistachio baklava, and so many other incredible treats, all made sweeter by the bees' hard work. I even bought a cute, hand-sewn patch from a girl selling them in the foyer. "Just Bee Yourself!" it proclaimed, with a little bee buzzing underneath, trailing a long trail of curlicues over the patch. I thought I'd use it to cover the hole in my work jeans, which had worn through on the right thigh.

Before I could even close the door to my trailer, Cleo busted in behind me, hugging me from behind.

"How was it?" she asked, obviously distracted.

"It was great, Cleo! I learned so much! The people I met were so cool, and the speakers were so awesome, and the food—you would have loved the food! All this stuff, made with honey..." I trailed off. "What's going on?" I asked her. She looked like she was going to explode with her own news.

"Shantel's GONE!" she declared, grabbing her hair with both hands and pulling in either direction, turning her to a disheveled Einstein.

"Oh—" I started, frowning.

"Wait a second," Cleo interrupted. "Did you already know?"

I nodded, hushed. "About her being pregnant?" Why was I whispering?

She nodded, hands on her hips.

"I swore I wouldn't tell anyone, Cleo."

"Wow," she replied. "I know who I'll tell my secrets to from now on. You didn't let on in the slightest! How long did you know?"

"I dunno, a few weeks, I guess," I shrugged. "I've had other things on my mind."

Suddenly the farm shrunk back down to exactly the same size it had been before my departure. Too small. Too claustrophobic.

"Where'd she go?" I asked, as much to confirm what I'd heard Dana and Craig saying as to hide my overhearing from Cleo. "What is she going to do?"

"Beats me. I never saw her leave. Aunt Dana told me she went home to be with her family until she could figure out what to do."

"Man. What does that do to the farm? Are Dana and Craig pissed?"

"Aunt Dana's not one to hold a grudge. She wants everyone to do what's right for them."

"What does Craig think?" I paused. Did Cleo even know the baby was Craig's?

"I imagine he's counting his blessings right now."

Of course Cleo knew it was his. We were around her all the time. Who else could she possibly have hooked up with?

"What a bastard," I said, shaking my head, though I didn't totally believe what she was saying.

***

At work on Tuesday, I watched Craig closely for clues as to his reactions, but he kept a stoic demeanor and focused completely on the work at hand. Actually, he was flying through the CSA harvest, moving faster than I'd ever seen, which is saying something, since his normal rate still outpaced me by at least double. Most of me wanted to slap him in the face, tell him to pull his head out of his ass, man up, and support the hell out of Shantel, but a small part wanted to reach out to him, to offer comfort, ask him how he was doing. I opted for following his lead and simply focus on my work, harvesting green beans, which was already growing tedious even after having done it only three times so far. You have to bend over for what feels like hours just to get a 5 gallon bucket full, and the beans kind of blend in with the foliage so it's hard to see them.

As I dressed for the Luscious Earth workshop that evening, my mind wandered back to the one early on, where Joshua had trailed behind and worked up the nerve to ask me out. As much as I didn't want to focus on him, I had to admit to myself I had a broken heart, and that was going to take some time to heal. If Joshua Murphy couldn't come around to trust me, I didn't want him anyway, or so I kept telling myself as I dressed in front of my tiny bathroom mirror. I chose a new, summery red dress I'd snuck away from the conference and bought from Repeat Boutique, my favorite thrift store. Growing up so near the city, with its mess of fashion-savvy city people who were always a step ahead of us "hicks" out in Salem, and who happily discarded their last-year's fashions in the bargain bins at the Goodwill, we never bought new clothes. We just pinched our pennies and headed into the city a couple times a year to hit the aisles at Repeat. The dress was a little lower cut than I'd usually choose, but I was feeling a lot more confident lately, and certainly I'd not be out of line for a Luscious Earth workshop. Hell, I swear Dana had been topless more than she'd been fully clothed at these gatherings. A little cleavage wasn't gonna turn anyone's head at this shindig, I was certain.

Dana instructed us to gather near the peach trees in the orchard where the "abundance of summer's bounty, offered forth from the generous earth," would be awaiting us. I came around the corner of the outdoor kitchen and saw the group of participants already forming.

Looming large off to the side, a head above everyone else, was Joshua. I panicked and crouched down behind the deck of the kitchen, peering under the picnic table at the crowd. At his side was a woman! A girl I'd never seen before. My heart raced as I watched Cleo and Jessi stride up, arms intertwined, to talk to Joshua. They reached out and shook the woman's hand. She stood a good several inches taller than me, rail thin, with short, styled, strawberry blonde hair. She looked quite hip, leaning playfully into him, and she beamed a radiant smile that matched Joshua's as they chatted with Cleo and Jessi. My heart sank.

Needless to say, I hid out in my trailer, crying my eyes out, rather than attending the "abundance of the generous earth" workshop. Not one of my finer moments.

***

When Craig announced the next day that Jessi and I were going to start switching off at the Portland and Salem markets in Shantel's absence, I nearly yanked my own arm off to volunteer for the first week. There was no way in hell I was going to stand across from Joshua and watch his new girlfriend come up and flirt with him right in front of me.

"Okay, Kelsie," he laughed. "With that show of enthusiasm, the position is yours for the week." He nodded at Jessi. "You'll be on for next week then."

On the way out of my trailer to pack for market on Saturday morning, I decided to send the painting I'd made for Joshua to market. It was my most cherished one so far, a close up of a goat nose and mouth nibbling on some pasture browse while a tiny honeybee drinks nectar from a clover blossom next to it. Who knows why I did it—to say goodbye? If that was the case, it worked like a charm.

The Portland market was a LOT busier than the Salem one, with the kind of crowd we in Salem had always referred to as Port-laliens. It seriously is kind of like another planet, Portland. It seemed like every other person who stepped up to the booth knew Cleo, and Craig wasted no time turning the charm on any young thing that didn't. He really was wretched. What had I been thinking?

We got back just as Dana and Jessi were finishing the unpacking, so they joined in to help us with our truck.

"Great news, Kelsie!" Dana said cheerfully. "You sold another painting!"

My heart sank. "Really?" I squeaked out. "Uh, which one?"

"That wonderful one with the goat and the bee!" she exclaimed, eyeing me.

I knew it. "That's great," I sighed. *I guess things really are over with him*.

"Oh, Kelsie," she started, calculating what she wanted to say next. She must have thought better of it, because she simply squeezed my arm and said, "Things have a way of working themselves out, you know."

***

Midweek Craig informed me my mom had called to make sure I remembered my sister's law school graduation party this Saturday. I gulped. I guess I'd blocked it out. Ugh. Just what I *didn't* feel like doing, driving all the way to Seattle with my family to sit around and be all fake and polite with Kirsten's posh friends, celebrating yet another of her achievements while my mom grills me about my life and when I'm going to get my shit together.

"I don't have to go," I told him wishfully, "if it'll leave you guys short-handed at market this week."

"While I appreciate your commitment to the farm, Kelsie," he winked, "I'm certain we can manage without you."

"All right," I grumbled, throwing a handful of cucumbers into my tote.

"Hey, watch it!" he admonished. "They're not the ones graduating from law school."

"Thank God," I said, cracking a smile. "That's the last thing we need around here—a farm full of cucumber lawyers."

My mom wanted us all to drive up together, so I met them at their house on Saturday morning after I'd helped load the trucks for market. I was mildly relieved to miss my week at the Salem market with Joshua, but a part of me wanted to see him. It had been several weeks since I talked to him, and even if he did have someone he was seeing, I still cared about him. At this rate, it'd be another two weeks before I saw him again. I pushed the thought out of my mind and trudged up the steps to the house.

When I entered, Mom and Dad were bickering.

"Are you sure you don't have them in your pocket?" she demanded.

"I already told you, no!" he bellowed, glancing in my direction. Kelsie!" his eyes lit up. "Hi, sweetie," he said, crossing to give me a hug. "I'm glad you're here." A resigned frustration laced his words. "We've—or, uh, *I*—have misplaced the keys to the Escort." He shrugs.

"Charles, damn it!" Mom yelled. "Quit fucking around and help me find the keys! You too, Kelsie," she said, glaring in my direction. "We're going to be late for Kirsten's party!"

Late? It's 8:00 am. What time does this thing start anyway? And Hi, *by the way. What's it been, 2 or 3 months since we've seen each other?*

"Mom, doesn't it start at two?" I offered calmly. "We have plenty of time to get there."

She threw her hands up in the air and leaned down to search the cushions of the couch, muttering. "Yes, there's plenty of time. We'll show up right at two and leave poor Kirsten to set everything up for her own party." I rolled my eyes.

"Has anyone checked the car?" I asked.

"Honestly, Kelsie!" she snapped. *Great.* It's going to be one of *those* days.

Dad's eyebrows raised. "It's worth a shot," he smiled at me.

I headed into the garage where the Escort sat, awaiting the happy outing. Opening the door, I saw the keys planted firmly in the ignition. I honked the horn, smiling.

In seconds, Mom burst into the garage with a scowl on her face. I jangled the keys so she could see them. Her face softened. "Good, you found them," she said matter-of-factly.

"Charles!" she screamed toward the house. "Kelsie found them in the *ig-ni-tion*!" she said, disdain dripping off each syllable. "Let's get moving!"

I slumped into the back seat alongside my graduation gift for Kirsten—a quart of honey and a small painting of a honey frame swarming with bees. I had no idea if she'd like it, but frankly I didn't care.

Mom relaxed a bit as Dad sped up the I-5 toward Seattle.

"Your friend Joshua came over the other day," Mom said casually, eyeing me in the sunshade mirror.

"What?!" I jerked upright in my seat. "What for?" I managed to stammer.

Mom raised her eyebrows. "He was looking for you," she said. My heart raced. *Looking for me?*

I don't get it. "Why would he be looking for me at your house?" I frowned. Mom faked a shrug, practically levitating her eyebrows off the top of her skull. "You tell me," she said.

I struggled to piece it together. "When did he come?" I asked.

"Last Tuesday," she said. "No, Wednesday?" she asked Dad, who shrugged.

"One of those," he said.

"That's helpful, Charles," she snapped. "It would have been Tuesday, because Wednesday we had that thing at the thing."

"Mmm hmm," he nodded, obviously paying no attention.

Joshua came looking for me last week?! I guess I hadn't been at market for the last two Saturdays. *But why at Mom and Dad's house? Why not at the farm? Of course! He heard Dana and Craig's conversation about Shantel, only he thinks it's me Craig got pregnant.*

23

"Did Joshua, um, say what he wanted?" I asked her, trying to sound casual.

Her expression softened a bit. "He just asked if he could see you, Honey."

My heart leapt. *Joshua wanted to see me? Even though he thought I was pregnant?* I wonder if he was angry.

"Was he upset?" I pressed.

"Honey, men don't exactly wear their emotions on their sleeves, as a general rule."

"I know, Mom, but...."

"He seemed," she searched for the right words, "pained and prodding. And scared as hell," she finished. "What made him think you were living at our house?" She seemed genuinely curious.

"I think he has me confused with someone else," I mumbled.

"Someone else he knows, also named Kelsie, who happens to be living at our house?" Mom asked, smiling.

My mouth twitched a little. "Mom!" I rolled my eyes at her.

"What did you tell him?" I held my breath.

"I told him I hadn't seen you in months," she stated plainly.

"Which is true, Kelsie. You haven't been to visit us in months!" she guilt-tripped me.

Oh not now, Mom! What did he want? I bet he thinks I lied to him about Craig, and he wants to call me out on it! That hypocrite! He's the one bringing his new girl around the farm! How callous can he be?

I sat fuming in the back seat the rest of the way to Seattle, and Mom had the good sense to let me be.

Kirsten's new house was, like everything else about her, perfect. As we pulled into the spacious circular drive, she came out the front door, waving, wearing a light sundress and looking as beautiful as ever. A tall, handsome man followed her out.

"Kirsten, it's *beautiful*!" Mom cooed, wrapping her into a hug before turning to her gentleman friend.

"Mom, this is Kevin," she said, grabbing him by the elbow. "He's an architect here in town. This is my mom, Peg, and my dad, Charles," she said as he moved forward to shake their hands. I shifted awkwardly in the background. "Oh, and my sister Kelsie," she added, smiling as she stepped toward me.

"Whoa, Kels!" she said, giving me the once-over. "You look fantastic!" She threw her arms around me.

"Uh, thanks, Kirst," I mumbled, practically shoving my gift in her arms as she released me. "And congrats."

"Ooh, what's this?" she asked eagerly, holding the amber jar up to the light.

"It's honey," I said, "from the bees I take care of."

"Bees? That's so cool!" She looked at the painting I gave her, studying all the little bees scurrying around over the canvas, attending to their chores, then back up at me. "Did you paint this?!" she asked incredulously.

"Yeah," I stammered, studying my shoes.

She showed Kevin the painting. "Keslie *painted* this!" she breathed, her voice oozing with pride. "It's so good, Kels!" she assured me. "I remember you painting when we were kids. I guess I didn't realize you'd kept at it."

"Yeah, I picked it up again this summer," I told her. "I really like it," I added. "I've, uh, been selling some paintings at our booth at the farmer's market." I saw Mom's eyebrows raise a touch.

"Wow! That's so cool!" She looked at the painting again with reverence. "Thank you so much for this! I have just the spot for it!" She grabbed my hand. "Come inside, guys! I want to give you the tour!"

Kirsten led us through the spacious, open, single-story house and onto the back deck, which housed a hot tub. "I thought we'd set up out here today," she said, "since it's so nice out." She'd already started getting ready for the party. Chairs and tables set up, and little vases of flowers on the tables. We busied ourselves helping her in the kitchen, getting the food out as her guests started to arrive. As I opened cans of olives and took the lids off the pre-packed vegetable trays, I realized that I hadn't actually opened anything in a can for months. Almost everything I was eating at this point in the season was coming from the farm, save some grains, salt, and olive oil.

"Kels, come here!" Kirsten called to me. She was standing around my painting and the honey, chattering away with several of her very well-dressed friends.

"I was showing them your painting and the honey you made!" she said with pride.

"I didn't make the honey," I reminded her. "The bees did. I just harvested it." They laughed.

"This is Jenn, Jamal, and Margaret," she said, introducing them all in turn.

"It's so cool you work on a farm!" Margaret said excitedly. The others nodded.

It took me a little by surprise, these well-to-do professionals so interested in the farm. "I guess it is," I said. "I really like it."

"How long have you been doing it?" Jenn asked.

"Just since March."

"What's it like?"

I flashed back to Craig spanking me in the fields, then to Cleo hoeing in her mock announcer's voice about getting in shape for bikini season. Dana's *chicas,* Joshua's goats, the bees, the exhaustion at the end of a long day, the amazing food.

"Aside from picking beans and raspberries, it's absolutely incredible," I answered honestly. "Life changing, for sure."

"You think you'll keep doing it?" Margaret asked.

The thought of *not* doing it sent a shudder down my spine. I'd found myself on the farm, and I'd be lost without it. "I can't think of anything else I'd rather do," I said, smiling.

"So how do you get the honey out of the hive?" Jamal asked.

The three of them grilled me for a good hour about all sorts of details about the farm, with other partygoers joining in periodically. They all seemed so intrigued by the idea that someone they knew could be doing what I was doing, getting dirty and sweaty all day, growing vegetables and sleeping in a trailer.

"It's just so *real*," one woman said, almost enviously. I hadn't given it much thought until then, but she was right. Their jobs in offices lacked a sense of connection to the real world, the one that sustains us, and there was a pang of sadness about that fact in their longing questions. Here they were, the best and brightest, up-and-coming professionals, and they were envious of me, digging all day in the dirt.

***

I was exhausted when I pulled into the driveway of the farm that evening. It had been a long day, a long drive, and I couldn't wait to climb into bed. As I approached my trailer in the dusky evening light, I saw an envelope sticking in the door. I gulped and grabbed it, hurrying inside. I flung myself down on the sofa and tore in, heart pounding.

Kelsie from Salem,
Missing you at market. Just signed the papers on the Johnson place. Would you join me for dinner tomorrow to celebrate? 6:00?
Joshua
p.s. I pruned the blackberries over the gate. So, should you choose to come, you'll have safe passage.

Joshua! My anger toward him dissipated into small bubbles in the soup of my mind. *He's been missing me! But what does he want? To scold me? To rub it in that he's got his dream place now? Is it one of those we-can-just-be-friends talks? Why couldn't his letter have been a little more explicit with regard to his intent?*

Ugh. I knew I had no choice but to go—I'd never forgive myself if I didn't at least go see what side of the fence he was on. Still, things seemed quite possibly beyond repair for us. *Would it be any worse to know that's true than continue with this horrible limbo?* I drifted to sleep in my clothes and woke up the next day with his letter crumpled at my side.

I spent my day off putzing in my little plot in the demo beds, harvesting the first few eggplants from my Black Beauty plants, and working on a painting of a squash bee bumbling out of an oversized male flower, weighted down with big yellow pollen blobs on her back legs. The whole scene was so garish, so abundant, this ostentatious flower offering an excessive amount of sperm-filled pollen to an industrious bee as she unwittingly aids the otherwise stationary plant in the act of copulation. I felt desire welling up between my legs as I thought of it. *She's a sperm bank with wings*, I chuckled to myself.

Dressing for Joshua's, I chose my gray skirt and *that* shirt—the one he'd popped the buttons off, then sewed back on again, all in the same, sexy evening. I slipped on my sandals, clutched my peace offering—a small cardboard carton of ripe peaches from the orchard—and stepped out of the trailer toward my unknown destiny.

I slipped through the gate, and took a deep breath, heading toward the house, but as I approached, the door flung open and Joshua emerged, carrying a pot of something, a towel on his arm. He wore a pair of loose-fitting jeans that hung nicely on his hips, and a pale blue t-shirt. His blonde curls gently lapping at his ears, his broad frame closing the door behind him. I gasped at the sight of him. I'd almost forgotten how incredibly hot he was.

Suddenly, he saw me standing there, and his preoccupied expression gave way to an unmistakable joy. He stopped in his tracks and took a huge gulp of air.

"Kelsie," he breathed, approaching me slowly. "You came."

I nodded shyly, my stomach tightening in a most greedy way.

"I wasn't sure if you would come," he said disbelievingly.

"I wasn't sure either," I lied.

"Well, ma'am," he said, his mood lightening. "You can follow this new *landowner* out behind the barn here for your surprise."

I grinned and followed him into his field. Coming around the corner of the bar, I saw his picnic set up in the pasture. White tablecloth, set with a vase of flowers, a glass jug of water, and two place settings.

"Oh, Joshua, it's beautiful!" I said, taking it all in.

"Please, ma'am, get comfortable," he offered, setting the pot down on the table. He pulled my chair out and waited for me to sit down. His hands brushed along my shoulders as he scooted me in toward the table. I set my carton of peaches on the table.

"Water?" he asked, shifting nervously. "Or, uh, wine?" There was a hint of hope in his voice.

"I'd love a glass of wine," I said, as it hit me. *He's still wondering if I'm pregnant.*

"Joshua," I began, fidgeting with the blue cloth napkin in front of me. "I don't know what all you've heard, but—"

"Kelsie," he interrupted, talking quickly. "I'm sorry to interrupt you, but I just have to say something." He took a big breath. "I know you're not pregnant. I thought you were. I—er—I overheard something that made me think that you were." He glanced up at me, scared blue eyes peering through blonde lashes. "At first I was devastated. I wanted that so badly someday for you and me. And I was so angry at Craig." His gaze darkened. "I was so angry at Craig," he whispered again. "More than anything I was mad that you felt like you had to run away from him, to run home, to your family..." I could tell the thought pained him, and I remembered with a start our uncomfortable visit to my parents' place. "That he wasn't going to take care of you." A tear came into the corner of his eye.

"Joshua," I started, reaching toward his hand across the table. He shook his head.

"I'm sorry, Kelsie," he said. "I gotta get this out before I lose my nerve." A lump caught in my throat.

"For a week I barely slept, just goin' over and over all this in my head. Then it all of a sudden became clear. I'm in love with you." His voice grew stronger. He tipped his head up to look me straight in the eye. "I'm completely in love with you," he said, his eyes shining. My heart seized up. "I realized there isn't one thing I'd rather do in this world than be with you, to build a farm and a family with you. And I came to your folks' place in Salem to tell you that."

He looked at me shyly, his large frame looking surprisingly small and childlike in his folding chair.

I let out the breath I'd been holding. "But I wasn't there," I said quietly.

"But you weren't there," he repeated.

An exotic, spicy smell emanated from the pot between us. I reached across the table again and took his hand in mine, encouraging him with my eyes to continue.

"I guess when your Mom said she hadn't seen you in months, I was worried. I'd specifically heard you'd gone home to live with them and figure out what to do with the baby. It didn't make any sense. So I called Miss Dana." He paused. "I just didn't know what to do," he finished.

My mind raced. "So, you came to find me and tell me all this even though you thought I was pregnant with Craig's baby?" I asked incredulously.

He nodded. "It's the only thing that made sense. Makes sense," he corrected himself. Tears swelled in my eyes. He squeezed my hand, holding my gaze steadfastly.

"And she told you about Shantel?" I asked.

He nodded, passion welling up in his eyes again. "I hope she's all right. Have you talked to her?"

I shook my head, embarrassed. I'd thought about reaching out to her, but everything had just been so crazy, I guess I hadn't made the time. "No, I should," I said dully, feeling guilty. How can Joshua be so good, so thoughtful? The light-haired model on his arm came into focus, and my expression soured slightly.

"You ok?" he asked.

I shrugged. "I thought you had a new lady friend," I said, surprised at how cold my voice sounded.

He looked at me curiously. "What made you think that?" He looked so bewildered I struggled to remember what I'd seen.

"At the Luscious Earth workshop," I said, quietly.

"You were there?" he asked incredulously. "I didn't see you there!"

"I hid behind the picnic table in the outdoor kitchen and watched you with a girl on your arm." The memory stung.

"Oh, Carissa!" his face broke into a huge grin. I failed to see the humor. "My cousin," he said sheepishly. "She was visiting from the east coast."

I froze, staring at him in disbelief. Slowly a smile spread across my face, too. "Your cousin," I repeated. "Cousin." I shook my head. "To think the torture I put myself through on that one!"

Joshua looked downright delighted at this news. "You *do* still have feelings for me, too."

"I said I was still sweet on you, and I meant it," I said, gazing steadfastly into his blue, blue eyes. This time I didn't feel scared of falling in. In fact, I welcomed it.

He picked up the bottle of wine, reaching for my glass, but changed his mind. Instead, he stood and came around to my side of the table. Stooping to take my hand, he pulled me up and into his arms, engulfing me in a hug. He picked me completely off the ground and spun me around, grinning like a fool, and set me back down, bringing his lips to mine in a forceful, almost desperate kiss. I gasped as he wrapped his arms around the small of my back and pulled me to him. I opened my mouth to meet his intensity, and felt the surge of passion as his tongue moved in to hold me, too. He was swallowing me whole, a delicious, full wholeness. He pushed me up against the barn wall, kissing me, squeezing, pinning me there. He let out small moans of pleasure as he brought his hands over my body, caressing, kneading, pleading. I felt his erection on my belly, and I groaned as he ground himself into me. He reached behind his head and pulled his t-shirt off, continuing to grope my breast with his free hand.

"Mmm," I mumbled, burying my face in his chest, inhaling deeply.

He smelled so good.

I ran my fingers up over his muscles and fuzzy fur, across his shoulders, and down his arms as he fumbled with the buttons on my shirt.

"Kelsie, you'd better do this quick, or there's not going to be a button left on this thing," he breathed between kisses.

I obliged, unbuttoning. He slid my shirt off my shoulders and stood back suddenly, gazing down at me with disbelief.

"You are so gorgeous," he said, shaking his head, his mouth hanging open slightly. My heart swelled and with a huge grin on my face, I unhooked my bra to free my breasts. I slid it off, holding his gaze, my nipples tightening as the air hit them. I unbuttoned his jeans and slid the zipper down slowly, grinning up at him through my lashes.

"God!" he exclaimed, grabbing me and lifting me up against the scratchy wood of the barn, pressing me into it, wrapping my legs around him.

I gasped, waiting, pinned there with his huge erection pushing through the fabric of our underwear. He reached down and freed himself, then moved my panties to the side and brought his thumb onto my already-swollen clit. "Aaah!" I groaned as he circled me frantically, bringing another finger to my wet, waiting opening. He pushed it inside me, and I cried out again, squirming against the rough barn wall.

"Kelsie, I need you so bad," he said, sliding his finger out and replacing it with his huge, erect penis. He eased himself into me, my sopping wet vagina sucking him in hungrily. I opened my mouth wide and he filled me with his tongue, bringing the full length of him inside, holding me there for a moment, as he mumbled approval through impassioned kisses. He began to move, steadily, confidently, in and out of me. As he pushed my panties further over to make room for him, they cut into my backside, and between that, the barn wall, and Joshua's slow rhythm it was all I could do to hold on. I clung to him with my legs and my arms as he picked up speed, nailing me again and again to the wall. Finally, I couldn't hold myself any longer. I tightened around him as he filled me completely, and convulsed my orgasm onto him.

"Oh, Kelsie," he breathed as I started to shake around him. He plunged hard and fast for a few thrusts, and then he lifted me quickly off him as he shot his own orgasm, splattering a line of cum over my thigh and my skirt. He brought me gently back to the ground. My weak knees barely supported me as he looked down into my eyes once more, sated and happy.

"Whoa," I whispered, a grin spreading across my face. "That was intense!"

His eyes sparkled. "Now that we're worked up an appetite," he said, motioning to the table. "We should eat before it gets cold."

I put my shirt back on and joined him at the table as he picked up where he left off, pouring me a glass of wine.

"Moroccan stew," he said, motioning to the pot. As he lifted the lid, that warm, exotic combination of spices filled the air again. He ladled me a bowl of the thick, rich-smelling stew, and I shook my head.

"I can't believe you did all this without knowing if I would even come over tonight," I said quietly.

He blinked, his eyes losing their sparkle momentarily. "You had to come," he responded. "You just had to."

Shaking his head as though to rid it of some awful thought, he changed the subject.

"So, I'm officially a landowner now," he said proudly, lifting his glass.

I raised mine as well. "That's so wonderful, Joshua. Congratulations." We clinked glasses and my eyes flitted away from him for a moment, struck momentarily by the real possibility that our futures could be intertwined on that land.

"Hey!" he said. "Seven years bad sex."

"Huh?" I asked.

"Eye contact. You've gotta make eye contact with every person you cheers with or it's seven years of bad sex."

I laughed. I'd never heard that before. "Well, I don't want to take any chances," I said, raising my glass again. "So let's do this over. To seven years of *good* sex," I said, staring blatantly into his eyes.

"Sounds good to me," he said as we clinked again, and dove into our delicious stew.

***

I helped him with the evening milking after dinner, and then helped him bring the dishes in from our picnic. When I stepped into his kitchen, I almost dropped my armload of plates.

There, hanging on the wall above the couch in the living room, was my painting of the bee and the goat. *His* painting. The one I thought had been sold at market.

I stared at him incredulously, unloading my armload onto the counter.

"Where did you get that?" I asked.

"Well, ma'am," he replied, grinning, "This nice lady at the market was selling it, and I just couldn't pass it up."

"*You* bought it? Seriously?"

"I know a good investment when I see one," he said with a shit-eating grin.

I smacked him in the arm. "No, really!" I said, "Dana said she sold it at market, but she didn't say it was to you!"

"The second I saw it I knew you had painted it for me," he said, taking my hand. "I just knew it. And even though I didn't know if we'd ever see each other again, I just had to have it."

I squeezed his hand. "I'm so glad you have it," I told him. "I was honestly pretty broken up about it when I heard it was sold, knowing I'd never have the chance to give it to you, if we ever did end up working things out..." I trailed off.

We stood there in his kitchen, holding hands, staring at it.

"You know what my favorite part about it is?" he mused.

"What's that?"

"When I look at it, I can see that all the stuff Miss Dana taught me, she's taught it to you, too".

"Yeah, totally," I replied, studying the tiny bee at work on her clover blossom and the happy goat muzzle grazing away alongside her. The perfect pair, content in their happy pasture. "She's completely changed my life."

The sun had long since set and I realized I should probably be getting back to the farm, to get to bed and get ready for the week ahead.

Joshua must have read my mind, because he pulled me around to face him.

"Want to stay here tonight?" he asked, a little sheepishly. I grinned.

"I'm not sure we'd get any sleep if I did that," I told him. "And we both have to work tomorrow."

He pulled me to him. "I reckon all we need is a couple ground rules," he said, smiling his easy smile and dipping down to kiss me.

"Like what?" I mumbled into his open mouth. He tasted like the peaches we'd had for dessert.

"Well," he said, drawing it out. "We can probably only make love two, maybe three more times tonight, and then it's lights out."

I laughed. "And probably just once more in the morning," I said, nibbling at his neck.

"Now that's pushin' it," he said, nibbling back. "I get up pretty early to milk."

"You're right, you're right," I conceded. "How about a maximum of two, uh, sessions, that can happen whenever we want them to between now and tomorrow morning?"

"Deal," he said, leading me into his bedroom. "I want to cash in on one right now."

***

Them months of August and September on a farm are tough, I learned. Right at the time when the garden is culminating in a gigantic bounty of produce, you're exhausted from a season of hard work, and you can barely muster the energy to harvest, let alone process the extra food and put the gardens to bed. Dana and Craig call it one of farming's dirty little secrets, noting that almost every intern who quit the farm did it during the last couple weeks of August. Shantel and her predicament aside, the rest of our crew kept it together pretty well. We kept our spirits up even when tempers were short, canning big vats of pickles and salsa in the outdoor kitchen in the evenings when we were done with our formal farm work, getting fall crops planted and cover crops seeded, and preparing for the fall festival.

I'd been dreaming and scheming with Joshua on his new land, too, as he prepared to move his farm there. The more time we spent together, the more comfortable I was with the idea of living there with him at some point. There was a spare room that I could use for painting, and a nice little plot for a vegetable garden. I could put my beehives next to the woodlot, so the bees could get a wide variety of wild flowers to drink from.

As the harvest festival approached, we turned our efforts to the beautification of White Oak Farm for the big celebration. We cleared the barn, brought in loads of straw bales from a neighbor's farm, strung lights from the trees and made long ristras of peppers and marigolds to hang from the rafters. Craig hosed down the tractor, planning to hitch it to the trailer and take folks for farm tours on it. Cleo had some friends from Portland coming out to play music for it, and Dana found a square dance caller, citing the importance of group dances in bringing community together.

An atmosphere of festivity and excitement permeated our days and evenings, mostly because of the party, of course, but also because of the symbolic ending of the season that the harvest festival represented. Although we wouldn't be completely done with farm work by then, we were damn close. All of the spring crop beds had been seeded with a fall cover crop, which was growing well, cloaking those areas in a soft blanket of green. That crop, Craig explained to us, acted like a blanket, protecting the soil from erosion during the wet winter months. In the spring, they would turn it under to feed the soil and start planting again. I recalled seeing that blanket when I arrived in spring, not understanding a thing about what it was for. My heart swelled with pride as I marveled at all I'd learned these past eight months, how shockingly different my life was now compared to when I arrived.

The day before the festival, we harvested the pumpkins and winter squashes. The morning was crisp but sunny, the unmistakable nip of fall in the air. We hadn't had a hard frost yet, but Dana and Craig wanted to get the squash out of the fields before the forecasted heavy rains hit. Craig revved up the tractor and we all hopped on the trailer and got our own little farm tour out to the pumpkin patch.

Dana explained how to cut the pumpkins swiftly from their

stalks with a large sharp knife, and stack them on the trailer so we could fit the most pumpkins possible in each load. As Craig drove slowly down the path next to the row, the four of us women cut and harvested and loaded hundreds of heavy squash, building the orange pile higher and higher.

I looked over just as Cleo, lugging an exceptionally large jack o' lantern, tripped over a vine in the field and stumbled, sending the blob rolling down her front and splattering open on the ground, spewing seeds and goo all over her lower half.

"Aah!" she cried out, jumping back, her black jeans covered with pumpkin ooze. "Damn, Pumpkin! Why you gotta be so clumsy!?"

We cracked up. "Happens to the best of us," Dana said, hugging two fruits to her chest, looking very much like she was clutching huge orange boobs.

The physicality of the work in the cool weather and the company of these women I'd grown so fond of over the year satisfied a deep yearning inside me, and I again counted my blessings for ending up here. After we'd unloaded the pumpkins, placing them strategically around the barn and gathering areas, we went back for the other squash, the diversity of which was amazing. Huge, warty, light blue hubbards; small, multi-colored sweet dumplings; red-orange kyaris; simple dusty orange Amish Pie Pumpkins; and, blatantly phallic, tan butternuts. We unloaded them into large wooden crates in the barn for storage.

After the long, grueling day, we relaxed in the weathered folding chairs in the doorway of the barn, looking with satisfaction at the abundance of hard work.

"All from a handful of seeds," Dana mused reverently.

Cleo approached from the outdoor kitchen with a cold six pack.

"Pumpkin ale," she grinned, handing us each a bottle. "I thought it would be apropos."

She took a seat between Jessi and Craig, reaching over to squeeze Jessi's knee, and took a breath.

"It's kind of a celebratory beer in another way, too," she announced, grinning. Jessi beamed back, putting her hand over Cleo's on her knee.

"We got a lease on a piece of ground on Sauvie Island," Cleo said proudly.

A collective *ooh!* circled the group.

"Cleo, Jessi, that's wonderful!" Dana exclaimed, leaning forward in her seat so enthusiastically it looked like she might tip out of it. "Tell us all about it!"

"Well," Jessi started. "It's 5 acres, just outside Portland. Been farmed organically for fifteen years."

"Vegetables?" Craig asked.

"Mostly. There's a small orchard, too, about a half acre."

"Ooh, an orchard!" Dana's eyes sparkled. "You could get some *chicas* to graze under the trees!"

"Water rights?" Craig prodded.

"Well water," Cleo nodded.

"Wow, that's so cool!" I jumped in. "Are you going to market?"

They eyed each other with a smile. "We're not totally in agreement on that yet," Jessi said. "As you know," she nodded at me, "I prefer CSA over market, but Cleo likes market better. So we're still debating."

"You could always do both," Dana offered. "And anyway, there's plenty of time for you to decide that stuff." She raised her bottle. "To Cleo and Jessi and their new adventure together!"

"Cheers!" we chorused, clinking glasses. I made sure to look each of them in the eye.

24

That evening in my trailer, I frantically hurried to put the finishing touches on two paintings for what would be my *bona fide* debut show. I had four already finished, and was planning on hanging them in the barn tomorrow morning. Accompanied by my new favorite band, the Be Good Tanyas, on my little stereo, and completely content surrounded by the chaos of my trailer-turned-studio, I hummed along with the lilting, feminine trio as I sat on my bed and painted.

As I dabbed the last fuzzy spots on a huge bumblebee drinking from a larkspur flower, her weight pulling the flower stalk down toward the ground as she drank, there came a knock on the door.

"Come in," I mumbled absentmindedly, the handle of a paintbrush in my mouth.

Joshua stuck his large head in the door, grinning. My heart skipped and I broke into a smile, removing the paintbrush from my mouth.

"Hey!" I exclaimed, moving toward the door to greet him with a kiss. "I'd invite you in, but I'm not sure you'll fit in here with all this mess!" He stood on the ground outside the door, which made me a little taller than him for once. I leaned down to kiss him and he hugged me around my waist.

"I'm sure I can manage to find an out of the way place, if you don't mind me watching you work for a bit?" he said, giving me a playful squeeze on the behind.

"Not at all," I said smiling. "I've finished this one, and I only have a little more to do on that." I nodded toward the nearly completed scene of a bee high in flight, blue sky and clouds behind her, scouring the fields below for tasty flowers.

I'd been hanging out over at his place for the most part, because of the state of my trailer, so he'd never actually been inside. He ducked low and climbed the two steps in, tipping his head to the side to avoid the low ceiling, and occupying pretty much every available inch of open space.

I laughed, reaching for his arm. "Joshua Murphy, you are positively larger than life in this trailer."

I shimmied around him to clear a spot at the small table for him to sit, and he grabbed my waist from behind as I did. I softened into his strong arms, groaning. "Mmm, Joshua," I mumbled, straightening to lean back against him. "I need to finish these paintings."

"Of course, ma'am," he said mischievously, sliding his hands up over my belly and toward my breasts. "I'm not here to distract you. I just came to watch the *artiste* at her craft." His hands rested on my ribs, just underneath the bulge of my breasts. My nipples ached for him to touch them. I wiggled my behind slightly against his leg, hoping to entice him to keep moving on up.

"Hey now, Kelsie 'Mixed Messages' Thompson," he teased. "Don't you have work to do?" He released his hands to my hips and pushed me gently forward several steps until he could reach the bench to sit down at the table. He did so, squeezing his large frame into the tiny seat, his knees occupying the entirety of the small hall between the bench and the sink, trapping me on the opposite side from my painting. He grinned at me, fully aware of the river he'd just created, that I'd have no choice but to cross.

"Joshua," I half-pleaded, whining slightly.

"Ma'am, I have no interest in standing between a woman and her work."

"You might not be standing between it, but you certainly are sitting between it!" I exclaimed, feigning exasperation.

He nodded, grinning wickedly. "Just sittin' here, behavin' myself."

Well, two can play at that game, I thought, taking a step toward him. I pulled my hair out of my ponytail so it cascaded down over my shoulders, tugged at my shirt so it revealed a substantial slit of cleavage, and took a wide, deliberate step over his leg, straddling him. I leaned forward toward him as I moved across, brushing over his arms, giving him a hearty eyeful of cleavage. I brushed my lips gently over his face, breathing in his ear as I passed, not stopping at his lips but rather brushing his nose above them. His breathing was sufficiently heavy and I grinned to myself as I passed over his head and prepared to dismount on the opposite bank.

To my surprise, he grabbed my waist to steady me as he threw his knees wide, pinning my legs wide open in front of him, so wide my feet nearly left the ground and I sat down abruptly in the void between us, suspended in air by my legs straddling his. I leaned against the cupboard below the sink to steady myself. His mischievous grin returned.

"Oh, Kelsie," he breathed, locking his eyes with mine and holding my waist firmly with his huge hands. "Now that I've got you here, there's so much I could do to you."

My lower half constricted sharply at his threat. My breathing quickened and my nipples popped through the fabric of my t-shirt, giving my arousal completely away, as if there was any chance of hiding it.

"But," he started, eyes clear and bright. "But I won't." My face must have fallen, because he quickly promised, "I want you to finish your work so I can do this proper, not hurried." I felt a blush spread across my face. "But I want that kiss you teased me with a second ago before you get back to it."

With that, he let go of my waist and took my hands, pulling me toward him. Our mouths locked and we kissed in the deep way that's become our normal lately, spilling passion into the other's mouth, drinking fully, sweetly.

"Whew, Joshua Murphy," I said as I pulled away. "You might not want to be distracting, but you most certainly are." I gave him another quick peck as I climbed off him and resumed my spot on the bed.

I studied the bumble bee. "She looks good to me!" I said, holding the painting up for his approval.

"Gorgeous," he said. "Honestly."

"Well," I said, offering the painting toward him. "I normally store the finished ones in the bathroom back there, but I'm not sure my resolve can hold up to another trip across the River of Joshua."

He chuckled, taking the painting from me and clambering to his feet. "Mine neither," he responded.

He ducked into the bathroom, setting the painting on the tub sill, perched over my mess of clothes occupying the tub.

"I didn't know I'd have such esteemed company here," I called to him as I situated the last painting on my bed-turned-easel. "Or I would have tidied up a bit."

"Looks great to me," he said, picking up a lacy black bra and swinging it around his finger like a lasso. I rolled my eyes at him, and turned my attention back to the painting in front of me. Just a little more work on the bee herself—it was a hard perspective to catch, from her eyes looking down, but also of her in flight in the air. Everything else looked okay, but she seemed slightly crooked somehow. I retied my hair to keep it out of the way and chewed on the end of a paintbrush while I concentrated, dabbing here and there with the brush to bring her into a full, comfortable focus.

"I could watch you all night," Joshua said softly. I looked up at him, where he'd resumed his seat at the tiny table and was staring at me with such a loving intensity I almost turned away. Instead I smiled fully at him. "I'm trying to make her look natural, not forced," I said, turning back to the canvas. "I think I'm almost there, but there's something slightly off about her...."

Joshua watched me work in silence for another hour, until I was finally satisfied. "I hope people like them," I said nervously as I rinsed my brushes in the bucket in the sink. He had moved to the bed, when I left it, and I hurried to finish so I could join him.

"Like them? Folks are gonna love them!" he assured me.

I wiped my hands on a towel and climbed onto the bed, snuggling up against him. "I hope so."

He shifted so he was leaning over me, stroking my hair off my face with his rough hand, gazing down at me with adoration. "They will. You'll see," he paused, his eyes twinkling. "You know, I've always wanted to see the inside of one of these mysterious trailers full of beautiful girls," he said, bringing his mouth toward me once again.

***

The day of harvest fest dawned chilly but partly cloudy, not raining, so we all took that as a good omen. Cleo helped me hang my paintings in the barn, making sure to locate them in an area where they'd have good light, and Caroline showed up early to help set up as well.

"Your big day!" she said as she climbed out of the car, hugging me. "Your first show! I'm so excited! Oh, hi Cleo!"

"Come see!" Cleo ushered her into the barn, where the paintings had been hung.

"Ok, Kels! They're beautiful!" she said, turning to face me. "I had no idea how talented you were!"

"Ladies, could I get your help with these tables?" Dana called from the outdoor kitchen.

We trotted over to help carry tables back to the barn, setting them up in an outer ring, so there'd be plenty of room for food but a wide open space in the middle for dancing.

Finally, at three, we retreated to my trailer to prepare for the evening's festivities. The party was to begin at four and go until folks went home, so it didn't leave us much time. For the potluck, Cleo and I had made some absolutely divine muffins, with winter squash, herbs, and Joshua's bleu cheese. I shared one with Caroline as we dressed for the party. I chose my new red dress, which had become a favorite of Joshua's. As I slipped it on, Caroline gave a low whistle.

"Kels, you look HOT in that dress!" she complimented. "Seriously, this farming thing has done you *so right*!"

I grinned back at her. "It totally has, Caroline. I seriously feel so grateful every day, especially since I don't have much more time here."

The thought pained me a little. Still, I had my own projects to look forward to, and what appeared to be a bright future with Joshua.

"I've been seriously thinking about applying for next year," she said shyly, gauging my reaction.

"Oh, Caro, you *should*!" I told her. "You'd love it!" The roughness of getting through the last month popped into my head. "Well, most of it, anyway," I assured her.

"I see what a difference it's made in your life. How happy you are, how grounded, how confident. It's quite alluring, really," she finished, zipping up her booty jeans.

She'd invited Cleo and Jessi over for a little celebration beforehand, and they knocked just then. She opened the door for them, extracting a bottle of champagne from her bag.

"I thought we should have a toast to celebrate Kelsie's first show," she said. "But I'm scared of popping the cork on these things," she laughed. "Will one of you do it?"

Cleo grabbed the bottle and popped the cork under a towel without a hitch, pouring us all a teacup full.

"To Kelsie and her bright career as a farmer-artist!" she said.

"Hear hear!" echoed Caroline and Jessi.

We clanked and drank. "Thanks, guys," I said gratefully, taking a long swig. I was getting pretty nervous. "Do you think there will be a lot of people here?" I asked them.

"Usually it's a rockin' good party," Cleo replied. "I have a bunch of friends from Portland coming down." She glanced over at Caroline. "Some pretty hot, single farmers, too!" she told her.

The four of us finished our glasses and made our way back through the demo beds toward the barn, where folks had already started milling around.

"Brian!" Cleo yelled, charging toward the skinny, heavily tattooed guy hauling a banjo case and mic stand into the barn. She leapt at him, and he gave her a big hug.

"I want you to meet my girlfriend Jessi!" she told him, leading him over to us.

"Jess, Brian farms on Sauvie Island too!" Jessi stuck out her hand to him.

"Cleo tells me y'all got that lease on the Beet's Knees ground?

Jessi nodded. "I love their name. I guess they wanted to scale up. I heard they got some land near Yakima."

"Well, it's awesome to have you two so nearby." He winked at Cleo. "Now we can really fuck some shit up."

"Yeah!" Cleo retorted, linking her arm playfully in his. I noticed he had a heart tattooed on his hand emblazoned with the words "Farm Hand."

"Hey, and this is Kelsie, an intern here, and Caroline, her friend from Salem," Cleo said.

"Cool, nice to meet you. I gotta go finish setting up, but I'll hook up with you later," he told us.

Caroline and I wandered into the barn to set our muffins up on the potluck tables when I heard my Mom's unmistakable voice.

"Charles, I don't see her anywhere!" she complained.

We turned and there they were, in the barn, on the farm. Caroline rolled her eyes slightly and we walked over to greet them. I gave my dad a big hug. "Welcome to the farm!" I said, turning to hug Mom.

"Oh we're so glad to be here, honey!" Mom said, a little over-enthusiastically. She looked around awkwardly. "Hi Caroline. Kirsten said she's coming down with some friends as well."

Kirsten coming to support me at an event—that was certainly a first. "Great!" I said, taking Dad's hand in mine and giving it a squeeze. "Thank you for coming. Would you like to, um, see my paintings?"

His eyes sparkled and he nodded.

"Of *course* we would!" Mom chimed in. "That's why we're here!"

I led them over to the wall, where several folks were already looking.

"They're *beautiful*, Kelsie," Mom gushed. I think she really meant it, too.

"Very good," Dad said appreciatively. Next to Mom, he always appeared a little understated.

A woman bystander piped in. "You painted these?" she asked.

I nodded shyly.

"Wow! They're great! Nice work!"

"Yeah, aren't they great?" Caroline chimed in.

"She's always been an artist, you know," Mom started in on the woman. "We have several of her pieces hanging in our home."

I smiled as I thought about that spot down by the river, the one Joshua had taken me to.

As if I summoned him out of thin air, I looked toward the barn door and saw him striding across the field toward us. He had a big bouquet of flowers in his hand. My heart leapt to see him.

"There's Joshua!" I said under my breath to Caroline.

"He's so hot!" she whispered. "I bet those flowers are for you!"

When he saw us, he grinned a big grin and sauntered across the barn to greet us, handing me the colorful bouquet.

"Congratulations," he said, leaning down to give me a kiss, then turning toward my folks.

"Mr. and Mrs. Thompson." He offered his hand to Dad and shook it heartily. "Good to see you again."

"Those are lovely flowers, Joshua," Mom said, eyeing me. "He's a good catch, Darling!"

Leave it to Mom to be blunt.

"So's Kelsie," Joshua and Caroline said in unison. Man, I loved my friends.

Just then, Dana's smooth voice rang out from the microphone.

"Welcome to White Oak Farm's 15th Annual Harvest Festival!" she called out to the crowd. "We welcome spirits old and new to celebrate with us tonight, to give thanks for the bounty of the earth, for good company and good food, and for the network of people who make this farm possible."

"No farm could function without customers," she continued, her strappy, rust-colored cotton dress highlighting her tanned skin and toned arms. She wore large silver hoop earrings and a big silver necklace, waving her bracelet-clad arms around as she spoke. "That you choose to put your hard-earned dollars into this small farm economy, to build a resilient regional food system, is invaluable. You could choose to shop anywhere, but you make the conscious decision to feed your families healthy, wholesome food. You are to be commended."

A chorus of applause rang out among the crowd. "The food that appears on those tables tonight is a gift. A gift from the earth, yes, from the rain and the sun and the soil and the seeds. It is also a gift from all those people who have put their hearts and their backs into the growing and cooking of it. It is all too easy to lose sight of the importance of people choosing to do this, to do the important work of growing our food. They are to be commended as well."

Another thunderous round of applause erupted from the crowd. Caroline let out a loud whistle, turning several heads around us. I elbowed her in the side, smiling.

"Each year, we host several bright, up-and-coming farmers, teaching them everything we can about the intricacies of this highly rewarding livelihood." Caroline beamed over at me, and Joshua squeezed my hand. "I'd like to bring them up individually, so you can see the human faces of the food you've been eating all year."

"First I'd like to bring up Kelsie Thompson, who joined us this season from Salem." My heart pounded as I took to the stage alongside Dana. She put her arm around me proudly.

"Kelsie came to us very much a greenhorn," she said, giving my shoulder a squeeze. "She didn't know much about farming, but Craig and I both recognized immediately that she had what it takes to become a great farmer—sincerity, drive, a good work ethic, humility. Through the season, she has blossomed into an invaluable asset on the farm, adeptly performing all farm tasks and taking on a formal apprenticeship in beekeeping. She's also the artist responsible for the breathtaking bee paintings that our old barn wall is lovingly showcasing tonight." Several cheers rang out from the crowd.

"Kelsie has assured me," she said, turning to me, "that she intends to keep farming upon her completion of the internship, particularly as a beekeeper, which is an occupation of the utmost importance in the face of the massive challenges bees face in our modern world. So," she said, nodding to Craig, who pulled a box out of the corner and brought it up on stage with us, "so we thought it fitting to equip you with your own tools as you venture out on this crucial work. Craig handed me the box, which I opened to reveal my own beekeeping suit, veil, gloves, hive tool, grips, and bee brush.

I beamed up at them. "Thank you both so much!" I said, tearing up. The crowd applauded again and I said softly to them amid the noise, "Thank you for all you've taught me. I—" I stumbled. "I could never repay you for all you've shared," I finished, choking up. Craig pulled me into a big hug. "You'll make a good farmer, Kelsie," he said in my ear. "And you'll make Joshua a very happy man." Dana wrapped me in a big hug, too. "This gift comes with the promise that we'll team up next spring to catch you some swarms, too, my dear," she said. "Now go enjoy your guests!"

I exited the stage to another round of applause, clutching my box of beekeeping gear. They called up Jessi, and then Cleo to the stage, congratulating them both on their land and praising their skills as farmers. They gave Jessi a mechanized seeder and Cleo a picnic table Dana said belonged to her grandpa. "Oh, the meals you'll make that will grace that table..." Dana professed.

When I returned to my family, Kirsten had arrived. "Keslie, this place is amazing!" she said, hugging me. I saw several of her friends that I had talked to at her party eyeing my paintings. "We're all so thrilled to be here!"

Bluegrass music twanged through the barn as Cleo's friend's band started in. Several people took to the dance floor immediately, old and young, swinging each other around to the music. I wanted to free my hands up for dancing, too, so I headed toward the barn stairs to stow my box of beekeeping goodies in the upstairs room.

"Hi Kelsie," I heard a shy voice beside me in the shadows at the darker end of the barn.

Shantel!

"Hey!" I greeted her, still clutching my box. "I'm surprised to see you here!"

"Yeah, me too," she replied, smiling. "I felt a little weird about it, but I really wanted to come up for the party, and Craig and Dana said it would be okay. Sorry I ditched out on you guys," she added.

"Shantel, given your situation, I think you had a pretty good excuse," I told her.

"Still, I didn't say goodbye to anybody, not that..." she trailed off.

I knew what she was thinking. *Not that anybody would care.*

"I was a little surprised to hear you had gone," I told her honestly. "But I totally understood." I glanced down at her belly, which now sported a small bump. "So, how are you doing?" I asked her.

"Oh fantastic!" she said, her bubbly personality returning. "I'm past the sick stage, and I've been feeling a lot more energetic this past month or so. I've been staying with my mom in Santa Barbara, getting everything figured out for the baby. I've had a couple of ultrasounds, and he's looking healthy!"

"A boy, huh?" I said. She nodded excitedly. "I just found out last week. Craig's pretty excited, too."

Craig?! Excited about it? "Really?" I asked.

"I really think so. It took him awhile to come around, but he did. He's pretty thrilled it's a son, I think, too," she smiled.

"So, are you going to move back up here?"

She laughed. "And try to make a family with Mr. Can't-Keep-It-In-His-Pants? No way!" She continued. "I'm going to live in California, near my family, and the little man will come up here for the summers, once he's old enough to be away. Craig will make trips down to visit every few months until then."

Interesting, I mused. *Not exactly the Cleaver Family, but I could see how that could work well for everyone.* "So you feel good about that?" I asked.

"I really do!" she said intensely. "For those first few months, I had no idea what to do. After he realized I was going to keep the baby, Craig immediately started in on how we would do this together. I'd live with him, we'd make it work. But I know him. He'll make a great dad, but he'd make a horrible partner. I needed to get out of here, to get away from him and make my own decision about what I wanted to do. And I realized," she finished, "that trying to be his partner isn't it."

"So is he ok with this arrangement?" I hoped I wasn't being to forward asking all this.

Shantel seemed relieved to be able to talk with someone about it.

"Yeah," she said. "It's a pretty good deal for him, really. He can keep farming, stay living here, flirting with all the ladies," she winked, "and still get to spend summers with his boy. And, of course, we'll visit each other a lot."

The thought of a young boy running around the farm with Craig and Dana all summer made me smile. "He'll have so much fun here!" I said to her.

"Yeah, totally," she replied. "I think it'll be really good for him. For all of us. My family is absolutely ecstatic," she added. "My sisters are nearby, and they both have kids, so he'll have a bunch of cousins to get into trouble with and, of course, Grandma and Grandpa to spoil him rotten."

"Ok, Guys and Gals, grab your partners!" we heard a voice boom over the microphone. "For the White Oak Farm annual square dance is fixin' to commence."

Shantel smiled at me. "You'd better set that down, and get out there with Joshua!"

"Right!" I said hastily, running up the stairs. "You gonna join in?" I asked her as I climbed back down.

"Probably ought to, since I came all this way," she said.

I spotted Joshua easily over the crowd as I rejoined it. *He's certainly hard to miss,* I giggled to myself.

He beamed at me as I approached him, and offered his hand. "Kelsie from Salem, may I have this dance?" He tipped his hat toward me.

"I'd be delighted," I smiled, taking his hand.

He led me out onto the dance floor, and we joined a square with Cleo and Jessi and an older couple I didn't know. A couple of Kirsten's friends joined us. I looked around for Caroline, and saw her a couple squares over, standing next to a cute guy wearing a flannel shirt and boots. She saw me and waved.

The music started up. "Bow to your partner," the caller twanged out over the melody. Joshua and I gave an exaggerated bow toward each other. "Now bow to your corner," he continued. I looked around for directions. *What's a 'corner'?* Kirsten's friends seemed equally bewildered. The older woman on Joshua's left grabbed him and turned him around to face her. "I'm your corner!" she laughed. I turned to Jessi, who was to my right. "Aha!" she said, figuring it out, and we bowed to each other.

"Now all join hands and circle to the left," and off we went, into a hilarious half hour of trying to follow along with the caller as we promenaded, do-se-doed, and circled round and round in our squares, laughing hysterically.

We danced and ate and chatted and drank the night away, until the stars shone over the fields and the music lilted off to sleep. Four of my six paintings were sold at the show, including one to Kirsten's friend Jenn. Marla, the owner of Heavens To Java coffee shop in Salem told me she'd be thrilled if I wanted to have a month-long show at the shop. But the biggest deal of all for me was that my parents bought one of my paintings! Mom chose the one of the bumble bee on the larkspur. As Dad took the painting off the wall, Mom gave me a big hug.

"I'm so proud of you, honey!" she said, wrapping me up in her arms. A lump caught in my throat. Those words sounded so, so good. "Thanks, Mom," I choked out. "It feels good to hear you say that."

"We had a lot of fun tonight, Keslie," Dad added, taking mom's arm in his free hand. We said our goodbyes and I watched them walk away, arm in arm, Dad carrying my painting. It was one of the best nights of my life.

"Are you ready to call it a night, Ms. Bigtime Artiste?" Joshua said, leaning over to kiss me on the cheek.

"I'm ready to leave this party, if that's what you mean, Mr. Bigtime Lover," I teased him. "Do you have any idea if there's a place nearby where a sexy farmer might offer a bed to an up-and-coming artist?"

"Funny you should ask, ma'am," he replied in his best twang. "I reckon there's a place just like you're lookin' fer o'er yonder through that fence." He took my arm. "Shall we?"

And with that, we headed off toward the gate through the blackberry bramble.

ACKNOWLEDGEMENTS

Well, it's finally done, thanks to the efforts of so many. A huge thank you goes out to all who kept pestering me about when the book would be out so you could read it. That as much as anything made me put down the hoe and make it a priority. After that, the biggest thank you goes out to Kelsey, my sister-in-law, who read and reread it, and who spent countless family gatherings helping me finagle sticky plot challenges. If you ever write your book, I'm ready to log some serious hours on it with you, Sister!

Thanks also to Mary McColl, my fantastic editor; to Amy Howa, grand cover designer; to Guy Hand, who took about 700 shots before getting the right one for the cover photo; to Matt and Abby, the betrothed who graciously posed for the cover photo (Matt even swapping pants with me because his weren't quite dirty enough); to Jesse Miller, botanist and lichenologist, for the detailed info on native plants in the Willamette Valley (and general enthusiasm for what he calls eco-erotica); to Brian Wood for farming wisdom and seasonality/timing logistics in Oregon; to Kurt Gindling and Carrie Jones for their goat milking insights; to Brandon Follett and Lori Bevan, who accompanied me on the epic road trip to the wilds of Salem; to the Idaho Writer's Guild; to Brent, who woos and supports his farmer/writer wife with as much gusto as any non-farmer, non-writer could; to Mom and Granny, who shared their vast insights from a lifetime of reading good (and not so good) books; and to all the beta readers who provided such excellent feedback!

ABOUT THE AUTHOR

Artemisia Rae writes and farms in southern Idaho. She's in love with the sexy interconnections of the natural world, especially how stationary plants pass on their genes by exploding with garish, irresistible flowers that lure in the bees, followed by incomprehensibly abundant seeds. This is her first novel.

PRAISE FOR WHITE OAK SUMMER

"There's something inherently sexy about life on a farm, where raw soil is transformed into swelling fruits that nourish life. White Oak Summer weaves together ecology and steamy romance through the progression of seasons and ripening crops, creating a lush landscape of images that stimulates the mind and body." Jesse Miller, Botanist

“You don’t need a college education to see the connection between growing vegetables and growing human relationships, You just need to read White Oak Summer. And what a hot read it is!” E.A. Kelly, Editor

White Oak Summer is a perfect blend of practical knowledge and steamy dirt digging, veggie-picking, dirt worshiping romance. Brook Dawn—Backyard organic farmer